THE LAST SHEPHERD

WILBUR SMITH

ISBN 978-1-64079-831-1 (Paperback)
ISBN 978-1-64079-832-8 (Digital)

Christian Faith Publishing, Inc.
296 Chestnut Street
Meadville, PA 16335
www.christianfaithpublishing.com

Printed in the United States of America

1

My name is Titus, someone said.

Excuse me, I replied.

I was sitting at a table outside one of those franchise coffee houses ready to enjoy an expensive cup of cappuccino in the warming sunshine of a perfect Southern California day, a type of day only early spring in California can produce.

I had closed my eyes briefly and it was during that time that the person had sat at the table across from me without my hearing him. He was a street person or a homeless guy or a bum or a hobo or maybe a hustler or someone I was wary of. His hair and beard were finger-combed, and he had a slight film of dirtiness on his face and hands. He smelled of campfires and old clothes and a kind of an animal smell, not unpleasant really, but like lanolin, like damp wool. He wore a nondescript greyish robe fastened at the waist with a piece of rope. But the striking thing about him was his bearing and his face which had high cheek bones, a hawkish nose, and a high forehead. He was olive-skinned. What held me were his eyes. The pupils were black, fathomless, ancient, his friendly gaze on me mesmerizing, stopping my anger at his sitting there without my permission.

Sorry, he said. I didn't mean to startle you, but you are the one who has been chosen to hear my story.

He sat across from me smiling at my reaction to him, and he was relaxed as though we were the best of friends. His lips were chapped and dry, and I offered him my container of ice water which

I had ordered with my coffee. He removed the lid with its protruding straw and took a sip.

I'm in kind of a hurry, I said. I have to get home before long.

Time is a relative thing, he answered. I said my name is Titus and my father named me that. Why, I don't know. I was born more than two thousand years ago, six years before Herod, King of Palestine, murdered his second wife, Mariamme, in twenty BC. That time is based on a calendar introduced by Julius Caesar a few years before that date. The BC stands for Before Christ, and the beginning of the new age is AD. That is Latin for *anno Domini*. I understand that modem scholars no longer use those appendages on time but rather use BCE or CE, meaning Before the Common Era or the Common Era. They have taken Christ out of it—out of time, Titus added dryly.

But I digress. I was born on the east side of the Great Sea, now commonly known as the Mediterranean Sea, in the hill country just north of Bethlehem, an old town even when I was born. My father had a small vineyard and olive grove and had sheep which grazed among the limestone slopes of the land of my birth. It was a good life because we stayed out of the affairs of our lord and masters, the priest and rabbi of our synagogue and mayor of our town and the aging Herod and the Roman governor and their soldiers.

He stopped speaking, took another sip of water, and looked at me quizzically.

Am I boring you?

No, I said.

His eyes held me and so did the notion that he was more than two thousand years old. I was captivated.

I may ramble some, he said, but my story is a complicated one with many layers, and it isn't all that easy to get started with it. But this is only an introduction to the main story anyway, so bear with me. As I said, my father had a flock of sheep, a modest herd that we kept at night in a sheep fold some hundred yards or so from our house. As I grew older taking care of the sheep became my responsibility while my younger brother, Joel, worked the vineyard and olive grove. Ours was a land of milk and honey, just like the old leaders said. We led a good life, except we were hemmed in by the laws of our priests and rabbis who tried to force on us the laws of how we were supposed to conduct ourselves according to the Torah and the prophets and the Mishnah, the oral traditions of purification and restrictions around the Sabbath and dietary laws. Can you imagine a day of rest on a farm? We were also caught up in terrible times of war and brutality and bestiality and greed and fratricidal godlessness which had been going on for the last two hundred years in my suffering country.

But there was hope for our salvation because prophets had written of a messiah, a chosen one, who would rescue the Jewish people in their darkest hour and deliver us from our enslavement back onto the path that God had ordained for us. The priestly mathematicians had arrived at a date for that event to occur sometime during the reign of Herod. And all of us were looking for signs so that we would know when the righteous one would appear.

I'll fill in more detail when I get to the story, but just to make it short, one night as my helper and I were keeping watch over our sheep, we had a vision of a heavenly angel telling us that the Messiah had been born in Bethlehem and that we should leave immediately and see the newborn baby. Bethlehem was only about two miles from our farm, so we hurried off scared out of our wits to do what the heavenly creatures had told us to do.

When we entered the grotto beneath the town's inn, we knew that something was different. The room should have been dark, but there was an eerie glow giving a low, bluish light showing the stabled animals and a man standing beside a woman who was sitting on a sack of wheat straw and holding an infant. Come, she said. You are our first visitors. Here is the child who will save the nation. We did as she bid us and bent over the tiny thing, just as the baby opened his eyes and looked directly into mine.

There was a quality in that gaze that I shall never forget. This child was like no other. I almost fainted from vertigo, a feeling of eons of time flashing by, that I may die from gazing on God himself just as Moses must have felt on that desert mountain. I knew at that moment that the proclamation of the angel was true. That the

Messiah had been born. I also knew at that moment that I would never be the same again, that I would be his servant forever.

Later, when we told others of our encounter, some were hopeful, others were doubtful, and many thought we were just ignorant shepherds who had had too much to drink. We made several trips back to see Jesus, the newborn child, then with his parents in a small home in Bethlehem furnished by some early believers. Each time I saw him I knew I was in a divine presence. I can't really explain the change. His father, Joseph, had begun working as a builder again to support the family, and his young mother, Mary, spent her time taking care of the new infant and doing her household chores and meeting guests who wanted to see Jesus for themselves.

During that time, three Persian Zoroastrian priests arrived in Jerusalem asking about the location of the birth of the new king of the Jews because they wanted to worship him. When Herod heard about them, he was furious and had his priests find the location of the birthplace of the Messiah. Then he met with the magi, the eastern sorcerers, and asked them to go find the child and after they did to return to him on their way home and tell him where the infant was so that he also could go and worship the newborn Chosen One, the savior of the Jews. The magi had a pretty good idea of what Herod really wanted, and they decided to not tell him of the location of the baby Jesus. Herod was seventy years old and ill and going increasingly mad and bent on destroying any hint of someone seizing the throne. They knew that if Herod could find the baby he would have him slain.

I could feel Titus becoming more emotional as he told about his encounters with the baby Jesus and Mary and Joseph. And as he began telling about the magi from the east coming to Jerusalem and involving Herod, his voice had become more hoarse. He had stopped fingering the container of water, and his hands had balled into fists.

What is well known, Titus continued, is that when Herod discovered that the magi had left the country without telling him where Jesus was located, in his madness he ordered the death of all the boy infants in and around Bethlehem two years old or younger. Being warned, Joseph and Mary fled for Egypt the night they found out about the order. What is not known is that my son and my wife, Esther, were slain by Herod's soldiers the day after Joseph and Mary found out about the order. My son had been clubbed to death, and Esther killed with a Roman spear by one of the Gauls who made up Herod's special guards. Our small home was located just above our family's olive grove near the sheep fold, and no one knew about their deaths until I returned later that afternoon. I saw both lying there with my son's s head broken and Esther's blood and his blood soaking into Judean soil.

I have a hard time talking about this, Titus said, his voice choking. I know she was killed trying to protect my son, slain with total indifference. I was filled with rage, and that night I cut the throat of one of Herod's soldiers in their camp near Bethlehem and fled south through Idumea into the Negev Desert and then westerly toward Gaza and the wastelands on the route to Egypt. I had no plan, but I knew I had to escape.

I confess I stole my way along because I had left with nothing, a water bag someone had left carelessly at a well near Charabim, a coat near Marisa, and any kind of food I could find along the way. I fell into the company of some other desperate men who had fled Palestine for their own reasons. I felt torn with guilt, but my anger drove me. I had become one of the outcasts--one of the robbers or revolutionists who tormented the leaders of the country.

One night we fell upon an encampment of pilgrims on the road to Egypt. They were in a narrow valley huddled around a small fire and totally terrified when we slipped in on them demanding food and money and their lives if they gave us any trouble. And then I saw Joseph and Mary, who was holding Jesus close to her. You can imagine my feeling of shame and guilt when I saw the holy family. I prostrated myself before the baby and begged for forgiveness. My fellow brigands were amused by my behavior but soon understood what had happened. When I told them about my experience on the night the angels had appeared to me, they understood because they also had been looking forward to the coming of the Chosen One, the Messiah. Jesus woke up from all the commotion and looked at us, the knot of dirty, ragged men standing in front of him and his mother.

They, too, knelt down beside me because they had also looked into his eyes. There was a quality in that young child that defies description, a mystery, God-like. A baby should have been bawling its head off being awakened by all the yelling and people moving around, but when he opened his eyes and looked at us he only smiled and seemed to welcome us.

What we didn't do was rob them, but what we did do was to escort the family to the borders of Egypt so that they would have safe passage from other desperate men as we had been.

Titus relaxed and took another sip of water. He turned his head slightly and noticed several people going into the coffee shop or coming out, all of them focused on themselves and most of them looking at their iPhones as they walked.

Miracles have occurred since I last visited your world, he said. What is that thing that man is holding? He seems to be mesmerized, and look at him tapping at it or swiping at it with his fingers. Almost everyone going into that shop is doing the same thing.

That is a phone, a camera, a computer, and other stuff all rolled into one, I answered. They can talk with other people, take pictures, send messages, look up information on almost any subject, and do other things that I don't even know about.

But they seem to be so alone, Titus mused. No wonder that I was ordered back during this age. If they all have so much knowledge at their fingertips, are they any wiser?

His question needed no answer, nor did he expect one.

Again, he fixed me with his gaze.

I know that you have many questions for me, he continued, and that the story that I am telling is one that you have heard often, that is, part of it is. I know that the apostles and their followers recorded the ministry of the Chosen One and of all of the miracles he performed and of his dislike of the Pharisees and of his death and rebirth. But I was there, living at the time and was involved in fighting against the corrupted Jewish leaders and the Romans. My story is about the lives of the common people, what life was like as the Messiah went about destroying the old order and establishing the new. The good news the apostles and their followers recorded focused on the ministry of the

Nazarene and not how chaotic the times were. If people really knew what life was like during that age, the message of the Messiah would be better understood.

I call myself a Christian, I said, but I see what you're getting at. I have no idea about the history of the age. The Gospels hardly mention anything about what was happening during those times except what Jesus was doing during those three years of his ministry. But it's hard to believe that you lived back then and went through all that and have been sent back as a messenger. Right now, I'm pretty well befuddled and skeptical.

Titus nodded. I understand, but things will become clear as I continue. Just as I am speaking as you do, for instance, should be a miracle to you, since my native language is Aramaic and Hebraic and I have never used the modem idiom of your language. But I need to finish my introduction to the story.

As I said before, I lived during that age and mingled with the crowds who followed Jesus and fought against the Herods and the Romans during that time as a Zealot. In the Messiah's last few days, I was captured and imprisoned as a criminal. I was one of the so-called thieves crucified along with the Nazarene on the hill of Golgotha. As we hung on our crosses, Jesus recognized me and forgave me. The Romans botched their job because they had to kill us and get us off the crosses before sundown since that day was the beginning of the Jewish Passover, and the powers that be knew that the people in Jerusalem would have rioted to have their most sacred ritual corrupted by having people alive but dying on the cross as we would have normally been. Jesus was impaled with a spear, and I and Gestus had our legs broken so that we would dangle and suffocate.

But the real story comes later. Now it is time to take another sip of water.

Titus sighed and took another drink and stretched himself. He was watching me with his haunting eyes, measuring my reaction to his story.

And then Titus leaned forward and began. Once upon a time . . .

2

A long, long time ago, maybe four thousand years or so, a man named Abraham led a small group of people out of Mesopotamia and headed west and south for a land promised to him by the one and only God. For years, he struggled to get a foothold in the promised land and finally settled near Hebron where his wife Sarah had a son named Isaac. The Lord told Abraham to sacrifice Isaac, so Abraham, his faith tested, took Isaac onto Mount Moriah and was about to sacrifice him on Oman's Rock when the Lord relented and told Abraham that he had passed the test. That hill is where the temple was located, and that rock was the location of the Tabernacle, the Holy of Holies. The Mosque of Omar now stands where our temple was destroyed by the Romans in 70 AD. It is the third most holy spot in the Muslim world.

About a thousand years after Abraham, King Solomon built the temple on Mount Moriah after buying it from the Jebusite Oman who had used the sacred rock as a threshing floor. By that time the Hebrew nation was strong and had a center for worship, a place to set the Ark of the Covenant, and a center for its life. Here was the resting place of Yahweh, the one true God. The city of Jerusalem grew beside it, and became the center of the Hebrew people, often scattered but always with the knowledge that they were a chosen people to lead all nations into the path of righteousness and that Jerusalem, the city of peace, the holy city, was the center of their life because of the temple.

Although originally there were ten tribes with different names for the Hebraic people, they became one family in Jerusalem and at the temple because of their sacred festivals centered there.

They all became known as Jews because Jerusalem was in Judah, or Judea as it was commonly called, so that is where the word originated. Actually, it helped to make them one nation instead of several and helped bind them together when they were in danger of being destroyed.

And they and their faith were almost destroyed several times. For them life was a constant struggle because they were almost always at war with their neighbors as they continued pushing into the land that they believed their God had promised them. In the return from Egypt, Joshua fought the Canaanites. Then through the years Jews battled the Moabites and the Ammonites east of the Jordan and the Philistines along the Mediterranean plus several other smaller nations. Through thousands of years that part of the world has been in turmoil with the struggles I just mentioned or with larger nations like Egypt and the Hittites and Assyria and Persia and Macedonia and Syria and then Rome fighting for control. And the Jewish people survived, hard-headed and stubborn, at times wavering in their faith but always returning to Yahweh and to Jerusalem and the temple.

Titus paused, looking at me a little amused. History can be tedious, he said. The farther away we are from events the less they mean. But they are what shape us. What is happening in Israel right now started back in those days thousands of years ago. Are you losing interest?

No, I said. You told me in the beginning that your story is complicated. But you do need to get on with it.

Titus smiled and continued. Jerusalem was off the easy path for armies moving north and south, but the city and the temple were sacked many times with the Jewish people always involved and being slaughtered and scattered. The Philistines and the Arabians conquered it in 844 BC and the Israelites in 782. The Babylonian king, Nebuchadnezzar, took Jerusalem three different times-in 607, 597, and finally in 586 BC when he took the leaders of the city along with him back to Babylon and maybe to have some peace in that part of the world.

Things really changed when Cyrus, king of Persia, defeated the Babylonians and took control of their empire. He allowed the Jewish people who had been held in Babylon to return to Jerusalem in 457 and ordered that the temple be rebuilt. Some believe Cyrus's action was because of his religion, that he was a Zoroastrian. In a hundred and thirty years or so, the Jewish people who had been left behind when their leaders had been taken captive to Babylon had forgotten about Yahweh and had married foreigners and even had begun worshiping Dagon, the god of the Philistines, and Moloch, the horrible god of the Ammonites and Phoenicians, both idols located in Jerusalem. It was Ezra, a strong and forceful priest, who began rebuilding the temple. He brought back with him the true god, Yahweh, and immediately demanded that all Jews who had remained in Palestine divorce their foreign wives and return to their true God. The work of rebuilding the temple and the wall around Jerusalem was finally finished in 445 BC by Nehemiah, who had been named governor of Palestine. He really finished the work that Ezra had started in re-establishing Judaism.

I am still amazed at how close it was that our religion could have been lost. It makes one remember that age-old argument of whether events shape men or if it is men who shape history. If it hadn't been for Cyrus and Ezra and Nehemiah, who knows?

Young Alexander, the Macedonian, took Palestine and Jerusalem in his vast conquest of that part of the world in 332 BC and introduced Greek culture, bringing along his anthropomorphic gods and the philosophies of deism and sophism. During this period through the next hundred years or so several non-Jewish cities were built, cities like Sepphoris, which was full of Greek influence, many of its citizens wealthy because it was a trading center filled with art and people from many different cultures. It even had baths and a theater. It is difficult to maintain a stem religion with the philosophy that life should be lived to be enjoyed. Many Jews were sorely tempted, and a group began fighting back with laws demanding strict obedience to God's commands. The Pharisees were the ones fighting against

Hellenism, but despite their efforts, Greek culture had an influence in Palestine from then on. How tempting it is to believe that pleasure is the greatest good.

The next time Jerusalem fell and the temple desecrated, the lives of Jews and the future of all people altered. Some events change history suddenly, violently, and when the Syrian ruler Antiochus took Jerusalem by treachery in 170 BC, life shifted violently for people living there. Antiochus plundered the temple, taking away all of its gold and ornaments and precious relics. Where the Ark of the Covenant had stood in the Tabernacle, Antiochus erected a statue of Zeus, the Greek god, and sacrificed swine to it. He slew many of the Jewish leaders and took about ten thousand captives as slaves. He outlawed the Jewish religion and forbade all of its practices like circumcision and reading any of its books or practicing the laws God had laid down for us. All sacred books were destroyed when they were found. He forced the Jews to build temples and erect idols to foreign gods in every one of their cities and demanded that they worship those gods. During this time, Antiachus also destroyed the temple on Mt. Gerizim, that the Samaritans had built to separate themselves from their fellow Jews. A hippodrome, a Roman gymnasium, was erected in Jerusalem, and even some uncircumcised Jewish youths participated in some of the athletic contests staged there. And it is said that the Jewish leaders who disobeyed the commandments of Antiochus were whipped and many were also crucified, and if infants were found circumcised they and their mothers were killed and the infants hung about the necks of the fathers as they hung on a cross.

Mattathias, a great-grandson of Asamoneus, a priest in Jerusalem, decided to fight back to save his people. Mattahias lived with his sons in Modin, a town on the eastern edge of the Plain of Sharon a few miles east of Joppa, at that time the most southerly seaport along the east coast of the Mediterranean. He was outraged and told his sons that it was better to die for the laws of their God and country than to live as they had been ordered to do. When Antiochus sent some representatives from Antioch to Modin to force compliance on his orders to sacrifice to pagan gods and when they asked Mattahias to make the sacrifices because everyone held him in high esteem and they would follow his example, Mattahias refused. But a traitorous Jew rushed in and made the sacrifice to please the Syrians. Enraged, Mattahias and his sons killed the fellow and Apelles, the king's general who had given the order, and the soldiers who had been sent along to enforce the law. Then Mattahias overthrew the idol and cried out, If anyone is zealous for the laws of our country and for the worship of God, let him follow me. Then he fled into the desert with his sons, leaving all of their possessions in Modin. Many people joined them, taking along whole families.

Several battles were fought with the Jews always being out-numbered but victorious because of their faith. Returning back into Judea, Mattahias began retaking cities and cleansing out the foreign idols and re-establishing the ancient laws of Yahweh, slaying those who opposed him and who were trying to stop him from begin-ning once again the practice of circumcision. After ruling for about a year, Mattahias knew he was dying and had his five sons come to him where he appointed them different tasks. He named Judas Maccabeus as the general of the army.

Judas began purifying the country, organizing an army, and casting out his enemies and putting to death his fellow Jews who had transgressed their laws. A Syrian general, Apollonius, fought against Judas near Modin. Judas rallied his forces and beat the Syrians and killed the general, taking his sword. Judas and his army defeated a second Syrian army near Bethoron, a village just a few miles south of Modin. Antiochus vowed to crush the Jewish rebellion and went east to Persia to replenish his treasury while ordering Lysias, governor of the kingdom, to rid the land of Judas and his army, enslave all of the people, and totally destroy Jerusalem and the temple.

A vast army of almost fifty thousand Syrians and auxiliaries faced Judas and his vastly outnumbered forces near Emmaus. But Judas gave a stirring speech to his men and made them vow to fight. The Syrian general tried a night attack, but Judas found out about it and took his troops away from camp but tricked the Syrians into thinking that they were still there and unaware of danger. Then early the next morning, Judas attacked the Syrian camp where the remaining foreign forces were not prepared for battle. He defeated them and chased the remaining Syrian forces as far south as Idumea.

Judas sent one brother north to Galilee to help free the Jews there from the Gentiles and another brother east across the Jordan to Gilead to bring home the remnants of the Jewish nation living there. He then took the citadel and reclaimed Jerusalem and began cleaning the temple, which had fallen into a deplorable state of ruin and neglect. After the temple was cleansed, they offered burnt offerings on the new altar and lit the candles and celebrated for eight days. He also began rebuilding the walls around the city.

Judas signed a mutual aid pact with the Romans who had begun taking possession of parts of Asia Minor. He admired their armies and their ability to administrate. But Antiochus and his successors continued their wars against the Jews, and Judas was finally killed in battle in 160 BC. His body was laid to rest beside his father in Modin, and he was considered a national hero.

During these times, religious fervor reached a peak with a renewed interest in the Torah, the five books of Moses that contained the law under which they were to live and worship. These were probably written sometime during the fifth century BC when Ezra restored the worship of God in Jerusalem. Books of the prophets were written during the time of Judas and of his brother Simon, who followed him as the leader of the nation, and Simon's son, John Hyrcanus, who also served as the high priest and was named king of Judea. The Psalms and the Book of Daniel were also written during this time. The Book of Daniel predicted the coming of the Messiah when the end of days or the last times had come, announcing the Righteous One, the one who would lead the Jewish people back into a proper relationship with God and establish a kingdom of God on earth for all nations. Some believed that events during that age were bad enough that the last days were surely upon them. Prophets like Isaiah and Zechariah and Jeremiah spoke of a savior of the people. Some of the writings showed him as a warrior king, others as a prince of peace. I suspect most people were hoping for a warrior king who would destroy all of their enemies and let them live in peace. The

Jewish people had struggled for generations against foreign invaders and foreign influence. They were ready for a real leader.

Titus stopped talking and stared off east into the darkening sky which was barely visible in the bright lights of the business and the parking lot. He seemed to pause for a more important part of his story.

It is a wonder that any of them survived, I said.

But people endure, Titus answered. They have to. Life goes on no matter what. One must choose to surrender or fight back. Enough of the Jews fought back for their way of life, for their God, that they did overcome horrible times, events almost beyond our believing, and all this time they were talking more and more about the coming of their Savior, the Righteous One.

I don't want to bore you, Titus continued, but after the death of Judas, leaders became so corrupted and incompetent that Jews began fighting one another, choosing sides by fighting along with Demetrius, king of Damascus and co-ruler of Syria. The king of Judea at that time was Alexander Jonathan, the grandson of Simon, Judas's brother. The Jewish people held Alexander in such contempt that during the Feast of the Tabernacle about 101 BC when he was on the alter and preparing to make sacrifices, people pelted him with citron in their contempt of him because he was not following the ritual correctly and they did not consider him worthy in the first place. Alexander was so enraged that he killed about six thousand of them. A few months later when Alexander took his Greek mercenaries on a campaign against Demetrius, several thousand of his Jewish subjects fought on the side of Demetrius against Alexander, their king. Alexander won in a battle at Bethome and took eight hundred of the Jewish rebels back to Jerusalem with him, and as he was feasting and watching, he had the men crucified, and as those men were hanging there in agony, Alexander had their wives and children brought in and had their throats cut in front of the husbands and fathers who were tied helplessly to their crosses. From that time on, the power of the Maccabees diminished.

And, of course, events like those only added to the chaos in the lives of ordinary citizens, who continued to endure the caprices of their masters. Alexander continued as king for another twenty-five years or so until he died and his wife Alexandra reigned in his place and then their son Aristobulus the Second became king until the Roman general Pompey sacked Jerusalem in sixty-three BC and began a new chapter in the history of the Jewish people.

3

Titus took a deep breath and sighed. After the Romans gained control and named Herod king of Palestine, he said, the course of events for the Jewish people changed drastically, and the desire for the Messiah grew stronger. But let's continue the history lesson, so stay with me.

Pompey had sided with Jonathan, the older brother of Aristobulus, and took Jerusalem and the Temple after a methodical siege and the death of about twelve thousand Jews. Pompey entered the Temple and the holy places where only high priests were admitted. He saw all of the riches like the golden table and the holy candlesticks and the rich spices and about two thousand talents of sacred money; but he touched none of it and then ordered the high priest to cleanse the Temple and allowed the Jews to practice their religion without Roman interference.

Pompey named Jonathan ethnarch and high priest and took Aristobulus and his family back to Rome. All of Palestine became a part of the Roman Empire after that, and Rome began collecting taxes from the Jews. This act was the beginning of tension between the Jews and their Roman masters that led to a horrible war about a hundred years later.

The woes of the Jewish people continued when Crassus, the Roman general in charge of all of Syria, which included Palestine, came to Jerusalem and sacked the Temple taking away at least two thousand talents of money and a golden beam which held the priceless sacred veils in order to pay for his campaign against the Parthians, a powerful kingdom south of the Caspian Sea. But Crassus's campaign was disastrous. He and his entire army perished. But Roman politics flourished, and Julius Caesar came into power. Antipater, king of Idumea, had a son, Herod, who helped the Romans retake parts of Syria that the Parthians had taken after defeating Crassus. Herod became a hero in Galilee after his campaign against the robbers who terrified that part of Palestine. As a reward, the Roman general Antony made Herod king of the Jews with a vote by the Roman senate in 40 BC. Herod went to Judea to wage a war against Antigonus, the last Maccabean king, took it, and returned it to Roman control and talked Antony into beheading Antigonus. As a reward in 37 BC., Julius Caesar confirmed Herod's position as king of Palestine and several provinces east of the Jordan and Idumea south of Judea. Many Jews, especially those in Judea, disliked Herod because in his campaigns many Jews fought against him and were killed. They did not consider him a rightful ruler because he was not a Jew, but an Idumean. They also disliked him because he was a loyal supporter of Rome's right to govern them. At that time, Herod was a good king and did many things for his people, but he had trouble in his family and with his several marriages. He sent away his first wife Doris and his first son Antipater when he fell in love with Mariamme, daughter of Jonathan, who had once been a Maccabean king of Judea. Mariamme held a grudge against Herod for playing a part in the death of Jonathan and the execution of Antigonus, the last Maccabean to rule. As a result of internal bickering, in 20 BC, Herod executed Mariamme, the only wife he ever loved.

Titus paused and took a sip of water, waited for a few moments while I tried to get more comfortable in my chair, and continued, his voice low. I have some memories of those days, he said. If you remember when I first began my story I told you that I had been born six years before Herod executed his second wife, Mariamme. The people who lived in my part of Judea were divided in their opinion of Herod. Some believed that he had brought some stability into their lives and that his close relationship with the Romans meant that they could live in peace. Others thought he was a tyrant and was too harsh on those who disagreed with him.

One thing Herod did that really helped the people is largely lost in history, and it can be argued that he did it to make himself better loved, but he helped the nation through a terrible drought that began two years after I was born and lasted for several years. The lack of rain had caused crops to fail, and when people had used up their reserves, starvation became rampant. Herod had shipments of grain imported from Egypt and gave it to people by using local synagogues as distribution points. He probably spent vast sums of money in those few years and saved many lives.

But he was an arrogant ruler and demanded that leaders swear obedience to him and doled out swift punishment for those who refused except to Pharisees who said they would give obedience only to God, and he allowed the Essenes to go unpunished when they failed to obey him. He ruled a kingdom of vastly diverse people, some who worshiped heathen gods. This caused the Jews who lived outside Palestine to resent Herod's handling of religious matters. Many resented the rapid growth of materialism and a growing divide between the rich and the poor.

Our synagogue was a place where people often met and talked politics, or they talked during the market day in Bethlehem about the rumors coming out of Jerusalem. Augustus Caesar, who had become ruler of Rome in 27 BC, made Herod procurator of all of Syria and bestowed upon him great honors. Some of the men in those tight circles of chatter thought that Herod would make them richer, that they would have easy markets for their crops or animals they produced while others said that he was turning the whole country into another Italy and that he was leading us away from the ways of our ancestors. The Pharisees in the community were very agitated about the growing laxity by many people in following the laws laid down in the Torah.

He is rebuilding the temple, one would say. Some say it will be more magnificent than ever.

I hear that he plans other projects that will please the Romans, another said. He is rebuilding the city of Samaria and renaming it Sebaste in honor of Augustus Caesar and plans to build a seacoast city north of Gaza and name it Arippeum in honor of another Roman.

You just wait and see. We are going to be taxed to death for all of his dreams of greatness.

Careful of what you say, a friend warned him. Some words may sound seditious to certain folks. Don't be too trusting.

As I and other youngsters played nearby or watched the goats or sheep our fathers had brought to market to sell, we listened to what our elders said, but really didn't pay much attention. The days were warm and full of light and of things for young boys to explore. For us the world was full of promise and not at all gloomy.

The one who spoke about increased taxes was correct. Herod did begin to collect taxes for extravagant building projects. He restored the fort on the north side of the temple, turning it into a royal palace for the Romans and named it Antonia, in honor of his friend Antony. He built a royal palace for himself along the west wall of Jerusalem and another palace for himself and his wives near Jericho among the date palm groves. The harbor he was building at Strato's Tower in Samaria was an engineering marvel. He renamed the city Caesarea in honor of Augustus and built an artificial harbor out of giant blocks of rock that would supply a safe harbor for several ships at once. He built a temple out of white marble for Augustus high up in the mountains north of the Sea of Galilee and named it Panium. The village there is Caesarea Philippi. He built other cities like Antipatris, named after his father. He built theaters and gymnasiums and called for games every five years and called them Caesar's games. He built another city north of Jericho and named it Phasuelis after his brother. He built a fortress as a memorial for himself on a mountain top south of Bethlehem and named it Herodium. He built two or three other palaces for himself and his wives near Jericho.

The heavy taxation of the people was the real turning point. Many people were taxed so much that many had to sell their small farms and became destitute, wandering the land trying to survive as day laborers or beggars or robbers, doing anything to survive. By the time my father paid the temple tax of ten percent and the tax imposed by the Romans and the tax demanded by Herod, our family barely survived, losing almost fifty percent of our possessions by tax collectors. No wonder that in a few short years the people turned against Herod, and he responded by becoming even harsher. He had spies everywhere and punished the most vocal critics by bringing many of them to the citadel Hyrcania just south of Jerusalem and having them put to death.

It was during this time that Herod began the reconstruction of the temple in 20 BC. The project was on a massive scale and involved thousands of workmen. The enlarged area covered about thirty acres, and the outer walls were immense with huge blocks of stones. Colonnaded porches were built along the outer walls, the south one named the Royal Porch and the east one named Solomon's Porch. A number of gates led in from the city. The Temple was built on the highest point in the north central part of the enclosed area. It had a wall around it that shut out the Gentiles and allowed in only the Jews, many coming from far-off lands to celebrate feast days like the Passover. Anyone could come into the outer courtyard, which was called the Court of the Gentiles. Nearer the Temple, steps led up to the Court of the Women and the money boxes. An entryway and steps led up to the Court of the Men of Israel, and more steps led up to the Temple area itself that only priests could enter. It was a magnificent building built out of white marble and had golden plates on the eastern front. It was 172 feet high and 172 feet long with a porch 172 feet broad. The Temple was finished in a year and a half, but construction continued on other parts of the temple area for seventy more years or so. The temple was a showplace, a drawing card for Jerusalem. Someone said that from a distance it looked like a mountain covered with snow.

But most importantly, it was a meeting place for the Jewish nation as Jews came to observe the different festivals. Just imagine you as a Jew seeing that magnificent building as you approach the city. Then inside Jerusalem you mingle with people from all over the known world speaking in different tongues, selling their wares, crowding the narrow streets. And then you go to the southern gate and go to the ritual bath and through the gate and up the stairs which lead to the Court of the Gentiles. It was thronged with people and with animals brought for sacrifice and money changers and speakers haranguing small groups in Solomon's Porch and people speaking in many different languages. And then you enter through the gate that separates the Jews from the Gentiles where you are suddenly separated from the world. You are family now, gathered together with your one God, separated from the world, speaking Aramaic and renewing old friendships-bonding. Coming home once again.

But all of that magnificence created a problem for Herod. The wealth of the temple and the rich clothing of the priests and Levites and Scribes wasn't lost on the poor people who couldn't afford to buy two doves for their sacrifice. Besides, as the poor mingled with other Jews, the differences became more evident because the wealthy ones wore much finer fabric in their prayer shawls and their loose white robes. The shawl was a reminder of the separation of the Israelites from other people.

History doesn't seem to be a smooth process, but rather it jerks along, slumbering for a stretch of time and then awakens by some off-hand incident. Even as an older boy and entering manhood through a ritual when I reached thirteen, I saw the differences between the poor and desperate and the rich merchants and wealthy landowners. Most of the rich had slipped into Roman habits and were disdainful of those who worked their lands or tried to buy from them. I could smell their perfumed bodies and oiled hair and see their hard eyes looking over the men who had come early in the morning to work as day laborers to harvest crops, the weak and older ones being pushed aside by those who would work for almost no wages. I know, because my brother Joel and I were in those crowds of desperate men jock-eying for position, and we were often chosen because young workers are much more agile and can climb into the upper limbs of an olive tree like monkeys. We both would work for others when we weren't tending to our own trees or vines or flock of sheep. We needed the money to survive.

And I listened to the hushed conversations of the poor as they told of the death of a wife or a child because of hunger or some disease brought on by starvation. The men talked of the old days and of the messages in the Torah of a coming Savior of the people, a Messiah, a Righteous One, who would restore them back to God. They would tell of a brother or a neighbor who had left and had joined with a group of other desperate men living off of whatever they could steal. And as they talked in hesitant, broken voices, they had to be careful of what they said about king Herod because Herod paid good money to informers. Even though he had built the temple, he did not trust his people.

Some thought that Herod was losing his mind as he aged. Rumors circulated about trouble in his family among his several wives and children. After he had executed his second wife, Mariamme, he had married another Mariamme, a daughter of Simon, the high priest. His fourth wife was Malthace, a Samaritan. His other wives were Cleopatra, Pallas, and Elpis. Herod had two other wives whose names have been lost. His first wife, Doris, was a real troublemaker, and her son, Antipater, was the one who spread the gossip about how some family members wanted to replace Herod as king. And he became ill and much more desperate about the intrigues of his family. In 7 BC, in his rage, he executed two of his sons, Alexander and Aristobulus, sons of the ill-fated Mariamme. He seemed to be punishing all of his subjects in his rage. Several whispered of revolt, but only faintly. If Herod was suspicious of anyone, he had them strangled and silenced.

And then in 6 BC the Messiah was born in Bethlehem, and I don't need to repeat that part of the story. What is apparent at that time was that Herod was approaching a critical time in his illness, which by what people were whispering was that he was rotting away inside. The arrival of the Zoroastrian priests looking for the new-born king of the Jews must have really triggered Herod's madness. Knowing that he was approaching death, he tried to kill himself, but his servants stopped him from committing that act.

But before I continue, Titus said, let's take a little break. What I have been talking about so far is mostly background material. From now on the events will be during the life of Jesus. And that is the main purpose of my story. Titus stood and stretched, and I also got out of my chair and looked about me. I tried a sip of my forgotten cup of cappuccino, but it was cold and unappetizing.

Did you ever see Herod? I asked.

Titus chuckled. No, I don't believe so. If I had been close, I would have had to bow. It is said that many people turned their backs when Herod passed. That must have enraged him. But if we have relaxed enough, perhaps I should get on with my story. I will begin with the death of Herod and the beginning of the end of the Jewish nation at the beginning of the modem era.

4

All of Judea was in an uproar with the antics of a mad and dying king, Titus said.

Knowing that he was dying, Herod named three of his sons to succeed him. Philip, the son of his fifth wife, Cleopatra, was to inherit Trachonitis and the neighboring countries. Antipas was to be tetrarch of Galilee, and Archelaus was to be king of Judea. These last two sons were of his fourth wife, Malthace, the Samaritan. The Romans had given him permission to name his heirs, but they wouldn't be official until the action had been approved by the Roman senate. And these were unpopular choices because the people resented being ruled by someone who was part Samaritan.

By this time, I had made my way back into Judea. I and the men with me had escorted Joseph and Mary and Jesus into Egypt far enough to ensure their safety, and then my fellow bandits turned back east toward Gaza while I boarded a boat shipping pottery to Joppa and worked for my passage back into Herod's kingdom. I wasn't worried about being taken for my crime because the country was so unsettled that an ordinary-looking person went unnoticed.

The roadway between Joppa and Jerusalem was crowded with people talking of Herod and his illness, and most of them were afraid because life had become so unpredictable for them. Who knew what their mad king might do next. Rumor had it that Herod was dying. But the winter rains had begun to show the first signs of spring with farmers sowing their fields between Joppa and Lydia, and the air was crisp and fresh as I followed the road into the hills toward Emmaus.

I slept overnight near Emmaus with a shepherd whom I had helped in birthing some lambs. We talked of the lives of common folk and how they were suffering from high taxes and the loss of land and how afraid people were of Herod and the Romans. I couldn't tell him of my family or of my recent trip to Egypt because I could trust no one to keep my secret. But it was comforting to be by the warming fire with him and see the brilliant stars, sleeping in the open with one of my friend's sheepskin blankets to keep me warm.

By early afternoon the next day I neared Jerusalem and could see the temple gleaming in the sunshine. The day was cool, the road crowded with people from many different nations making their way to the holy city. Jerusalem sits on the crest of a hill about 2,500 feet above sea level, so the air had a different quality than that on the plain east of Joppa. I entered Jerusalem at the Joppa Gate and was swept along in the crush of people busy with their markets or trades, arguing loudly over deals, beggars pleading with passersby, the air suddenly heavy with the smells of cooking foods and unwashed bodies and human waste.

I made my way into the temple by taking the bridge across the Tyropean Valley and through the West Gate and into the Court of the Gentiles and through the stalls of the money changers and the merchants selling doves to poor people who wanted to offer sacrifices. Suddenly the mob of people shifted toward Solomon's Porch on the east side of the temple, and I followed, curious to see what the hubbub was all about. I squeezed my way through the crowd until I was opposite the east side of the temple and went under Solomon's Porch in back of the pressing bodies. Some young men had let themselves down by ropes to a golden eagle that hung above the great door of the Temple. They were chopping away with axes at the supports holding the golden eagle. Two men were standing beneath them with their arms upraised ready to address the crowd.

That is Judas, son of Sepphoris, and Matthias, son of Margalus, someone said. They are great teachers of the Torah and the laws. They teach young men every day at the Royal Porch. That must be some of their students cutting down that abomination.

Now hear me, sons of Israel, Judas yelled, quieting the crowd. These young men are doing the work of God. You all know that it is against the law to display idols in the likeness of animals or men, yet our king had this placed here above the doors leading to the Tabernacle, our most holy and sacred place. As we talked with these young men about this statue, they pleaded with us to let them act, to rid the holy place of this idol, this very image of the Roman empire. They said it would be a glorious thing to die for the laws of their God and country.

People yelled their approval when Judas had finished and had turned to look up as the golden eagle came crashing down at his feet onto the Court of the Priests. We who were watching could see it all because the Temple is raised above the level of the Court of Gentiles. Other young men rushed in and began cutting at the fallen statue. By that time soldiers had come rushing in from Fortress Antonio and were clubbing their way through the crowd of onlookers. Some of the young men fled back among those watching, but Judas and Mathias and about forty of the young men stood beside the fallen idol defiantly facing the guards.

Our actions are just, Matthias said to the captain. Those of us standing here admit that we have acted justly in accordance with the laws of God. Take us to your courts of law and we will plead before the Sanhedrin, our legal recourse since King Herod has died, as we have been told.

King Herod lives, old man, replied the captain. And we will take you and your followers to him at Jericho for punishment. About half of the soldiers surrounded their prisoners while the others faced the crowd of people cowing away from the clubs and drawn swords. I stood where I was, my back against the massive outer wall of the temple compound, letting my gaze shift from the soldiers to the defiant knot of young men with their two teachers.

Disperse the crowd, the captain ordered, and soldiers began clubbing the nearest people while others fled with me among them. Some of those clubbed were lying senseless on the paved ground or holding broken arms. Judas and Matthias and the young men were being bound together for their trip to Jericho, a distance of about fifteen miles.

I hurried out the North Gate and took the road to Jericho, getting away from the rabble heading for the west gates or those to the south. By this time it was a little after noon, and I should have been hungry, but I had no appetite. I knew the fate of those two great scholars and their young followers.

Two days later Herod was carried into the theater in Jericho where he had assembled the principal men of Judea to act as a court. Herod was so feeble that he lay on a couch and told them of the act of Judas and Matthias and their followers and then began recounting all of the great things that he had accomplished in Judea like the building of the temple that he hoped would be a memorial to his rule.

These men tried to affront me by their act, he said hoarsely between gasps, struggling to breathe. What they did was sacrilegious and against the wishes of God. So judge them. He glared at the assembly, trembling in anger.

The frightened leaders said that what Judas and Matthias and their followers had done was without their knowledge or consent. Herod, hardly able to speak, ordered that Judas and Mathias and the young men who had lowered themselves down by rope to cut off the golden eagle would be burned while the others would be executed in the usual way. The order was carried out that evening, those to be burned tied and thrown onto a huge stack of precious wood, where some of the young men screamed in agony and where the voice of Judas could be heard praying until the flames stopped him. That night there was a full eclipse of the moon, and as I understand it, Titus said, that eclipse has allowed your scholars to date the event. Our nation's heroes died on March 13, 4 BC.

Herod's anger continued unchecked. He sent letters to all of the leaders of every village, town, and city in Judea to assemble with him in Jericho. When they had all gathered, he had them arrested and taken to the hippodrome in Jerusalem where he ordered them held and asked his sister, Salome, to have them all killed when he died. Do away with them so that people will have something to really mourn about when I die, not just pretend at the passing of their king, Herod said with tears in his eyes. Those listening promised to obey.

Then Herod, near death's door, tried to kill himself with a knife that he was using to pare an apple, but a cousin stopped him. Upon hearing that his father had killed himself, his son Antipater went about trying to make himself king in his father's place. Herod, when learning of Antipater's plans, had Antipater put to death as Caesar had suggested. Five days later, seventy-year-old Herod died after serving as king of Palestine for thirty-seven years.

Salome and her husband went to Jerusalem and released Herod's prisoners from the hippodrome and told the guards that Herod had changed his mind, and after the leaders had fled their captivity, Salome told the guards about Herod's death. Next, the people assembled in the theater in Jericho where Herod's new edict about his successors was read to the assembly. Archelaus, was the new king of Judea, and people promised him that they would accept his rule and wished God's blessing upon him. According to Herod's will, Archelaus was to rule Judea, Idumea, and Samaria. Philip was named tetrarch of Batnaea, Trachonitis, and Aurantis north and northeast of Galilee. And Antipas was tetrarch of Galilee and Perea. Perea is east of the Sea of Galilee.

The funeral Archelaus held for his father was fit for a king.

Herod's body was dressed in a purple robe, and on his head he had a diadem and above it a golden crown and a scepter in his right hand. He was carried on a golden bier with purple cloth embroidered with precious stones draped upon the sepulcher. His sons and relatives walked beside him. His army went at the head of the procession in a regular military manner, and following his relatives came his regular guards of Thracians, Germans, and Gauls. Following them were five hundred of his servants and the important people of all of Judea. The caravan of mourners went from Jericho past Jerusalem and Bethlehem to Herodium, Herod's fortress home, where he had demanded that he be buried.

And many of us common folk tagged along, careful to stay away from the armed guards but hoping for some stray tidbit from the rich procession. We were awed, yet angered, at such a show of wealth, our stomachs growling for the lack of food. We knew that according to custom the funeral rites would last for seven days and that Archelaus would have to feed everyone, including us. He was really trying to placate us and win us over to his side.

And because of his desire to be popular, after the funeral he made his first of many blunders.

Archelaus dressed in white and went to the temple where he tried to please the people following him, and then he sat upon a golden throne and asked them to tell him of their grievances against his father. I am not your king, yet, he told them, until it is approved by the Romans, who have control of our affairs, but I will listen to your complaints and do what I can do. Those crowding before him asked that he ease their tax burdens and get rid of duties on the goods they imported. And they asked that he release those imprisoned by his father. He agreed to their demands.

When the mourning period for Herod was over, the day for observing Passover had come, and as usual Jews from many parts of the country arrived and filled Jerusalem. During the period of mourning, more and more voices cried out for those put to death over the cutting down of the golden eagle, and for the deaths of the two great teachers and the young men and their rabbis. People protested against Joazar, the high priest that Herod had named, because of the cutting down of the golden eagle. The cries spread from the temple area to all of Jerusalem.

Archelaus sent his general and his troops into the temple area to calm the crowd, but the crowd threw stones at them, so the soldiers withdrew. Sensing a victory, the people became more clamorous in calling for a new high priest and justice against those people who had approved the deaths of those who had cut down the hated idol. In order to stop the growing rebellion, Archelaus sent his whole army against the protesters, his cavalry into the surrounding hills, and his foot soldiers into the city and the temple. About three thousand protesters were killed, some in the temple as they were offering sacrifices. The Passover riots were hardly over before Archelaus went to Rome to claim his right to rule Judea. He left his brother Philip in charge of things back home, which was a big mistake.

Varus, the Roman governor of all of Syria, had brought a legion of soldiers from Antioch to Jerusalem anticipating further trouble when Archelaus left for Rome, and trouble erupted fifty days after Passover. Many Jews from Galilee and Idumea and Perea and other areas east of the Jordan had stayed around Jerusalem to continue their protest against the slaughter of their fellow Jews and to observe the Festival of Pentecost. They began setting up defensive positions to fight the Romans and the army of Archelaus. One of the most fierce battles occurred in the temple area where the Jews fought the Romans to a stand-still by getting on top of some of the cloisters and shooting arrows down onto the Romans. But the Romans set the cloisters on fire and burned the defenders. Seeing parts of their new temple area burning enraged the Jews even more.

The rebellion had spread into Galilee and parts of Samaria and Idumea to such an extent that Varus decided to stop the non-sense. He sent another legion from Galilee though Samaria where he destroyed several towns and went on south into Judea where he burned Emmaus and several other towns and took Jerusalem. And to show he meant business, he had two thousand of the leaders crucified. The Arabs, out of their hatred for Herod, had fought with the rebels in Idumea, but the Romans took over there and sent the Arabs back home. When conditions had settled down, Varus left a part of a brigade at Jerusalem and went back to Antioch.

Unrest continued for the next several years because small groups of men attached themselves to self-proclaimed messiahs and went on different missions in trying to seize control of the country. It was during this time that Joseph and Mary had brought Jesus back to Nazareth. And I am sure that the family saw Sepphoris burning. A young hothead by the name of Judas, a son of Hezekias, who had revolted earlier and had been killed by Herod, had attacked Sepphoris and had broken open the Roman armory there and had armed his rebels. A little later, a Roman captain had recaptured Sepphoris, set it afire, and had taken the Jews in the city captive and had sent them off as slaves. All the holy family had to do was walk up the hill just north of Nazareth and look north to see that lovely city burning.

I have a hard time keeping all of these Judases straight, I interrupted.

It was a popular name back then, Titus answered. Remember, Judas Maccabeus is one of the most loved people in Jewish history. Do you know that Jesus had a brother named Judas?

One of Herod's slaves, a tall and robust fellow named Simon, declared himself king and put a diadem on his head. He raided near Jericho, burning the royal palace at Jericho, and allowed his followers to carry off plunder. He then went around the country and burned several more of Herod's palaces. Simon's career was cut short, literally, when his army was destroyed and his head cut off by a general of Archelaus's army. A man named Theudas led a group of rebels and burned Herod's royal palace at Amathus by the river Jordan.

There were dozens of uprisings in Palestine and especially in Judea, but I'll cut it short by telling about just one more. Remember my telling of staying overnight with a shepherd near Emmaus on my way back to Jerusalem and home? His name was Anthronges, and he was a tall, strong man with a royal bearing, a quality about him that set him apart from most common folk. He and his four brothers rebelled against the foreigners coming into Judea to quell the uprisings. In the beginning, I became a part of his group. He fought against the Romans and Archelaus's soldiers with real daring, not caring whether he lived or died. But after a few weeks he put a diadem on his head and declared himself king and held counsels about what we should do for the people. I remember once we attacked a company of Romans bringing food and weapons to the army at Emmaus, and we defeated them and killed a number of them. But I left Anthronges when he began establishing trials for Jews who he believed had sold out to the foreigners. The shepherd was turning into a tyrant himself.

The people were leaderless. Conditions were chaotic with more and more people becoming homeless and desperate for food and shelter, fighting one another over the bits of grain or fruit left over after harvest, begging pitifully along roadways or at the gates of cities, dying from starvation, especially the children and the old.

It was during this time that Augustus Caesar made Herod's decisions about his sons ruling Palestine official and sent Archelaus back to Judea to assume rule over his restless people. Archelaus, angered over how his subjects had rebelled, treated them so harshly that the people from Judea and Samaria sent ambassadors to Caesar asking for relief. Caesar brought Archelaus back to Rome and exiled him to Vienna, an outpost city in Gaul. He then took control of the government in Judea and sent Coponius, a member of the equestrians, the most influential group of extremely wealthy Romans, to rule Judea as procurator. The year was 6 AD. It was the same year that young Jesus stayed at the temple after Passover to learn from the temple's famous teachers while his mother, Mary, and his father, Joseph, searched for him, worried sick about him, of course, because of the uncertain times, leaving their other children with their traveling friends while they searched for their blessed son.

And it is at this point that my story attempts to show you what times were like during the Messiah's growing years and on into his ministry. If you know what his world was like during his lifetime, you would have a better understanding of what and why he taught and ministered to the people he loved.

Titus leaned back in his chair and closed his eyes. The memories seemed to be draining him, so I went back into the coffee shop and bought another cup of coffee for myself and brought back another cup of water for him. What he had been telling me about conditions in Palestine before Jesus was born and during his stay in Egypt and his return to Nazareth was difficult to follow, terrible. How could people treat one another so? And then I thought of our recent and current history.

5

Titus closed his eyes, remembering.

The Roman baggage train stretched a hundred yards winding its way up the road from Joppa to Emmaus to bring food and weapons to the small garrison there. Titus crouched behind a wall along with several other bedraggled men in Anthronges's army. The night air was cold, the moon down. A shift of wind carried a whirl of dust with it. His mouth was dry That always happened just before a battle, he thought. He carried a lance and a short sword. Some other rebels with him had only staffs or scythes. They weren't really prepared to fight a disciplined force, but God was on their side, they believed. He could hear the creaking wheels of the loaded wagons and the soft curses of the soldiers having this duty when they could be in camp resting.

"Let them come nearer," Anthronges whispered. "Be patient. Pass the word." Anthronges had scouts following the wagon train and had been delighted when he had seen that it had not camped at Gazara but that its commander had decided to make it to Emmaus with a forced march. He had decided quickly to attack the contingent of drivers and guards that night and had brought along only two dozen of his faithful followers. The soldiers were really Syrian conscripts dressed in Roman uniforms and trained by Roman officers.

The lead wagon and a few guards passed the first part of the Jewish rebels, the tired oxen straining to pull the heavy wagon up the steeper incline. Titus, in the middle of the line of attackers, ducked lower behind the piled rocks. When the lead wagon was even with the last of the rebels, Anthronges let out a wild yell, ululating like a native from the land of Sheba. They all screamed as they leaped from cover surprising the Syrian troops. The oxen stopped gladly, moaning for air, and the drivers leaped for cover leaving the fighting up to the guards.

Titus attacked the nearest soldier who had turned, surprised at the screaming and rushing bodies. The soldier was dressed in a Roman helmet and had on a breastplate and shin guards, his short cape swirling as he turned. Titus thrust at the Syrian's throat while chopping with his sword at the soldier's arms and hands. The soldier had left his small, round shield on one of the wagons, and so he was at a disadvantage in the surprise attack. Titus had only a small area of face and throat that made a target, but like most shepherds and farmers, he had a keen sense of direction when using a staff, a lance in this case, and he scored quickly, catching the Syrian just below the chin with his first thrust. The soldier twisted, gagging, and clutching at the fatal wound before Titus ran on into the battle and left the soldier in the road on his hands and knees and then falling forward.

The battle ended quickly, and Anthronges had some of his men become drivers of the abandoned wagons. They did not pursue the drivers who had fled their loads because they were natives of some coastal town near Joppa, not enemies. They left the road quickly and followed a wadi south and west, some of the men following the wagons and the main group brushing out tracks. They would have to hide what they had captured before daylight because they knew they would be pursued by Roman forces. Anthronges had lived all his life in the area, so he knew where a grove of sycamores was located that would give them some cover for a few hours. All Titus wanted was a place to sleep.

Titus still had his eyes closed when I returned with my coffee and his water. Did you have a nice nap? I asked, handing him the water.

You caught me dozing, perhaps, but I was just remembering, he said, taking a sip of the cold water. This tastes good, he said. Better than the water from Siloam.

Did you ever go home again? I asked.

Yes, Titus said. After I left the shepherd's army, I wandered through the land working at odd jobs and avoiding military patrols. I went home again when I was thirty-two, slipping into our farm during the night because I didn't want someone around Bethlehem to recognize me and turn me in to the authorities, which some desperate person might do, someone in need of some food, perhaps. My brother, Joel, didn't recognize me at first, but then we had a joyful reunion. In those ten years since I had been home, my mother had died and my father had become infirm, leaving most of the work up to Joel and his sons.

Titus knocked softly on the door after hesitating for a few moments. He was afraid of what he might discover, almost sorry that he had decided to return home. No one answered. He knocked again a little louder and then heard some noise inside. Then someone unlatched the door and opened it a crack. Behind the partially opened door, Titus could see a middle-aged man, looking at him suspiciously.

"Joel, is that you?" Titus asked.

"Titus." Joel opened the door wider and threw his arms around his brother. "Titus, oh, my brother. Blessed be the most holy I thought that I would never see you again. Come in, come in and out of the night air."

Joel lighted a lamp so that they could see one another better. Bodies began stirring in the far corners of the room because of the sudden light. "As you can see," Joel said, "my family now lives in the main house since Mother died two years ago talking of you with her last words. Father isn't well, so we take care of him, and I have a son living in your old house and another in mine, but yet to find a bride."

"I cannot stay long," Titus said. "The authorities would like nothing more than to arrest me for what I have done. But I will stay the night and tomorrow but leave the following morning."

"These are troubling times, my brother. We have all prayed for your safe-keeping, and our neighbors hold you in high regard and still mourn for your loss as we all do. They will remain silent."

"I want to visit the graves of my wife and son now," Titus said. "That is one of the reasons I have returned. How often have I thought of my actions those ten years ago when I left Esther there on the ground and my young son Benjamin, killed by that old and evil king."

"We gave them a proper burial in the sight of the Lord," Joel said softly. "I will take you to them now." They walked through a portion of the vineyard and through the olive grove to a ledge of limestone rocks. There was enough moonlight for them to see dimly where the graves were marked. Titus could smell the rich loam and the sheep fold on the pasture area above the ledge.

"I know you want to be with them for a while," Joel said. "I will wait for you at home. We still have much to talk about."

I visited the graves of my wife and son and mother, Titus continued. Joel and his family were prospering because of the Roman garrison at Fortress Antonia. The Syrian forces that Varus had left there were given two pounds of meat and grain a day per man. So it was a relief to see that the grief the Jewish people had suffered the last few years had hardly touched my family.

But my brother told me that in two days he had to go to Bethlehem and report to a Roman official at the synagogue. All Jews in Palestine who owned property were to be entered into a census and their holdings recorded. Joel would have to declare the amount of land our family owned, the number of trees in the olive grove, the size of the vineyard, the number of sheep and animals, and the number of buildings. The census was one of the first orders issued by Coponius, the Roman procurator, and the Jews were furious about the order. A census was a form of subordination, and above all else, the Jews demanded freedom, which made them quarrelsome and contentious. We like nothing more than a good argument, Titus said, smiling at his memories. I knew there would be trouble.

My brother was outraged because the tax collector would be a Jew, a publican. But I knew that Coponius and his Roman garrison would enforce the law without mercy. Several years before, Varus had put down a series of revolts throughout the country and crucified people by the hundreds. Each town in Judea that had been the center of a revolt witnessed those executions. I remember the scene near Emmaus where my good friend, the shepherd, was crucified along with a number of his followers. He lasted for more than a day before the ravens moved in. The rebels were left to rot where they hung. I will never forget the smell.

I talked with Joel about what I had experienced and that he needed to obey the edict no matter how much he may resent it, that conditions would change and that perhaps the prophecies of the Messiah would come. He knew of my experience twelve years before when the Lord had revealed to me the true Messiah, Jesus, newly born and being held in his mother's arms in that simple room, a stable beneath the inn in Bethlehem. And I told him of meeting the family on the road to Egypt and of my involvement in helping them on to Egypt. The prophecies are being fulfilled, I told him. Be patient and we will live to see our people free.

The next day while Joel and his sons were working, I hid inside and visited with my father.

Titus could sense that his father was dying. Eli was an old man, his body twisted and racked with pain, his fingers crooked, the knuckles swollen. But he was alert and hugged Titus when Titus bent over him. "My son, my son, why did you stay away so long?" Eli whispered.

"I have sinned in the eyes of the Lord, Father, and wanted to bring no harm to you or the family," Titus answered. "And I dare not stay and shame you further. Forgive me."

"When have I not forgiven you? What you may have done was caused by others. Our God is testing us to see if we are worthy of salvation. I believe in the Messiah, the Righteous One, who will deliver us from our enemies. You told us of your encounter with the Blessed One, and I believe in him and in you, my son." Eli looked at Titus and touched his cheek. "You also are to do great things, Titus. Your destiny is before you."

We talked of many things, Titus said.

Before daylight early the next morning, I left my family and slipped by Bethlehem and entered a narrow valley which flows east to the Dead Sea. The way down was steep and narrow and difficult because it was dark and the sandstone cliffs closed in, making the way down the dry stream bed even more difficult. I had brought along a water bag and some dried figs, so I was in no hurry. Occasionally I had to climb over huge boulders that had tumbled down into the ravine, but just before sunrise, I made it out to the sandy stretch between the towering cliffs and the Dead Sea.

The rising sun made those sienna-colored cliffs glorious, but I knew the late summer heat would be almost unbearable because the sea is 2,600 feet below sea level, the air oppressive. It always amazes me at the sudden change in geography in that area. Just a few miles east of Bethlehem the land changes from green trees and fields to desert with only some thorn bushes clinging to the barren hills. The Desert of Judea, on the east side of the hills running through Palestine, gets only two or so inches of rain a year while Bethlehem gets fifteen or twenty.

But I stopped for only a few moments, ate some of the figs and drank some water and hurried north to the entrance of the Kidron Valley, which flows from Jerusalem to the Dead Sea. I was taking this route because I wanted to avoid Roman patrols. I was using a trail only the desperate would follow. I was beginning to tire because the journey from Bethlehem to the Dead Sea was about fifteen miles and the distance to Kidron Valley was about five. The way up the valley was steep because it rises about 4,000 feet in twenty miles.

By noon I began looking for a shallow cave or someplace where I could find some shade and spend the rest of the day before going on up to Jerusalem. The chalk and sand cliffs were dotted with splits, weather-worn depressions, and I found a place where people had left the valley floor and climbed upward toward a ledge about sixty feet above the valley floor. There I found a shallow cave and shade. People had been there before me, but I decided to rest there, hoping no one would join me.

The day was almost unbearably hot, but I was in shade with my goatskin of water and waited patiently for the sun to set behind the ridges. No one traveled that valley pathway all day long. Early the next morning I left my cave and clambered down to the valley floor and began my fifteen-mile climb up to Jerusalem. Near the top of the valley and just before it flattens out south of the city, a series of tombs had been dug into the rock walls, stones covering the entrances, the final resting place of rich Jews. A small cluster of houses was on the slope of the hill forming the eastern slope of Kidron which went on up the east side of Jerusalem.

Before long, I went through the rich gardens where the Kidron and the Hinnom valleys joined together just south of the city walls. At the Fountain Gate, I was stopped by a tax collector and a Roman sentry who stood guard beside the table. They stopped me and made me prove that I was bringing nothing into the city to sell. Tolls were collected on all products or salable items going into or coming out of Jerusalem. It was at that moment that I knew I had to be careful because the Romans were serious-they were going to establish law and order throughout the entire area. They let me pass, and I went on up the Tyropean Valley and by the King's Garden, which was watered by water from the Pool of Siloam. As I went on up the road, I bought a melon from a vendor. Beyond the garden the west slope of the Tyropean Valley was filled with houses of working families. The rich people lived on up the hill and west of the temple.

My main purpose of entering Jerusalem instead of bypassing it was that I needed water, and I wanted to visit the Pool of Siloam, a holy place in Jewish history. The pool was dug into a slope with the north wall solid rock. It was about seventy-five feet long by seventy-one feet wide and walled. A few steps led down into the pool area. An arcade had been built around the west and east sides that helped shade the pilgrims who came to see and use the pool. A tunnel had been dug into the north wall from which water flowed into the pool itself, which was about fifty-eight feet long, eighteen feet wide, and about nineteen feet deep but never filled. Steps led down to the water.

The tunnel had been dug long ago to connect Siloam with Gihon Spring, which was outside the east wall of Jerusalem and upstream. An ancient king of Israel, Hezekiah, had ordered the tunnel to be dug because he knew that Jerusalem needed a better source of water inside its walls to withstand a siege. An Assyrian army had invaded the land and was threatening Jerusalem. The tunnel had been dug through solid rock and was more than 1,700 feet long, twisting and turning, maybe to bypass the royal tombs or to follow easier digging, but workers had worked from both ends, joining in the middle. For most of the way, it was large enough that a person could walk through it standing up.

The area around the pool was crowded with pilgrims, some gathered in groups talking loudly, agitated. Others were down by the water dipping into the pool, some praying. Several beggars were working the crowd. Near the east end of the pool several workers were removing blocks of dressed stone, some of the men chest deep in water attaching nets to some of the blocks that had tumbled into the pool. I made my way through the people and went to the north end where I found a dipper for people who wanted to drink the water flowing from the tunnel. I drank my fill, filled my water bag, and then joined some men under the west arcade. The arcade shaded the area, and it was pleasant.

"Welcome, stranger," a man said, indicating that Titus could sit beside him and join the group. "Have you traveled far?"

"Some distance," Titus replied. The stranger's question was a little presumptuous, but Titus didn't mind. "What are the workers doing?" Titus asked to change the subject.

"Several months ago a watch tower beside the outer wall of the city that you can see there going up the Ophel where it connects with the wall of the temple collapsed, and some of its blocks came crashing down into the pool and killed several people. It was a terrible thing to be worshiping here by this sacred water and be crushed while praying. Priests spent days purifying the area." The man was a citizen of the city and knew all the latest gossip. Titus cut up the melon that he had brought with him and shared it, which made him a more accepted member of the group.

"Are you going to pay taxes on what you make?" one of the men asked another. "You work all day in that shop of yours making pottery, and now when you sell it part of the money goes into Roman pockets."

"It's the law," the man answered. "I don't like it any more than the rest of you, but there is nothing I can do about it. The rich and powerful make all the rules, and we have to live with them."

"Not all of us do," another said. Up in Galilee a man from Gamala named Judas is stirring up a revolt. He says that if we pay the taxes, we are slaves to the Romans."

"I am no man's slave," someone replied hotly.

"What is the penalty for not paying?" another asked. "Prison. Or they can take your property."

"So what choice do we have?"

"It all depends on whether or not you want to survive," an older man answered. "We all remember the battle that shook our city several years ago, the one that weakened the tower that those men are dredging out of the pool."

"These are terrible times," his friend said. "The prophets predicted that our people would be saved by a messiah, someone who would cleanse the land and deliver us from what we are suffering right now. The High Priest, Joazar, says we should pay."

"Don't count on a messiah rescuing us from the Romans. We all remember those crucified rebels outside our city walls, strung out along the road to Joppa. Some of them had called themselves messiahs. Look what good it did them or us."

The group was huddled together and getting louder in their conversation. Suddenly a worker in the water began choking and coughing, struggling to breathe. He had been under water fastening the net to a block. Titus and his group rushed to the edge of the pool as did others around the area. A worker pounded the choking man on the back helping him to get back his breath, and then they both began laughing.

"I'm fine, brothers," he shouted to the onlookers. "And ready to celebrate. This is the last stone we are hauling out of the pool. Our work is almost done."

Titus and the others went back under the arcade and continued their conversation. "Now the priests can purify the pool once again and get it ready for the Feast of Tabernacles that will be with us in a few weeks." Water from the Pool of Siloam was used on the last day of the feast when Levites came to the pool with a golden pitcher to bring water back to pour over the sacrifice in memory of the water from the rock of Rephidim, the rock that Moses struck and brought forth water for his thirsty people.

It was at this time that Titus saw a brown, skeletal hand reaching in behind them to grab some of the melon rinds the group had thrown aside. The ragged, starving man was gnawing on the green flesh, sucking and chewing. The man tried to pull away when Titus turned to him, but Titus grabbed the man's skinny arm, restraining him.

"Don't be afraid, neighbor," Titus said. "We aren't going to harm you. Besides, there is no nourishment in what we have thrown away."

"Food is food when you are starving," the beggar replied.

"Here is something better," Titus said and handed the man a handful of dried figs from his pouch. "God go with you and protect you."

"Thank you, thank you, and may God bless you also for your kindness."

Titus stood and said goodbye to the group and made his way out of the pool area.

The men were all citizens of Jerusalem and had all the latest gossip, Titus said. From them I learned of a new revolt in Galilee led by Judas, a Gaulonite from Gamala, a city on the east side of the Sea of Galilee. He had crossed over into Galilee and had gained many followers. I decided to go to Galilee and learn more about this revolt against Rome and its new taxes.

6

I left the pool and took Herodian Street north to a street just south of the temple wall and exited at the Horse Gate where a tax collector and a guard searched me for any possible merchandise leaving the city. By then the hour was getting late, so I followed the path down into the Kidron Valley and went north. I decided to stop at the orchard at Gethsemane and help myself to any fruit that may yet be on the trees. I was able to find some figs by climbing a tree, and I gathered several pomegranates by searching through the fruit for the ones ripening, but most were still not ready to harvest. They had several weeks to go. That night several people slept with me in the garden, huddling away from one another. Travelers had to be alert because they became easy targets for robbers.

The next day I joined some others going down to Jericho, the road looping down quickly and the air becoming more humid as we began approaching the Jordan River Valley. Later that afternoon I helped some workers loading bunches of dates onto a wagon, and they gave me a sackful for my work. The Jordan Valley was the most productive area in Palestine, well-watered on both sides. I spent the night at the ford of the Jordan east of Jericho with other travelers, and the next day crossed over into Perea and headed north on the east side of the Jordan. Jews did not travel through Samaria back then because to do so would make them unclean, and being purified was a complicated process. Besides, it was dangerous.

Grapes were usually harvested during the time of the Feast of Tabernacles, but fruit doesn't ripen at the same time, so some of the bunches were being gathered. I helped harvest grapes for two days. At one of the vineyards, the owner fed his workers a bowl of hot lentils and some bread, a most generous gesture. I spent four days making the journey up the valley to the ford near Ennabris. Back then the Jordan had only two easy crossings, one just south of where the river flowed out of the Sea of Galilee and the other several miles north of the Dead Sea, a natural barrier against invasion most of the way. From there I went west and up a valley north of Mount Tabor and spent the night at Darbitta, a small village clinging to the north slope of the mountain.

The next morning, I saw how unique Mount Tabor is. The early sunlight showed the mountain at its best, like an upside-down tea-cup with no ridges leading up to it except a low line of hills going off westerly towards Nazareth five miles away. Tabor is about 1,800 feet tall and symmetrical, its slopes steep and rocky, and back then topped with the ruins of some ancient fortress.

I followed the valley as it went west and a little north heading for Sepphoris, the most important city in Galilee. I wanted to go there because I had heard that Sepphoris was one of the leading centers of the new movement that had been started by Judas. During my journey up the Jordan Valley and even last night in the small village of Darbitta I had heard all kinds of stories about Judas and his Zealot movement. Someone told me that his followers were very dedicated, and they had a password and an oath that they used. No lord but the God of Abraham, Isaac, and Moses, no tax but that of the temple; and no friend but a Zealot.

After about two miles I decided to cross the ridge and go to Nazareth, not really out of my way, because I wanted to see the village where Jesus lived. At the top of the hill I could look south and west at the vast Plain of Esdraelon, one of the most fertile areas in all of Palestine. Off in the distance to the west I could see Mount Carmel where it juts out into the Mediterranean. Its western face drops off almost vertically six hundred feet to the sea while the eastern side of the 1,700-foot mountain ends on the southern side of the rich land that lay before me where ancient battles had been fought. I could see fields dotting the plains and orchards on the tops of the low-lying hills. Several small villages were off on the southern edge. I went on down the hill and headed west and north where I could begin to see Nazareth.

As I took a path between the fields, I spoke to some of the more friendly farmers who were beginning to plow the fields where barley and wheat and flax had been harvested last spring or where they were staking up bean and pea and lentil bushes to dry in the late summer sun, securing the bushes. The seeds in the pods had to be completely dry for storing. I did not ask about Joseph or his family.

Closer to Nazareth, the fields gave way to gardens where onions and melons and other vegetables were planted. Some older boys were busy in them searching for the riper melons. Onions had already been harvested and were hanging in braided bunches from the rafters in the homes I could now see clustered on the south side of a hill, higher than the ridge that I had followed from Darbitta.

Nazareth was a cluster of several dozen homes, typical of most small villages in Palestine, but as I got nearer I could also see that it was cleaner and probably more prosperous than many I had seen in Judea. Several of the houses formed around a courtyard, probably filled with relatives, extended families. Most of the houses were made of mud bricks, the walls whitewashed. I don't really know what I was expecting from Nazareth where Mary and Joseph were raising their growing family. I suppose I thought that the home of the Messiah would be somehow different, but it wasn't.

There was no wall around the village. Gardens and vineyards grew next to the outlying homes, and paths wandered haphazardly through the clusters of buildings, evidence that it was typically Jewish and had not been built by Romans or Greeks. Their cultures demanded order, not the arrangement that could have been found in tent settlements around oases of the wandering tribes of my ancestors. I walked on through the settlement going up the slope, and as I went, I passed women and their older daughters grinding grain and getting ready to bake the bread for the evening meal. They did not look at me directly but averted my gaze, most gathering their shawls more tightly around their faces. Strangers were to be avoided. The small courtyards they were busy in had the usual flock of chickens pecking around and jars lined up along the walls of their homes ready for storing the beans and late grain after they had been threshed. Some of the homes on the upper slope of the hill had been partially dug into the side of the hill. At that time of day, all of the windows and doors of the buildings were open, and ladders leaned against the homes because families spent the evenings and nights on the roofs enjoying the cool breezes.

North of town, scattered through the drying grass and thorn bushes, were the village animals, being tended to by children from the village. Goats and a few sheep and a donkey or two nibbled at the bushes or the grass. Some of the boys were practicing with slingshots, probably bored, but also glad that they were not out in the fields with their older brothers and fathers. On top of the highest point of the hill was Nazareth's synagogue. A cliff forty or fifty feet tall was on the east side of the hill. It may have been the site of a quarry where workers had dug out the layers of limestone. As I reached the crest of the hill, I could see Sepphoris gleaming whitely on top of a hill less than two miles away.

I turned to look down at Nazareth and then on south to the far line of hills running east and south from Mount Carmel forming the northern border of Samaria and joining the main range of hills and mountains running south from Mount Hermon through Samaria and Judea. How could such a beautiful country harbor such chaos? I stayed there for a few minutes enjoying the view, and then I went north down the hill and across the valley and up the steeper hill to Sepphoris, a city that contrasted completely from the simple village I had just left. Parts of the city had been destroyed by Caius a few years ago and its citizens sold into slavery, but I had heard it was being rebuilt by Herod Antipas, tetrarch of Galilee, and I wanted to find out more about the Zealots.

The city had been built by Greeks and then rebuilt by Roman city planners. Its streets ran in straight lines, some of the avenues broad enough for several chariots to pass. Several of the homes were luxurious, walled with marble. Through an open door of one I could see an interior courtyard with watered plants. Workers were busy restoring some of the mansions which had been damaged by the rampaging Romans. The main road ran east and west through the city, and in the center crossed a major north and south street. The center of Sepphoris had a plaza paved with blocks of limestone.

Titus joined a group of workers who had left their tools and were relaxing in the shade of the wall which they were rebuilding. Some had brought along something to eat while others had nothing. All of them drank from jugs or skins they had brought with them. Titus had helped himself to a few cucumbers in a rich garden near Nazareth and shared them with some of the laborers who had brought no food. They were reshaping some stones piled beside the wall, the outer wall of a Roman villa. The men were dressed for hard work and were still sweating, but they soon accepted Titus into their group. The food he gave them helped.

"How many of you live in Sepphoris?" Titus asked.

The question got a laugh. "Are you kidding?" a worker answered, smiling at such a stupid question. "Do we look like we're rolling in money? This town is made up of the rich and their slaves and servants. Romans, Greeks, Syrians, Phoenicians, Galatians, rich Jews, people from all over the land live here sucking life out of us who have had our roots in this country for generations. The house we're working on right now is owned by a rich Jew, a man making his money by buying farms from families that can't pay their taxes or the money lenders. He owns several farms south of here around Nazareth, and he has overseers running them."

"I just came through Nazareth," Titus said. "It looks prosperous to me."

"Don't be fooled by appearances. Some of that land you came through is being taken care of by the very men who used to own it. Day laborers now, they and their families being taken care of by their relatives. It's only a matter of time before they will be forced out of Nazareth and starving on the road. Much of that food and grain and fruit you saw growing around Nazareth is feeding the bellies of these rich people living in this town."

"Don't say too much," a friend warned him. "The Romans and Antipas have spies everywhere."

"That may change," the man answered. "But to answer your question," he said to Titus, "we are Jews from Ruma just north of Sepphoris. Over there working on that building across the street is a group of workers from Nazareth."

Titus saw several men and three boys resting, huddled together talking. "Do you know them?"

"Of course. We are all builders doing the same things, working with wood or metals or stone as we are doing now."

"Is one of them Joseph?" Titus was looking intently at the Nazarenes but could not recognize the man that he had helped ten years ago.

"Yes. See that man in the cloak with the blue stripes? That is Joseph, and that is his son Jesus that he is sharing that fig cake with."

"The young scamp that gave his parents fits last Passover by staying behind in the temple," another man interrupted. "But he is a great worker. Smart as a whip."

Titus saw the two the men had indicated, and he did begin to remember Joseph, but he would not have known Jesus, now twelve. Jesus was laughing at a joke someone in their group had made.

Jesus looked just like any other boy, Titus realized.

At that moment, a town messenger stopped in the street a few houses down from the groups and prepared to read from a script. He was accompanied by two Roman soldiers. "Hear all of you to this command. By the order of Quirinuis, governor of Syria, and by Augustus Caesar, ruler of Rome, a trial will be held at the theater at the eighth hour."

"That is two hours from now," a man beside Titus whispered.

"All citizens of Sepphoris and all visitors will attend. Workers and their overseers will continue working. These orders will be obeyed." The messenger rolled the sheet of paper and turned down another street, continuing with the command.

Titus looked across the street and saw that Jesus was stricken, shocked at the command.

He knows what is to happen, Titus thought. Joseph put an arm around his son and pulled him close to comfort him.

Titus had stopped talking for a few moments, closing his eyes. He took another sip of water, looking at another person entering the coffee shop, and then back at me. About noon, Titus continued, I had lunch with some men rebuilding a mansion, and they pointed out Joseph and Jesus across the street from us with a group of men working on the wall of another home. At first I didn't recognize Joseph nor Jesus because ten years had passed since I had last seen them. About then, a messenger came by announcing a trial that was to be held at the theater and that all but workers were to attend. I wanted to talk with Joseph and his son, but I didn't really know what to say. And, frankly, I didn't know how to approach the Messiah. Should I kneel and bow to him? How would a twelve-year-old boy react to adulation? What would the workers and his father think?

I decided to leave the group and go to the trial that was to be held at two o'clock.

> Titus wandered through the city, past the ruined forum being rebuilt, past the renovated baths, and by the palace that Antipas would occupy in a few years. As he walked, he began to see men heading for the theater, most in small groups talking earnestly, waving their arms. When he arrived, most of the terraced seats had already been taken, but he squeezed in among the spectators near the back row. The theater was typical of other Greek and Roman theaters. The theater was built on the eastern slope of Sepphoris in a semi-circle with the terraced seating descending so that all spectators had a good view of the stage. A small level space was in front of the stage which was about four feet above the ground, its floor paved. Pillars on both ends supported a roof Several hundred men had assembled for the trial. There were no loud conversations, but a steady hum of whispers was more ominous.

> On the hour, a person walked onto the stage from a side entrance carrying a staff and a scroll.

He stood in the center of the stage waiting for silence. Then when the whispering had died, he thumped the floor three times with his staff and cried out in a loud voice, "Men of Sepphoris and all assembled here, this tribunal is now open to try before you a man accused of sedition against a lawful order of Rome. Anyone assembled here who causes a disturbance during these proceedings will be arrested." The messenger looked at the entrance from which he had come and nodded. Four slaves carried a heavy chair onto the stage and placed it near the front center and then scurried off, followed by the official who had just spoken. The crowd shifted uneasily.

Then four soldiers led a man who had been stripped of all his clothes except a loin cloth and stood him in the area below the stage. The man's hands were tied behind his back, which was still seeping blood from a whipping that he had received earlier. The soldiers faced him toward the stage and stationed themselves on either side of him and stood at attention.

After the prisoner had been positioned and a dramatic minute or two had passed, a Roman officer walked onto the stage followed by two guards and a scribe. Two slaves came with the scribe, one carrying a small table, the other a chair. The scribe had them set his table and chair off to one side of the chair the Roman judge had stood before. Then the Roman took his seat and smiled at the crowd and looked down at the prisoner. He knew that he was presenting a drama, a deadly one, a lesson to all of those people sitting out there focused on him and what he was about to do.

The Roman spoke in a clear and controlled voice. "Men of Sepphoris and you gathered here as witnesses to this trial, I am Caius, a captain in the Tenth Legion, duly appointed to hold this tribunal and to pass judgment upon this prisoner, who has been accused of seditious acts against the Roman Empire. We will question him and allow him to answer freely. We expect no interference from you sitting as witnesses. I will now proceed."

Caius looked down at the prisoner and smiled. "Citizen, what is your name?"

The man looked up at the captain, his gaze steady but filled with hate. One eye was swollen shut, and blood flecked his beard. "I am Reuben, the rope maker of Sepphoris."

"The charge against you is that you refused to pay your taxes, duly assessed by Rome and that you repeatedly refused after the publican had given you several chances to recant your position. Is the charge correct?"

"It is. There is no lawful tax in all of Israel except the tax of the temple."

"I hear that is a position taken by Judas, the Gaulonite," the captain responded.

"The Jews pay the temple tax gladly because that is the command of Yahweh, the God of our ancestors."

"You live in a world of men who have established laws and given codes of conduct so that men may be governed in a social order. Men are elected to rule over others, to see that these laws are obeyed, to establish peace and maintain discipline. Taxes must be paid in order to build roads and bridges and harbors so that commerce may be handled efficiently," Caius said, no longer smiling.

"We have no lord except the God of Abraham and Isaac and Moses. Moses led us out of Egypt and gave us our freedom. We are slaves to no one." Reuben's shrill voice and his message made the witnesses shift uneasily. Some of the richly dressed Jews looked embarrassed, ashamed, their eyes shifting away from the man testifying to their faith.

"You are under the protection and laws of Rome and have your own governor, Herod Antipas, tetrarch of Galilee. There is a difference between religious and civilian lords." The captain was beginning to lose patience with the prisoner.

"We accept no lord but God," Reuben answered.

"Then how do you respond to the charge?" Caius asked.

"I freely admit that I refused to pay the unlawful tax imposed upon us by the Romans," Reuben answered, "and I tell you that all Jews hate the tax and hate those who impose their laws upon us. We were born free men, and some day we will regain our freedom."

The captain was furious, his face red. "Are you a follower of the rebel, Judas?"

"*I am.*"

"Are you ready for sentence to be passed upon you?"

"I am, and may God have mercy on you and upon my soul." Reuben sagged, supported by the two guards.

Caius stood and raised his voice. "The act of not paying taxes is a crime against the state and is punished by the confiscation of property or imprisonment. But Reuben, the rope maker from Sepphoris, is charged not only with a failure to pay the lawful tax required by Rome but also with being a follower of Judas of Galilee, a rebel against Rome and the governor of Galilee. Therefore, it is the sentence of this court that Reuben will be executed, a just form of punishment for sedition. By the power given to me by Augustus Caesar, I pass this judgment. The prisoner will be crucified tomorrow morning outside the city on the road to Legio."

The Roman soldiers dragged the slumping prisoner away while Caius glared at the audience for a few moments and then walked stiffly off stage followed by his attendants and the scribe and slaves. The seated Jews were quiet, awed by the bravery of the Zealot and ashamed that they lacked the courage to disobey the Romans. Then some of the foreign citizens of Sepphoris began to leave, satisfied that the sentence was just. After most of them were gone, the Jews followed, their heads downcast. After a few moments, the remaining witnesses began to file out of the theater. Titus was one of the last to leave. He could hardly function because of his emotions, taken by the bravery of an ordinary citizen. How could a man go through what Reuben had faced, knowing that his testimony was his death sentence, admitting that he was a follower of Judas?

The trial was terrible, Titus said. The prisoner was accused of not paying his taxes, but during his testimony he admitted that he was a follower of Judas. By doing that, the man was sentenced to be crucified, the usual punishment for sedition, a rebellion against the state. After the trial, I decided to go to northern Galilee to find Judas, the leader of the Zealots, a man who could command such loyalty.

7

Titus rubbed his hands together with a washing motion and then relaxed them on the table, palms down. His face looked a little drawn and sad, emotions stirring as he recalled what had happened two thousand years ago.

They hanged the Zealot the next morning on the west side of Sepphoris on the road to Legio, a main road being built by the Romans, Titus began. The road was being extended to the south as far as Sebaste in Samaria. The Romans were great road builders for commercial and military use. As the road went south, it passed just west of Nazareth. Can you imagine all the farms that were destroyed because of those straight-running roads? The old roads meandered between property, not through it. Anyway, back to my point. I knew that Jesus and the builders from Nazareth would see that hanging body as they went back to their work in Sepphoris that morning. I also realized that Jesus had known what the man's fate would be. I remembered his stricken face the day before when the trial had been announced.

I did not see Reuben crucified.

I went on to Cana, a village about five miles north of Nazareth and stayed the night, sleeping in a grove of almond trees. The air was mild and the stars bright. The land seemed at peace, ageless, not troubled by the current violence. Through generations it had seen armies come and go, indifferent, surviving. The presence of God is in all that he has created. It is man who chooses to disobey his laws.

The next morning, I entered Cana and found a day's work helping with an olive press, a sensitive job because the oil had to be taken from the fruit without crushing the nut, which would turn the oil bitter and ruin the batch. The people working with me knew what had happened in Sepphoris the day before but were very careful in expressing their views. Jews made up most of the population in Galilee, but through generations that northern country had been the first invaded by more powerful nations. As a result many Gentiles lived among them, and the rich Jews had become more extravagant and had begun to be influenced by Roman and Greek culture, but the average Jew, the small land owner and craftsman, was fiercely independent, for the most part, following the laws in the Torah and those laid down by the Pharisees, but they were not as rigid in their practices as those living in Judea. Most Galileans believed in Judas and his campaign to rid the land of Roman rule, but they were careful not to say too much. Informers could report them.

When I left the village later that afternoon, to the north I saw the range of hills and mountains that ran mostly west and east, counter to the north/south hills and mountains anchored on the north and west by Mount Lebanon and east of it Mount Hermon, both high peaks snow-covered. The land was much greener than that in Judea. The southern slope of the hills and mountains in Galilee are terraced, not with a regular slope, but stepped so that Galileans had planted fruit and nut trees in those areas. The higher crowns of the hills were covered with trees, oaks at the lower elevations and pine and fir and cedar higher up. Galilee back then got about thirty inches of rain a year, the streams and rivers flowing to the Mediterranean, but were usually dry by late summer. Some hemlocks grew along the bank of the stream in the valley at Cana. The land was fertile and productive. Back then there were more than two hundred villages in Galilee.

For the next several days I followed the roads going north into upper Galilee, being careful not to attract the attention of Roman patrols who were stopping travelers, searching for Judas of Galilee and his followers. I would hunch my shoulders and shuffle along and tell the soldiers that I was on my way to visit some relatives in Capernaum. I was lucky the soldiers could not detect my Judean accent. Galileans knew I was from Judea the moment I spoke. I knew that desperate men hid in the caves on the steep, eastern faces of the mountains in the Mount Lebanon range, and I believed that I could possibly find Judas there.

> Titus faced the cliff, looking for the dim trail that he had been following from the last of the almond groves high on the face of the mountain. He was resting on a bench about ten feet wide. The trail had disappeared among the stone rubble, but he could see that someone had come this way before him and had probably followed the bench where it curved out of sight around the cliff about fifty feet ahead of him. Through an opening in the pine trees he could see off to the east the range of hills and peaks that went south from Mount Hermon, now glowing in the late afternoon sun, its snow-covered peak standing out from its granite slopes. Far below he could see the valley and the low range of hills that marked the western edge of the Jordan River plunging down into the Sea of Galilee.
>
> He placed his rolled-up shepherd's coat beside him as he sat on a rock looking off east, enjoying the beauty of the country. No shepherd would be without his coat because it served him in cold weather and became his bed and blanket when he would have to be with his flock during the night. He also had his goatskin water bag with him and drank sparingly from it. Titus enjoyed the stillness with only an occasional breeze stirring the tops of the pines or some bird singing in the trees. A sharp contrast to the teeming valleys below, he thought.

He looked more closely at the rock-strewn bench and noticed some of the rocks had been shifted by people walking along this way. The path hadn't disappeared after all, he realized, but had merely spread out some as the trail here had become easier than the nearly vertical climb that he had just made.

After resting for a few minutes, Titus gathered his coat and water bag, put their straps over his shoulder, began walking slowly along the bench staying near the face of the cliff, and looking closely for signs that he was still on the path. The caves on the east face of the Lebanon mountains had been used by desperate men before, and several battles had been fought in them in the last few years, so Titus knew that he had to be careful, that he was walking into danger, that he might not be welcome if he did find the hideout of Judas and some of his followers. Just ahead of him the bench narrowed to less than two feet because some past earthquake had caused the rest to slip and fall into the valley. He shifted his coat and water bag to his outer shoulder and began cautiously to walk ahead, not looking down into the void. After about fifty yards, the cliff changed to a more gradual slope, and Titus followed the path, now more visible, upward at an angle.

Titus was stopped by two men a few hundred yards farther. They had been hidden in a closely packed stand of fir trees, guards posted there by someone. Judas, I hope, Titus thought. Both were tough-looking men, one of them short but stout and well-muscled, the other taller and wiry. They both carried short swords and staffs. The taller one had a bow and a quiver of arrows, not that those would do much good against Roman armor, but they looked dangerous to Titus, unprotected against a well aimed shot.

"Looking for someone?" the taller one asked, shifting his staff to his right hand.

"Someone who might hate the Romans as much as I do," Titus answered, not wanting to admit that he also hated the Herods.

"Listen to this man," the short one said. "Do you hear the way he speaks? He's from Judea, and a long way from his flock unless he stole that shepherd's coat. Only someone from there drags out the language like that."

"I was a shepherd there a long time ago," Titus answered. "But I lost my flock and my home and family and have no love for a politician. I have been outside the law of the Herods and the Romans for more than ten years."

"Anyone can tell that story," the tall one sneered.

"I am looking for Judas," Titus said. "If he is your leader, take me to him and let him judge me. If he is another man, say so, and I'll turn around and return to the valley."

"We have our orders," the short one said curtly. "No one is to pass."

"I am only one person, easy to dispose of if I prove false. Let Judas decide."

"So now you assume our leader is Judas, a brave thing to do." The tall one chuckled. "Since you seem to be a sincere pilgrim, I'll take you along and let someone else decide what to do with you, since you already know where our hideout is."

The short guard stayed behind while the other one took Titus a few hundred yards farther along to a giant crack in the granite cliff face. The passage inside the cave was narrow for a short distance and then opened up into a larger room lit with several candles, leaving most of the space farther back in darkness, an eerie place, one that troubled Titus, who was used to the hills of Judea where one could see for miles.

The guard took Titus to a man who stood almost six feet tall and was well-muscled, broad through the shoulders, a full beard and piercing eyes, a regal air. "This man tried to pass our guard post," the guard explained. "He said he was looking for you."

Judas studied Titus through hooded eyes, judging him. Titus looked directly back at Judas, calmly, knowing that the next few minutes meant he either lived or died. "So you have found me," Judas said, his voice deep. "What brought you here? Is it Caius, the Roman captain, the killer of Jews, or is it Antipas, the Herod governor who likes to kiss Roman feet? Or have you heard stories of our resistance to Roman rules and Roman desecration of our religion?"

"I have no love for either the Romans or the Herods," Titus replied. "Ten years ago, Herod's soldiers killed my wife and son when they murdered the innocent children at Bethlehem. I killed one of Herod's soldiers because of that and fled the country Several years ago, I joined a group of rebels led by a shepherd in Emmaus and fought in a battle against an armed wagon train bringing supplies to the garrison stationed there. I have heard throughout Judea and Galilee of your stand against the Roman taxes that have been imposed on us. I wanted to meet the man who would arouse a nation as you have done."

As Titus spoke, Judas had listened carefully and had studied Titus's face looking for any deception. "Now hear me," he said to the fifteen or twenty followers, some highlighted by the flickering candles, others indistinct in the deeper shadows. "I believe this man, and we will treat him as a friend unless he proves otherwise." Then Judas grabbed Titus by the shoulders and pulled him to him with his muscled arms. "Welcome, and may God be with you."

"And also with you," Titus answered.

"Let me introduce you to my close friend and co-leader of our movement," Judas said, as he took Titus by his arm and pulled him along. They stopped in front of a man dressed in a striped gown, cleaner than the others. He had a trimmed beard, well oiled, and eyes that were restless, but he had been watching the exchange between Judas and Titus closely, judging.

"This is Sadduc, the Pharisee," Judas said. "He is a keeper of God's laws and hates the Hellenized Jews as much as he does the Gentiles."

"I am Titus, the shepherd," Titus said, looking at Sadduc.

"I know," Sadduc answered. "I heard your conversation with Judas."

The three of them talked of conditions in the country in general terms, Judas and Sadduc questioning Titus about his journey from Judea to Galilee and about conditions in Judea, but Titus couldn't tell them anything that they didn't already know. He told of displaced people crowding the roads and the mad scramble of gleaners rushing into fields and orchards to pick up the last bit of grain or fruit left by the growers, a tradition still being followed by Jewish farmers but beginning to be ignored by Gentile land owners.

"Conditions are worse in Judea than in Galilee," Titus said. "Much worse."

"Of course," Sadduc said. "They are ruled by Coponius, a Roman; and our high priest, Joazar, has told Judeans to pay Roman taxes. But we have people even there talking of resistance. We will not be ruled by Romans forever."

Two men carried a large bucket of water into the lit room from the darkness back in the cave. Men began the ritual washing of their hands and faces preparing for a meal. The cave must go back to other rooms, Titus thought, as he went through the ritual, accepting their routine. After several minutes had passed, some men brought a large pot of soup and sat it in a space cleared by the men who had moved to the walls. Two other men brought in a large, woven platter stacked with flat bread. The aroma of the soup made Titus realize how hungry he was.

Six men sat cross-legged around the pot and began dipping into it with pieces of bread that they had torn off. One or two had gourd ladles. The rest of the group stood aside patiently waiting their turn. As was the custom, they used their right hands for dipping into the pot.

Judas and Sadduc invited Titus to eat with them as the last group. "We believe that those who lead should be the last," Judas explained to Titus. "In the new Israel, all Jews are free men, and those who lead are servants to those people entrusted to them."

"The soup is delicious," Titus said. "I haven't tasted better."

"Those who cooked it wanted it to be special," Judas explained. "Tonight is special because we have Sadduc with us, and later he will give us a special report."

"I do have many things to talk about," Sadduc said.

The soup was made of onions and leeks and beans and other vegetables. Added to it were bits of fish, which gave the soup a rich flavor, and unusual because soup rarely included meat. "Some of our men put out nets this morning to catch the fish that we are enjoying," Judas said, as he reached into the pot to extract a piece with his right hand. "They wanted to keep busy. The bread we are eating was given to us by some villagers below. A dangerous thing for them to do."

After they had all eaten and the pot carried away, Judas stood before the seated men and looked at them, remaining silent until he knew that he had their full attention. "Men, the soldiers of God," he began, "we have struggled against our enemies as did our fathers before us. Since the time of

Abraham and Isaac and Jacob, our people have fought to keep what God had given them. Those old shepherds and their sons were free and formed a covenant with God that they would abide by his laws. When in later years they were held as slaves in Egypt, God sent Moses to bring them back to the promised land. And they returned and reclaimed what God had given them. Later the Babylonians took our people captive, but once again our land and our God were returned to us by Ezra and Nehemiah. Others have defeated us, but we have always been led back to victory by great men like Judas Maccabeus. Now we are enslaved by the Romans and betrayed by our leaders who submit to them. But we shall be free once again. We shall show the people the way because God is on our side. He gave our people this land and freedom generations ago, and we must fulfill the covenant." Judas raised his arms and shouted, "Freedom!"

The men, stirred by his speech, responded, yelling, "Freedom!" The chamber echoed.

Then Sadduc of Gennesaret stood. "I have just returned from Scythopolis where Herod Antipas holds court, not even in the land of Galilee. Perhaps his wife wants to live closer to her father, the king of Arabia. There I learned that Antipas plans to build a wall around Sepphoris and make that city the capital of Galilee."

"He should do that," Judas interrupted, "but he needs to build the wall high and strong." Sadduc stopped for a few moments in his report while his listeners muttered agreement with Judas. "I was also told that Coponius, procurator of Judea, plans to replace our high priest, Joazar, with Annas, a priest of his own choosing."

The men roared at that news, and Judas jumped to his feet, shouting and waving his arms. "We elect our high priests. He can't do that. Roman law says that they will not interfere with our religion."

"Right now he can do whatever he pleases," Sadduc said. "As you all know, the ceremonial robes of the high priest are kept in the Fortress Antonia along with a whole garrison of Syrian troops dressed as Roman soldiers. We must be careful in what we do, but we must fight against our enemies who treat us with such contempt." Sadduc paused for a moment and smoothed his beard. "In many of the towns and cities through-out Palestine, we have Pharisees who believe in our cause. They are afraid that the leaders of the people are beginning to follow the ways of the Romans, are more concerned with easy living than the will of God. As a result, Pharisees are becoming even more zealous in demanding that Jews follow the laws laid down by God. Laws of cleanliness, diet, relationships, observing the Sabbath and the festivals, and the other ones that guide us in proper living and keep us together as a family, forming a center for our scattered people. But some realize that merely demand-ing obedience from their followers in the law is not enough. They must somehow break the total control the Romans have over us right now."

"Do they have any suggestions?" Judas asked.

Sadduc smiled thinly. "I am afraid not. Right now we are at the mercy of the Romans."

"We will have our revenge," Judas growled. "Reuben of Sepphoris was executed because he believed in us. That murder will not go unpunished. Caius has patrols out looking for us, but we will not be stopped."

"I was at the trial," Titus interrupted. "Reuben could have saved his life by saying that he knew nothing of you, but he spoke in your favor knowing it would cost him his life. He was a brave man."

"He was a true follower," Sadduc said. "God has a plan for everything. Maybe he is testing us again by the Roman occupation, as he tested us in the past, but God also gave man the power to choose. If we could not choose, we truly would be slaves. He gave us minds and the ability to think, to reason. How we choose to act is important. If we choose wisely, we gather the fruit. If we choose foolishly, we suffer the consequences. The soul of man is immortal, and after death it goes underground with the body. There the soul is either rewarded or punished by the choices made during its life on earth. If the choices were good, then the soul will live again. But if the choices were bad, the soul will remain underground and live in everlasting pain. Those of us who oppose the Romans and die in the service of God will be born again. That is why Reuben chose to testify the way he did He will live again, and he will be known as a hero of the people."

Judas stood and hugged Sadduc, indicating that he wished to conclude the meeting. "Well said, old friend." Judas spread his arms and scanned the room, catching the eyes of all the seated men, awed by what Sadduc had said. "All of us are soldiers of God," Judas began, "willing to lay down our lives for our cause. We could stand the taxes the Romans demand That is not the point. What matters is that we are controlled by them against the will of God, who gave us our freedom. We must resist. We must fight back We are Zealots as the sons of Abraham, who was willing to sacrifice his son for God. Rise, warriors," Judas roared. "Repeat our pledge." He raised his arms higher. "We have no lord but God." The men chorused the words. "We pay no tax but that of the temple." The men repeated. "We have no friend but a Zealot," Judas roared, ending the meeting.

"We have no friend but a Zealot," the men shouted back and began hugging one another.

Titus had stopped talking for a few moments, and then took a deep breath and began again. I did find Judas and Sadduc, the Pharisee, and some of their freedom fighters high up in the mountains west of Julius. I stayed the night and was impressed with their cause, but I knew that I could not join them because the commitment would be binding. I told them of my seeing Jesus, the Messiah, and that I had decided to stay near him, watch him grow into manhood and lead the Israelites to freedom. Judas and Sadduc were skeptical. Several false messiahs had led their followers to death against the Romans in the last few years, so their attitude was understandable. As I had watched their meeting the night before, I believed that they had awakened the Jewish people, but that they, too, would fail.

Before leaving, I joined the group for a morning meal of a hot brew of herbs and bread. We tore off pieces of bread and dunked them into the cup, an invigorating way to start the day. I followed another trail down into the valley and took a Roman road heading north toward Lake Huleh. I intended to return to my home in Judea, but first I wanted to see more of upper Galilee and perhaps visit the Essene commune near the lake. The road was well traveled, and once again I was stopped by several Roman patrols. I noticed how the people who were stopped by the patrols acted, accepting the searching and questioning, their faces averted not wanting the Romans to see the hatred in their eyes. It was early in the morning when I first entered the road, and as I walked north, I passed several bodies lying off the road, in some cases families huddled around them. Disease and starvation were becoming more common in this rich land.

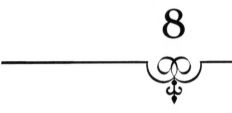

8

Lake Huleh is about eight miles north of the Sea of Galilee in a fertile valley. A village, Thella, was located on the southwest side of the lake, and the Essene camp was a short distance north nestled in a pocket of land with low hills on three sides with the east sloping down to the lake. It was surrounded with fields and gardens and orchards.

I stayed there through the winter, Titus said, working as a potter's helper. He closed his eyes, remembering, pausing for a moment.

> Titus was struck by the beauty of the area. Lake Huleh, about a mile long and half a mile wide, sparkled in the bright sun. Three fishing boats were near the shore, the fishermen pulling in their nets, working together. To the north and slightly west Mount Lebanon anchored the line of hills on the west side of the lake, its summit snow-covered because its peak is almost ten thousand feet. To the east of Mount Lebanon, Mount Hermon, its peaks also snow-covered, looked blue-green. A shallow valley ran from a flank of Mount Hermon to the lake and broadened into the area that Titus had entered. Titus knew the Jordan River flowed into the lake.
>
> When Titus walked past a line of low east-west hills, he could see the Essene camp nestled in its

small valley. Instead of houses or huts, there were four tents on the outer edges of a compound and a larger structure with the bottom half of stone and the upper half of adobe. It was fairly large but low, about ten feet tall. Its roof was flat but slanted so that water would run off Titus found out later that snow sometimes covered the land in winter, and because of that, the roof could not be flat because of the weight of snow. Fields covered the land between the camp and the lake, the fields now brown with stubble because the wheat and barley and lentils and beans and flax had been harvested. Grapes were ripe and ready to harvest on the north slope of the valley; and, higher, Titus could see groves of fig and olive and almond and pomegranate and mulberry trees on the sides of the hills.

As he walked through the fields toward the camp, he passed gardens where the men grew herbs and onions and leeks and melons. The camp was immaculate. As he entered the compound area, he noticed no sign of animals, which was highly unusual, he thought. A tall man in a linen cloak came out of the door of the building, the meeting hall, and smiled at Titus greeting him. His beard was long, his hair black and also long, combed but not oiled.

"Welcome to our valley, pilgrim," the man said, his voice deep, the accent slightly different from the Galileans. "We are a group of men who have separated ourselves from the rest of Israel in order to find the true way. Most of us are Nazoreans." Titus knew of that group of Jews who had long ago come back to Judea from their Babylonian captivity. In the second century BC, they had separated themselves from changes which had been made in worshiping God, sticking to the laws of Moses, had been persecuted, and had moved to northern Palestine and nearer their desert roots.

"I have heard of you," Titus replied, "and of the Essenes who seek to live righteously in the laws of God. If you would have me, I would like to stay here and study and learn. Of course I will do my share of work and abide by the laws of the group."

"You may stay with us and get closer to God, but you must obey our rules, and we will judge you and your worth. It is our custom. My name is Jesse, the priest of our order."

"My name is Titus, from Judea. I have no home, but family near Bethlehem."

"From your coat, I would suppose you were a shepherd," Jesse said. "A long time ago," Titus answered. "I see you have no sheep."

"We live without animals, nor do we eat meat," Jesse answered. "We wear linen, and we use leather shoes only in winter. The rest of the year we like the feel of God's great earth as we walk upon it. We live simple lives, avoiding corruption."

"The community looks well tended," Titus said. "It tells much about the community."

"We provide for ourselves and try to help those who need us," Jesse replied. "We have isolated ourselves for meditation and as part of the rem-nant that will redeem Israel, but we go out into the world of the Gentile and the wayward Jew to trade and to help the poor and the widow and the orphan. Our real mission is to study and prepare the way for the coming of Righteous One, to overthrow the Kittim who now control us." Titus knew that Jesse was referring to the Romans when he used the term "Kittim."

Another man walked around the corner of a tent and approached them. He was stocky, muscular, frowning. "This is Samuel," the priest said, "the guardian of the camp. He will be in charge of you and look after your welfare and be your instructor."

"I am Titus," Titus said to Samuel, introducing himself. "I am from Judea and have lately been in Sepphoris."

"The city of sin," Samuel said curtly. "We have heard of the execution there of someone who refused to pay the taxes imposed by the Kittim. They do not tax us."

"Guardian, if you would show Titus his quarters and begin to instruct him, I will return to my studies and prepare for this evening's gathering," Jesse said. He turned and walked back into the meeting hall.

"Come," Samuel said and began walking toward the tent on the west side of the compound.

Inside, Titus could see in the dim light that the tent was primarily used for storage, stacked with jars of grain and jugs of olive oil and dried onions hanging in bunches from a rafter. In one area near the door was a lone pallet. The floor was packed earth. The smell of grain and onions was pleasant.

"That is the habitation of Abner, who is in his second year of becoming a son of Zadok, a member of the remnant that will save the nation, one of us," Samuel said. "We live in groups of ten. The other tents have ten sons in each of them, and in our community are twenty sons of Zadok and Samuel, the priest, and I, the guardian, and right now the administrator, taking care of the finances and the operation of our farm. I will allow Abner to explain how we function and some of our rituals because he is proving to be worthy of us and has my trust. You may prepare a space for yourself on the other side of the entry" Samuel indicated a space near a stack of jars. "Right now, Abner is in the library memorizing some passages from the Law of Moses. I'll send him to you. Abide."

In a few minutes a young man entered the tent distracted by the sudden change from bright sunshine to the dimness of the tent. He saw Titus and smiled, glad to have someone staying with him. He was short and wiry and full of energy, his beard just beginning to show some growth.

"My name is Abner," he said, "from Bethsaida, but that part of the town which is east of the Jordan, and in Gaulanitis, under the control of Herod Philip." Titus knew that the town was located where the Jordan flows into the Sea of Galilee and that Herod Antipas ruled the western part of the town, the eastern one prosperous and growing, the western one a town of fishermen.

"Greetings, Abner. My name is Titus from Judea. Will I be a problem for you?"

"No, not at all. It is well that I have someone I can talk with, since Samuel, the guardian, has given me permission to introduce you to the camp and our routine. Come, I will show you part of it right now."

Abner went back out the entrance followed by Titus. They went west up the narrowing valley, slanting upward quickly toward the westward ridge. "You can see our groves here on either side. Farther up are our spring and bathing pool on the south side of the valley, and on the north side we have our station where we relieve ourselves," Abner said as they walked briskly beside the narrow stream of water. They followed the well-worn path by a low outcropping of limestone, and then Abner turned left and went up a steep rise to a leveled area. After they had passed some bushes, Titus could see the spring flowing from another layer of limestone. It had been walled and a rock bottom installed. Water flowed from a notch on its north side and was channeled to the stream bed below. Water had been piped from the south side of the pool to a basin surrounded by bushes. As they walked to the basin, Titus could see that it was about four feet wide, four feet deep, and six feet long. Water flowing from it was directed away from the stream bed and toward the grove of fruit and nut trees below. The area around pool and basin was shaded with oak trees, cool now under the lowering sun.

"This is where we bathe," Abner said, indicating the basin. "Our Rule says that we must be clean in body as well as spirit. Only one member can bathe at a time," Abner explained, "because it is against our Rule for one brother to see the body of another. The Rule also states that the water must be chest deep and clean. That is why our bathing place is built the way it is. We have privacy, and the water flows in and out."

Titus was somewhat amused by Abner's fervor.

Abner turned and plunged downhill and across the narrow ravine to the north slope, following a path up among another stand of oak trees and bushes. Before long, the land leveled once again, and Abner showed Titus the camp's comfort station. It was a pit about ten feet long with a log on their side of the pit. Dirt from the pit was on the opposite side. "This is where we relieve ourselves as nature intended," Abner explained. "Each brother has a spade, and after he uses the station, he throws a spade-full of dirt into it. We will get you a spade later. Right now you can use mine if you have a need."

Titus nodded, and Abner handed him his spade and walked back down the path. Titus was grateful for his thoughtfulness. He was impressed with the camp's system and that the station area had no smell, only the musty odor of rich soil. Titus joined Abner near the bottom of the narrow valley, and they walked together back to the camp.

On the way downhill, they met several of the members going up to bathe or get water or use the station. Abner introduced them to Titus, but Titus could not remember their names. Most of them were friendly but some reserved. The Essenes considered themselves set apart, chosen by God to redeem the nation, and, as a result, they were serious men, some fanatics. The Greek word for Essene was *Hosios*, which means "saint."

And their order made them live up to that standard. As a result, they were careful of outsiders, Titus knew.

A little later Titus and Abner returned to the bath for their ritual cleansing before the evening meal. The water was cool and invigorating. Titus wrung out his hair as he emerged and put back on his shepherd's cloak. He thought that he would probably have to change to linen, the type worn by the other men in the community.

As they returned to camp, Abner explained the roles of their leaders. "The Priest must be between thirty and sixty years old," he said, "and an expert in the Torah, which contains the Law of Moses, as you know. We are all ruled by him. He is the one who blesses the food before we eat, and he presides over our assemblies. He presides over legal functions when one of us, a son of Zadok, is charged with misconduct or some crime. After he turns sixty, he can no longer be the Priest."

"A very responsible position," Titus replied.

"The Guardian studies the Law of Moses continually and concerns himself with the right conduct of men toward other men. His chief duty is to teach us the Law of Moses and the path of righteousness. He interviews all men who wish to join the group. He teaches The Rule of the Community to prospects like me. He instructs the congregation about the works of God. He examines every man entering his group about his past deeds, transgressions, understanding, strengths, abilities, and possessions. No one else can admit another person in place of the Guardian. He must be between thirty and fifty, and have mastered all secrets of men and the languages of all clans. He admits all newcomers and ranks them. He handles all suits or judgments.

"The Overseer," Abner continued, "is the administrator of the camp, and that position is also filled by our Guardian, Samuel. He oversees all of our activities like the farm or other industries in the camp. He is in charge of finances, and he provides for the camp's material interests and needs. The other members of the community are called Sons of Zadok, who was a faithful chief priest to David."

The two entered the camp just as the sun reached the western ridge. "It is time to assemble," Abner said. "No one speaks but the Priest unless he invites someone to comment. You must sit in the back with me, and as a visitor you are not allowed to speak unless you have had permission from the Guardian." Several men were standing outside the entrance to the meeting hall, and Titus and Abner joined the group. Most of the men examined Titus but remained silent. "It is almost time," Abner whispered.

Just as the sun was about to be hidden by the ridge, Jesse walked through the group and entered the hall. He was followed by Samuel. The other men began entering according to their rank, as Abner had previously explained to Titus. They sat in silence around a long table with Abner and Titus at the far end A cup and a round of bread was set at each place. Two men carried in a large pot of stew, another brought in a jug of wine, and two others brought in gourd bowls and cups. After they had taken their places at the table and everyone was looking at Jesse, he raised his arms and blessed the food and the wine.

"Blessed is this bread we are about to receive," Jesse said, his deep voice resonating around the room. "May it nourish our bodies so that we may be your faithful servants. And blessed is this wine that we may drink in remembrance of all that you have given us. We thank you for this bread, the staff of life, and this drink in remembrance of all that has been sacrificed for us."

The stew of beans and onions and squash was ladled out and passed down the rows of men until everyone had food and drink. Then Jesse tore off a piece of bread and dipped it into his bowl.

After they had eaten, Samuel went to a stand with a scroll on it, unrolled it until he reached a passage for the evening's discussion. He squinted at the text in the dim light of a candle, frowned at the men, and began reading. "From the Law of Moses given in the Book of Leviticus. 'When an alien lives with you in your land, do not mistreat him. The alien must be treated as one of your native-born. Love him as yourself, for you were aliens in Egypt. I am the Lord your God.'" Samuel looked up at the assembly, the men uneasy, the passage clearly in conflict with how they felt about the Gentiles living in their land.

"This is a law of God given to Moses during the trials of the people in the desert. It clearly states that you should love your neighbor. Does anyone care to speak about the passage?"

One of the older men sitting near the leaders cleared his throat. "You may speak," Samuel said.

"Another passage in Leviticus addresses the issue about those aliens who live with us and who now govern us. I may not be quoting the law exactly but it says that if anyone takes the life of another, he must be put to death," the man said, his voice becoming louder as he spoke. "If anyone injures his neighbor, whatever he has done must be done to him, an eye for an eye, a tooth for a tooth. Whoever kills a man must be put to death. You are to have the same law for the alien as for the Israelites."

"Well said, Brother," Samuel replied. "The Kittim must be dealt with since they have violated all the laws laid down by God. We must be careful not to think of all the Gentiles who live among us as blasphemers. God loves all of his children whether Gentile or sons of Israel. Each must be judged on his works. However, the Teacher has written a War Rule, and we have received a copy of it from the scribes at Qumran. It is a secret directive instructing us on how to cleanse the land of the Kittim and prepare the path for the Righteous One, the Messiah, who will become the lord of all nations. You must remember that we Essenes are the remnant of Israel who are keepers of the Law of Moses. Many of our fellow Jews have been led astray by foreign ideas and customs. We are the elected ones to do God's will. God singled out Abraham's people to be His people. Then God formed a covenant with Moses on Mount Sinai when he revealed to Moses the way, the Law of Moses, and he ratified His way with him. Our salvation is adherence to that covenant, to the law and the spirit of the law. We must have firm trust in God and believe that He will reign triumphant over the entire world."

Samuel sighed and rolled up the scroll, signaling the end of the lesson. He concluded the meeting by saying, "We believe that the One God chose the Israelites to be given His laws and by obeying them to be an example for all men. Israel would be a state of perfect obedience to the Will of God, but our people have often gone astray, and they were punished, as we are being punished now, by wars and famine and pestilence. The Israelites were brought back onto the path of righteousness by prophets and leaders like Ezra and Judas Maccabeus. Our job is to prepare the way for the Righteous One, who will lead all people back to God. And now to business. Tomorrow we shall all prepare the southeast field for this next spring's planting. May God be with all of you through the night."

And then Titus continued. The group was very strict in keeping to their laws as written in their Community Rule guide. They all worked for the good of the community and helped the poor and needy in that area as part of their service. One of the first things I did there was to join the other men in hoeing a barley field, turning the soil with heavy hoes since they had no animals in their camp. They ate no meat, and I became used to their diet and routine. In the morning, we had a hot drink laced with herbs, and at midday we had a cake of figs pressed together with almonds and sesame seeds which had previously been blessed by the camp's Priest. The evening meal was always at sundown, the Priest blessing the food before we ate. After we ate, a leader gave a lesson from the Torah and led a discussion.

The potter had a shelter on the east slope of the northern hill where there was a vein of excellent clay. In the wintertime, it was very cozy inside the shed with the kiln blazing away to strengthen the jars that we made on potters' wheels in the same shed. Some of them were sold to outside merchants.

The camp's Guardian invited me to become a member of their group, but I had no intention of binding myself to their laws. According to my roommate, who was in his second stage of admission, before being admitted, one had to be an Israelite; be scrutinized by the Guardian for mental and moral capacities; be fit to enter the Covenant of God in the presence of the whole community; pledge himself to a binding oath to every commandment of the Law of Moses with all that had been revealed to the Sons of Zodak, the keepers of the covenants and the seekers of God's will; and for admission if found adequate, take instruction for two more years. For instance, in the first year he could take no part in sacred ceremonies of the council such as solemn meals prepared in special ritual purity. In his first year, he retained all his money and possessions, but in the second year he handed over all his belongings to the overseer. Once accepted, he was ranked and his property was turned over to the group, and he pledged to accept any judgment of the community. He was then able to share all of the sect's secret doctrines. It was his duty to set himself apart from the habitation of unholy men and to help prepare the way of the Lord through study and contemplation of the scriptures. If he or any Son of Zodak transgressed any law of Moses either deliberately or carelessly, he was expelled immediately.

The Essenes had separated themselves from other people in their attempt to save the nation, but I knew that their movement was doomed. They looked backward instead of forward and had even hatched a plan to defeat the Romans. I left the Huleh camp in the last few days of February. Even though the valley was just a little over two hundred feet above sea level, the days were cold and blustery, and I was glad that I had kept my shepherd's coat. It had snowed several times there during the winter.

9

I went north following the Jordan River intending to find the main road to Tyre because I was curious about that industrious seaport and the Phoenicians, or Canaanites, as we called them. I was also curious about Moloch, one of their gods, a subject brought up by the Guardian during one of our lessons in the camp. The Jews had a deep hatred for the rituals held for Moloch, and one of the Law of Moses stated that any Israelite or alien living in Israel who gave his child up to Moloch would be stoned to death.

When I reached the road, some travelers told me that they were going to a new city being built by Philip at the sacred Pool of Phiala, a pool fed by a fast-flowing spring, the water from the pool forming one of the tributaries of the Jordan River. Philip, the Tetrarch of Gaulanitis, had named it Caesarea-Philippi in honor of the aging Emperor Augustus. Since it was only about six miles farther, I decided to join the group. We passed Daphne, the magnificent palace that Herod had built for Augustus, located along the small, clear-running stream that was the beginning of the Jordan, and had a great view of Mount Hermon. A mile farther, we entered the small village of Paneas that was being tom down and rebuilt as Philip's tribute to the emperor. Caesarea-Philippi was being built as a resort, a city where the wealthy could go to relax and have a good time, to get away from a harsh religion and a demanding God.

Two days later, I headed west for Tyre and the Mediterranean coast. On the summit of a pass through the hills running south from Mount Lebanon, I could see the Mediterranean in the distance, bluer than the sky, and feel the warming breeze coming off the sea. The hills were green with grass and early leafing trees and evergreens, a verdant land. I could also see part of Tyre on the island where the older city of Tyre had stood for centuries before Alexander destroyed it in 332 BC. He had sold the thirty thousand residents into slavery, but the Phoenicians had rebuilt the present city, which also extended onto land using the causeway that Alexander had built to conquer the city, and it was flourishing more than it had before, the most important city along the eastern coast of the sea. I and the people I was traveling with hurried on, eager to reach the city about ten miles away.

Titus could feel the change in people as they hurried toward Tyre, some with carts loaded with wool or dried fruits or honey or other produce to be exported to Egypt or Athens or Rome or other ports around the Mediterranean. All of them seemed happy, freer somehow, some singing. It was the last day of February, and the day after tomorrow the ban on shipping would be lifted. The Romans had ruled that no shipping was allowed on the Mediterranean from November until March because of sudden storms during the winter and the danger of being driven ashore. Phoenicians were the major merchants affected by the rule, their ships transporting goods throughout the area, and Tyre was one of the major ports. A large wagon loaded with olive oil had stopped along the road just short of the city, the driver cursing at his bad luck and kicking at a wheel sagging, split by the heavy load.

The main road bisected the city as it headed for the docks and warehouses ringing the shoreline. Titus followed it into the city, through the outskirts of crowded housing where the workers lived and on into the center of town where there were better walled homes and a theater and a bath and a market place on the east end of a plaza that Titus entered. The plaza was small, less than a hundred yards on a side. It was paved, and in the middle was a raised platform, tiered until it stood about six feet tall and the top tier about ten feet square. On the west side of the plaza was a line of warehouses and merchant stalls which were receiving products to be sold. Some of the carts that had entered the city with Titus were parked at the different stalls, their Jewish owners haggling with the merchants hoping for good prices but knowing that they had arrived late and had little room for bargaining. To the north Titus could see the tops of two temples. He would find out later that one was the temple of Diana, the goddess of fertility, of crops and green-growing plants, and the goddess of women who worshiped her, praying for children and easy birthing. The other temple was the home of Bacchus, the god of fruit and of the sea. The Romans had lately started worshiping him as the god of wine and debauchery, but the eastern cult was still more closely associated with Dionysus, the god of fertility that drove women into ecstasy.

Titus crossed the plaza and followed a street through warehouses to the docks along the harbor. From there he could see that the island part of Tyre now had the homes of the wealthiest citizens around the heights while the harbor section contained more docks. The harbor was filled with ships being loaded by lighters that were lined up along the docks and being filled with goods to be shipped to ports all around the Mediterranean.

Titus went into a hostelry for some food and hopefully for some lodging. He had slept outside since leaving the camp at Huleh. The room was filled with sailors from many different nations, laughing and drinking and speaking in many different tongues, none of which Titus recognized Some were at a table gambling, rattling and throwing different-colored stones or riffling through a deck of cards. Little chance of getting a room, he thought.

He walked to a stall where a man was pouring some wine into a cup for a sailor who was cursing him to hurry. "Do you speak Aramaic?" Titus asked.

"Now why would you want to know that?" the innkeeper joked, looking Titus over and recognizing him as a Jew, one of those serious, conservative, one-god people from Galilee or Judea. "Did you just sell a load of wool to some exporter, and you want to celebrate?"

"No, nothing like that," Titus answered, smiling. "I'm just a lonely traveler looking for some food and lodging and maybe a captain of a cargo ship heading for Egypt so that I can work my way back home."

"This is the beginning of a busy time for us," the innkeeper said, waving a hand at the crowded room. "As you can see, we are busy, and sailors are all looking for work, most of these already hired for tomorrow's shipping."

"I don't mind sharing a room," Titus said.

"I have them piled on top of one another now," the innkeeper laughed, "but I should be able to squeeze you in somewhere. One more shouldn't make a difference."

"Have you food?" Titus was hungry since he hadn't eaten anything but some nuts all day.

"Eel and eel broth stew," the innkeeper said. "Pay me now for the room and food, and find a table. I'll have someone bring you the food as soon as I can."

Titus paid him two shekels. "Double that, and we've got a deal," the innkeeper laughed. "This isn't the temple."

Titus dug in his pouch and came up with the other two coins, also noting that he was running out of money. He was angry that the man had made a bad joke about the temple, but he kept his temper and thanked the man and found a table in a corner of the room where several other men were already seated.

"Is this seat taken?" he asked.

"No, stranger, fill it if you like," one of them replied. He was a large man with massive arms and a barrel chest, his beard tinted red. "We haven't had the company of a Jew for a while. What port are you from?"

Titus knew that his gown was used as a symbol of his religion, the stripes along the border marks of identification. He was amused at the large man's use of a nautical term. "From Judea," he said as he sat on the bench.

"Brought a load of wool to market, did you?" the man asked, noting Titus's shepherd's coat.

"No, I'm just traveling through and hoping to find a boat going south. I want to work my way back to Judea."

"A shepherd and a sailor, are you?" the huge man joked. "You look strong enough to work the ropes or the cargo, I'll say that. I am cargo master on the Ibis leaving day after tomorrow for Egypt with a cargo of oil. We will be stopping at Caesarea for some more goods. If you want to work for your passage, I'll allow it. My word is bond."

"Then it is settled," Titus said. "I will gladly work my way and will do what I am told to do to make the cargo safe. What time should I be dockside to help load oil?"

"Early morning, the first hour. If you're late, forget the deal." The cargo master smiled.

"I'll be there before that time," Titus promised.

The other men at the table were also sailors. They had already eaten and now were drinking wine. They were talking with one another in a language that Titus could not understand, but the huge man translated for Titus. They had talked of their voyages to far lands even beyond the Pillars of Hercules into the vast Atlantic and north to Cadiz, and one of them said that he had traveled to the Island of the Celts for tin. Journeys to Carthage and to Italy and Greece were routine. They considered themselves the masters of the seas.

The plate of stew with chunks of eel in the middle arrived, and Titus· ate without even caring that he had been unable to wash before eating. Breaking the Law of Moses was easy in Tyre. As he ate he didn't notice the change in the conversation at the table until the cargo master began to explain to Titus what the men had been talking about.

"There is a festival tomorrow asking Moloch to make the seas safe for shipping. It will be worth watching because it does not happen every year. There is a saying that the god of the underworld knows when Poseidon, the god of earthquakes and the sea, needs to be appeased I saw the ritual once in Carthage. It is something I will not forget," the man finished soberly, his voice showing the change in his emotions.

The conversation at the table shifted to local gossip, where one could get the best food and drink and lodging and the comfort of followers of Diana, plying their trade for rutting sailors. The red-bearded man told Titus that a rumor from Galilee was circulating that the chief of the religious fanatics called the Zealots had been killed by a Roman patrol.

"Was his name Judas?" Titus asked.

"I believe it was," the large man said. "Yes, Judas, the Galilean. He was killed along with several followers when they 'attacked' a Roman patrol on the Plain of Gennesaret, wherever that may be."

"A beautiful valley on the west side of the Sea of Galilee," Titus answered.

"He must have been a good man fighting against the Romans," the man said.

"He was a brave man fighting for his people. I considered him my friend."

Titus left the table and went outside and to the wharf. He had known that Judas would lose his battle for freedom from Roman rule, but hearing about his death in a roomful of drunken Gentiles was upsetting. He had been warned that being outside alone in Tyre was dangerous because of roving bands of robbers, but the smell of the ocean and the moored ships in the harbor and the occasional light from the homes on old Tyre were comforting. The air was fresh where he stood looking west, and he dreaded the thought that he would be sleeping with a roomful of strangers. Much later he went back inside, unrolled his wool coat for bedding, and slept that night on one of the tables.

Early the next morning Titus strolled through the city impressed with its wealth, a city known throughout the world for its purple dye, used by royalty for their robes. The dye was extracted from cuttlefish, a shellfish found only near Tyre. Also, Tyre and Sidon to the north had the two best ports on the eastern side of the Mediterranean, almost a monopoly on shipping. The new port city of Caesarea in Samaria or the limited port at Joppa in Judea had not taken away too much of the import-export business in Palestine. Titus bought some bread and hot broth from a food vendor at one of the market stalls along the plaza and found a place to relax and wait for the festival that the cargo master had told him about.

Some slaves were busy sweeping the plaza, preparing it for the event, and on the raised platform in the center of the plaza several men were lifting into place a bronze statue, struggling because of its weight, about that of a camel, Titus judged. The statue was seated on a box, his forearms extended on his thighs with the hands cupped, palms up. Its hollow body was that of a man with a bull's head distorted to look somewhat human.

"They are preparing Moloch to receive the sacrifice," someone said. "See, even now they are bringing in the wood for the fire."

Two cartloads of wood were being wheeled in as the person spoke. Titus watched as the workers placed kindling in an opening between Moloch's thighs and arms and poured on them some oil and then stacked in wood and lit the fire. Titus could see smoke pouring from the seven orifices: its gaping mouth, nostrils, slanting eyes, and short, almost human ears.

The box upon which the idol sat began to glow, and then the entire statue became red hot, yet the workers continued to stoke the fire. Titus could imagine that he could see the eyes of Moloch glowing. The workers poked and prodded the glowing coals inside the box, and when they settled, the men put in more wood until the carts were empty. In a few minutes, as though on a signal, the fire makers picked up the handles of the carts and left the plaza, which was beginning to fill except for an aisle from the main eastern street to the platform. That space had been made by rows of people dressed in orange robes lining either side. On their heads they wore wreaths of woven almond branches that showed the green of new leaves. Titus stepped upon the bench that had been his seat so that he could get a better view, but he did not want to push forward through the crowd, now a solid mass of people.

On the third hour, the sound of drums began off in the distance. Bells and cymbals and flutes joined the rhythmic beat, and the music became louder as a procession entered the plaza from the main street. Dancers preceded the musicians, twirling light cloths about their bodies, their bare feet flying with the tempo of the music. Following the dancers and the musicians, a priest appeared carrying a child, a baby boy about a year old. The baby was wrapped in a red cloth. On either side of the priest were the father and mother of the child, dressed in purple robes and wearing yellow crowns. From what Titus had been told earlier, parents fought for the privilege of giving up their first-born son to Moloch. For one year, the priests of Moloch treated them like royalty as the priests prepared the parents for their sacrifice. A group of twenty or so devotees made up the main body of the parade. The mass of people whistled and waved their arms, delighted with the show. Titus tried to turn away from the ceremony, feeling sick, but he seemed transfixed unable to leave.

At the base of the platform holding the glowing god, the musicians and the dancers moved to either side, allowing the priest and infant and parents room on the east side of Moloch. The priest began to chant, offering prayers to the god as the drummers picked up the rhythm of the priest's intonation. The baby watched with glazed eyes as though it had been drugged, as had its parents. It began to wiggle in the priest's strong grasp. The priest's words became louder, more urgent, as the drummers picked up the change and beat their drums louder. Then the priest held the infant out at arm's length in a gesture of giving, pulled it back to his body, and took the two steps up to the front of the fiery statue.

Once again, he raised his voice and stretched his arms out to the god, and then placed the baby onto the lap and arms of Moloch, stepping back quickly as the child screamed once and then was still. Titus could hear the sizzling sound of the flesh on heated brass, and he saw the instant stiffness of the child and then saw it drop down into the fiery box upon which Moloch sat. A sudden burst of black smoke emitted from the seven orifices of Moloch's head. The crowd cheered at the conclusion of the ceremony, and Titus could see that the mother had wet herself, water puddling at her feet. Moloch's gaping mouth seemed to leer, still belching smoke.

Titus found an opening and fled the scene.

I have to stop for a moment, Titus said. Most of my memories of Tyre are not pleasant ones. He took a sip of water and closed his eyes. I could tell that whatever he had been thinking had disturbed him.

And then he began again. Tyre was a cosmopolitan city, sophisticated, urbane, tolerant of all religions and all people, rich, spoiled, open to every vice, any debauchery. I could hardly wait to enter it. I could hardly wait to escape it two days later. I watched a child being burned alive as a sacrifice to Moloch. The citizens in the city were overjoyed that shipping would be safe for another year, their profits secure. I cannot blame them for their beliefs. All of us are products of whatever we have seen and touched and been taught. People brought up in the country have one view of life, those in the city another. Our brains are imprinted with our first impressions. As a Jew, I was brought up to believe in one God, to follow his commands, to live in the world a certain way. I could not change who I was, nor would I want to. Born a Jew, I am a Jew. You are a product of the society into which you were born. I know that you are white, that you live comfortably, that you have said you are a believer in Christ, and I assume that you have accepted his teachings. It was probably your parents who took you to church as a child and taught you what was right and wrong, and your community shaped you also. And where you lived either with long sweeping views of the land or hemmed in by tall buildings, cramped, also shaped you and your attitudes and beliefs. Of course, some attitudes can change and lives take different directions, but it is as though our brains are hard-wired for certain things, and when we try to change the shape of those principles, the basis of being, we are in danger of losing ourselves and the inner harmony that God intended for us.

While in Tyre, I also learned that Judas and some of his followers had been killed in a battle with a Roman patrol. His death only made his followers more zealous to rid the land of their efficient conquerors.

I left Tyre on the second day in March when the shipping lanes were opened for the season and worked my way south on a ship carrying olive oil for Egypt as the cargo master's helper. The few days on the Mediterranean helped heal my soul as I watched the bow of the vessel forming whitecaps and bottle-shaped fish pacing us as they swam joyfully, diving in and out of the water.

I left the ship at Caesarea and walked south through Samaria and back to my home, not realizing until then how much I had missed my family and my land. I needed the comfort of a structured life.

10

I was eager to return home, Titus explained, but I took the Roman road east to Ginea, the southern-most city in Galilee. The road I traveled joined another Roman road heading south into Samaria. I stayed overnight in Ginea. In the morning I went south through a country full of meaning for the Jews because at one time it had been the center of the nation. The ancient city of Samaria, chosen by Omri to be the capital of Israel, had been destroyed by Alexander but rebuilt by Herod, who had renamed it Sebaste. It had become a thriving city once again. From Sebaste to Jerusalem is thirty miles. I would be home in two days.

Several miles south of Sebaste was the city of Shechem where I decided to stay for the remainder of the day because the city is near Mount Gerizim, a mountain sacred to the Samaritans and also to Israel. Blessings were read to the Israelites from the top of the mountain when they first entered the promised land of Canaan. Also many believe that it was here that Abraham almost sacrificed Isaac instead of at Moriah. Jacob built an altar on the mountain top and dug a well at its foot. Ezra and Nehemiah refused to let the Samaritans help rebuild the temple in Jerusalem when the Jews had returned from their captivity in Babylon, so the Samaritans built their own temple on Mount Gerizim. That temple was destroyed in 128 BC by Hyrcanus, the Jewish king and high priest. I wanted a closer look at the mountain. I wanted to see the land and feel the events that caused the Samaritans and the Jews to hate one another so deeply that it would cause both groups to violate the Law of Moses.

In the morning, I could see Gerizim clearly in the bright sunlight standing about eight hundred feet above the valley floor. The ruins of the temple were clearly visible, and the path to the top was worn smooth by worshipers making the ascent for hundreds of years. I went to the top of the hill to where the outer walls of the temple had been, but I did not approach the altar, a sacred spot to the Samaritans. Also several priests were at the altar conducting some ceremony. From the top of Mount Gerizim I could look west to the Plain of Sharon and to the east see the hills hiding the view of the Jordan Valley. It was a great place for worshiping God.

Then I continued walking on south and stayed that night in Borceas, the first town in Judea on the road to Jerusalem. Somehow it felt good to be back on Judean soil. Instead of staying in the town, I spent the night with a shepherd and helped him with some late birthing, the ewes panting and struggling in the process and then imprinting their smells and motherhood on the new-born lambs, a kind of miracle that was comforting to me. Titus paused for a moment to collect his thoughts.

> The next day about four in the afternoon Titus walked into his family's olive grove where his brother Joel was working after the usual afternoon pause from labor. He was up in a tree trimming off a dead branch when he saw Titus.
>
> "Hello, up there," Titus called out, laughing at seeing how startled Joel was as he almost lost his grip on a limb when he turned and looked down.
>
> "Titus! My brother, home," Joel said as he scrambled off the tree and came running, his arms extended.
>
> "Wait. Wait," Titus shouted. "Don't touch me. I am unclean."
>
> "Then I shall be unclean with you." Joel ignored the warning, and the brothers hugged, filled with

emotion. "It is so good to have you home again, Titus. We have much to talk about;" Joel added as they parted and held one another at arm's length.

"It is good to be home," Titus said. "I have seen much and have experienced many things that are affecting our land. It is indeed the age of tribulation. Hearing of events is one thing, but seeing them is another. But the first thing that I must do is go through the cleansing ritual."

"Then you must obey what God commands."

"I will stay near Esther and Benjamin during the night and leave tomorrow for Jerusalem and the first stages of atonement," Titus said. "You may bring me my supper," he added, laughing. "I don't mind ordering my younger brother around."

"Father is there now also," Joel said. "We buried him this last winter. His last thoughts were about you."

Titus was expecting the news, but it still hurt him to know that he had left his ill father to follow his deep longing to know his country and see for himself its afflictions. "I should have been here."

"No, Titus. Somehow, I feel that you have a greater destiny."

The next morning at sunup, Titus left for Jerusalem with one of Joel's helpers carrying a lamb which Titus was taking to the temple as a sacrifice, the first step he was taking for purification. The two of them shared the work by trading off about every mile. By the time they approached the Fountain Gate, they were both tired, and the lamb was struggling, bleating occasionally, its mouth gaping. Titus remembered the child in Tyre and was sick of the process, one that he knew he had to endure.

When they reached the south gate to the temple, Titus allowed the lamb to stand with the helper holding it while he entered the public room made for ritual washing before entering the temple area. Then Titus picked up the lamb and entered the gate where a temple guard stood watching those who entered, and the other man turned to return to the farm. Titus walked up the long flight of stairs which passed under the Royal Porch and entered the Court of the Gentiles, the main plaza, and then went through the gate of the wall separating Jew from Gentile, through the Beautiful Gate, through the Women's Court and to the Court of Israel, the men's court, to the Priest's Court, the lamb now quiet.

"I have brought this innocent one as part of my atonement for breaking the Law of Moses," Titus said as he stood the lamb for the priest to inspect before accepting it.

As the priest examined the lamb for any defect, he looked at Titus closely, looking for any deception. "Did you sin unwittingly?" the priest asked.

"No, I knew what I was doing, but I was on a journey to Galilee and Caesarea-Philippi that Philip is building. I went from there to Tyre, crossing onto Gentile land, knowing that I was breaking a Mishnah law. I consorted with Gentiles, and while there supped on some eel and eel broth without knowing that it was eel until after I had eaten. On the way back from Tyre, I went from Caesarea into· Samaria and through that country home to Judea. I am deeply repentant for my transgressions, and I am asking Jehovah for forgiveness."

"Because part of your sinning was accidental," the priest said gravely, "God will accept the sacrifice because you must make your peace with him. For those sins you committed knowingly, you must ask God for forgiveness from your heart and soul. Only he can cleanse you of your grave errors."

Other sacrifices were being made on the altar, and then when it came time for the lamb to be sacrificed, Titus watched as it was ritually slaughtered and bled with some of its blood splattered on the altar and then watched as the flames destroyed its ritual parts, deeply sorry that he caused the sacrifice, a strange feeling which brought back the scene in Tyre, the hideous Moloch, the scream of the baby.

Titus left the temple and went to the Pool of Siloam. It was about midday with several people in the pool. He entered the cool water and waded to an area where he was somewhat alone. He stood about chest deep intoning his prayers asking for forgiveness, and then he ducked under water and washed his hair and face, scrubbing vigorously. He washed his clothing as he washed his body and immersed seven times, washing his hair and face each time before leaving the pool and standing in the sunshine until his clothes and body were partially dry. The process made him feel better. Returning to the laws was good because he knew that guilt could destroy him.

When Titus returned home, Joel met him at the family home, his wife, Marianne, standing beside him. She was holding a basket that she had brought to the door when Joel had told her that Titus was walking up the path. "We were expecting you, Titus," Joel said warmly. "You have gone through the most important part of purification."

"Yes, in six more days I hope I have cleansed myself and will be worthy of God's mercy."

"We have cleansed the other house for you, and Marianne has prepared your supper." She handed the basket to Titus.

"I am grateful for your kindness," Titus said. "I will accept your offer of my old home, and I will help care for the sheep. I have missed that."

Then he took another sip of water.

Joel and his family welcomed me home, but before I could live with them I had to go through a purification to cleanse myself according to our laws. After seven days, I could begin to eat with them and enter their home and become a part of the family. Joel and his wife, Marianne, and their children had moved into the main home to take care of my father who died after I had begun my journey north. I stayed in the home that had been mine and Esther's, and I stayed there the next few years waiting for Jesus to begin to reveal himself as the Messiah. When that happened, I was determined to follow him and listen to his teachings. All of Israel was crying out for a savior, someone who would cleanse our land and bring us back to God.

During those years, several events happened that deepened the longing for the Messiah. In the year ten, the Samaritans became so angered with the rule of Coponius as the Roman governor of Judea and Samaria and Idumea that they fouled the temple that houses the Tabernacle. Part of their anger came from the control that the Romans had over the high priest of the temple. Soon after Coponius had become procurator in the year six, he had dismissed Jozar, the high priest who had been chosen by the Jews and had replaced him with Annas, a man selected by the Romans to fill that position. The Romans knew that if they controlled the high priest they could control the Jews. They also knew that they had introduced a political system into our religion because if the high priest wished to remain in that position he would have to follow the orders of the Romans. Annas had insulted some of the Samaritan priests concerning their rituals at their temple on Mount Gerizim, and they came up with a plan to pay him back.

> The Samaritans struggled with the two loaded carts, the loads covered with baskets and cloths. That evening they left the road and entered an olive grove just south of Bethel to rest and to wait for the proper time to enter Jerusalem and the temple. At midnight the gates to the temple would be opened because it was the beginning of the first day of Passover, and the group planned to enter the temple at that time. They had left Shechem the day before, and they were weary but determined to carry out their plan.

> "Our load may begin to smell," one said. "I hope the evening cools."

> "We will succeed. We have the blessing of our high priest. Annas, the Roman lackey and high priest of the temple in Jerusalem, has insulted us by saying that our altar on Mount Gerizim is not a holy place, not sanctioned by Yahweh. We will foul his nest," another answered.

> Later they continued their journey south to Jerusalem, the road becoming steeper near the city. Just after midnight, the hooded men entered through the Sheep Gate on the north side of the temple, two hooded men supporting a third

between them, telling the sleepy guard that their friends were ill and desired choice spots for the coming festivities.

The Samaritans smuggled six dead bodies inside the temple and took them south across the Court of the Gentiles to the cloisters of the Royal Porch and threw the bodies into those cloisters where Israel's most famous rabbis taught. They then fled down the passageway beneath the Royal Porch and out the south gate.

You can imagine the uproar the dead bodies caused. Israelites from around the world had come back to Jerusalem to take part in Passover, the feast of unleavened bread, but then the temple had been contaminated and would have to go through the ritual of purification, which took a week. Annas and other priests worked through the rest of the night devising a plan to cleanse the temple and at the same time bypass the Law of Moses. Passover had to occur as scheduled. You might say tourist season was in full swing. Shiploads of Jews from Rome and other parts of Italy and from Greece and Damascus and Alexandria and Cairo and cities from Asia Minor had arrived by the thousands. Jerusalem, a city of thirty thousand, swelled to more than a hundred thousand during Passover with pilgrims camped around the city. There would have been a revolt if Passover in the year ten had to be canceled.

Annas solved the problem by placing guards around the affected cloisters in the Royal Porch to prevent anyone from entering that area, said nothing about the incident, and carried on with the festivities. When word leaked out about the dead bodies, Jews were outraged at both the Samaritans and Annas-angry at the Samaritans for polluting the temple and angry at Annas for not declaring the entire temple area contaminated. Those who had worshiped in the temple during Passover that year felt betrayed. There were strict rules in the Torah about dead bodies, and those commands had not been followed by the high priest. He seemed to be more interested in filling the temple treasury.

From then on, Annas ordered that no Samaritan could enter the temple. Many Jews living in Samaria considered the temple in

Jerusalem as their place for worshiping God during the various festivals, and they were angry because of that edict. Jews were angry at all Samaritans for what a few had done. Animosity grew into hatred. Jesus would have been fifteen at that time. I wonder if he were with the group from Nazareth that had traveled to Jerusalem for that Passover?

Other events in the year ten added to the general unrest. Herod's sister Salome died that year, having deeded her land to Julia, Augustus Caesar's wife, instead of to the Israelites. They were small parcels, only a few square miles, but they were symbolic. Rome now owned a part of Judea instead of merely governing it. One bit of land was Jamnia just south of Joppa along the Mediterranean. Another was Phasuelis and its surrounding land. That town had been built earlier by Herod a few miles north of Jerusalem in honor of his brother, Phasael. The third parcel was Archelais, a magnificent palace also built by Herod and given to his sister along with some of the richest palm groves along the Jordan River. Resentment grew against the Herods as well as the Romans. Whatever would Julia do with those trinkets? She was already satiated with riches. She never visited Palestine.

Herod Antipas had finished rebuilding Sepphoris and the wall around it in the year ten, and he moved the capital of Galilee to that city but still spent much of his time in Perea, living in Machaerus, his fortress on the east side of the Dead Sea.

Political leadership became a little unstable in Judea that same year when Coponius was recalled to Rome and Marcus Arnbivius became procurator of Judea. He served two years before Annius Rufus replaced him. Both of these procurators retained Annas as the high priest. In the year fourteen Valerius Gratus became procurator and replaced Annas with Ismael, who lasted one year. Gratus appointed Eleasar, a son of Annas, as high priest but soon replaced him with Simon, who lasted a year. In the year sixteen, he named Joseph Caiaphas, a son-in-law of Annas, as high priest. Caiaphas was able to work smoothly with his Roman masters and served as the high priest for a number of years. Spiritual leadership for the Israelites became highly unstable because of the changes in the most important position for the Jewish religion. The high priest was the only one who could enter the Holy of Holies, the inner sanctum of the Temple, the House of God. In that sense, he communicated with God and was God's messenger on earth. The people resented the control the Romans had over their high priest, but they felt they could do nothing about it. During those years, Rome had total control over Palestine. There were sporadic uprisings by the Zealots in Galilee, but they were quickly put down and the leaders crucified.

Augustus Caesar was a harsh ruler but one who treated his subjects equally. There were very few dishonest people appointed by Augustus to rule in the Eastern Roman Empire. Those few who tried and were found out were dealt with quickly.

When Augustus Caesar died in the year fourteen, Tiberius Caesar became Emperor of Rome. He was a son-in-law of Augustus, having been forced to divorce his wife and marry Julia, Augustus's daughter. Tiberius had had a brilliant career and had won many battles for Rome, but he was fifty-six when he became emperor. But corruption, long controlled by Augustus, began at that time, and the Roman Senate was busy with many trials.

In the year seventeen, Tiberius sent his adopted son Germanicus Julius Caesar to take total control of the Eastern Roman Empire, an empire that was becoming politically unglued. Germanicus quickly crowned Zeno as king of Armenia and reduced Cappadocia and Commagene to the status of provinces. In the year nineteen he traveled to Egypt out of curiosity without authorization. For some reason his action offended Tiberius. A chain of events followed. The same year that Tiberius had sent Germanicus to the eastern provinces, he had appointed Gnaeus Calpurnius Piso to be governor of Syria. He wanted Piso to assist Germanicus in cleaning up the politics in the east. However, soon after Germanicus had returned to Lebanon, he died of poisoning. People accused Piso of poisoning Germanicus. Piso returned to Rome to defend himself, but while there he committed suicide. Politics in the east became unsettled, Tiberius became less and less interested in governing, arid in the year twenty-six withdrew to his magnificent palace on the Isle of Capri and turned the affairs of Rome over to the Roman senate that was controlled by the equestrians.

After Tiberius was named emperor, Herod Antipas began building a city on the west shore of the Sea of Galilee in one of the most beautiful sections of the west shore and named it Tiberius after the newly-appointed emperor. In the year twenty, he moved the capital from Sepphoris to Tiberius. Many of its citizens were Greeks and Romans, and their epicurean ways offended the Jews.

And the Jewish people suffered. More and more people were being displaced and joining the desperate ranks flooding the roads. Ancestral land dating back to the land program of Judas Maccabeus was being lost and taken over by rich Jews who were beginning to violate the law that set aside part of the harvest for gleaners, those less fortunate. And more and more of the affluent Jews were living in luxury, imitating the life styles of the Greeks and Romans, ignoring the laws of God given in Exodus and Leviticus and Numbers, only putting on a display of repentance during the holy festivals. This condition caused the Pharisees to be even more harsh in their demands for the people to follow the Torah and the oral laws which had developed concerning proper conduct. Religious sects were beginning to splinter the people-the Sadducees advocating living for the moment since there was no life after death; the Pharisees demanding strict obedience to God's laws; the Essenes separating themselves from their corrupted brothers to live strict lives while waiting for the coming of the Righteous One, the Messiah; and the Zealots also demanding strict obedience to the laws but also demanding an end to Roman domination. And Caiaphas, the high priest, was more interested in helping the Romans keep the peace than he was in healing the religious wounds of his people.

And the people suffered, praying for the promised Messiah to come and deliver them from their oppressors. God was punishing them, they thought, testing them as he had done through the ages.

And I was waiting for Jesus to reveal himself. I stayed on the farm, traveling back to Galilee several times to find out what I could about the Nazarene. I believe that he had visited the Essene camp at Huleh several times and had turned over most of his family's affairs to his younger brother, James. His father Joseph had died during this period, and Jesus seemed to be preparing himself for his work ahead. Even then Jesus was well aware of his destiny. He was preparing himself by living with the people in all parts of Galilee, seeing their desperation. At the camp in Huleh he was able to read the Book of Enoch and the writings of Hillel, a liberal Pharisee who taught that God was a loving God and wanted his people to live in harmony willingly, not by obeying strict laws.

Jesus knew that he had to reach a certain age before he could begin his ministry, and he knew that he had to wait for the right time. That time came in the year twenty-six when Sejanus, speaking for Tiberius Caesar, named an up and coming politician, Pontius Pilate, to be the new procurator of Judea. Sejanus hated the Jews for their argumentative nature and for the dispensations that had been given them by the Romans. He believed that they should have to serve in the Roman army as did other people under Roman rule and that they should have to pay due obedience to the Roman gods. Only fools, he believed, could worship only one god. Pilate shared those views and brought them along with him to Judea. He had nothing but contempt for his subjects and the obsequious high priest, Caiaphas. Pilate had a plan. He would rule Judea in such a way that Sejanus back in Rome would reward him with a higher position and would recall him back to Rome away from this boiling pot.

Pilate's actions did cause that pot to boil. His contempt for Jewish tradition began two years before Jesus met his cousin John at the Jordan River. The time for the Messiah had come.

11

Pilate and his wife, Claudia Procula, moved into the procurator's palace in Romanized Caesarea surrounded by Roman guards. Caesarea had been built by Herod sixty or so years before in honor of Julius Caesar, and he had built all the comforts of home for the Romans like baths and a theater, a gymnasium for Roman games, and shrines for pagan gods, but Pilate wasn't too interested in those attractions. He wanted to establish his authority in Judea.

Pilate had been told that he must appease the Jews and that he was responsible for his actions. Jews could not be conscripted into the Roman army, the only conquered subjects exempt from that duty; Roman coins used in Palestine bore symbols instead of the image of Tiberius; Jews could not be called to court on their Sabbath; and Roman soldiers could not carry images of Caesar on their shields and banners. He sat in his palace and looked westward at the Mediterranean and dreamed of Rome and brooded and hatched plans.

The Roman soldiers in Fortress Antonia overlooking the temple in Jerusalem were Syrian troops led by Roman officers. In the year twenty-seven, Pilate decided to send his crack Italian soldiers to Antonia to garrison them near the temple and place his foreign troops along the eastern borders of Palestine. He considered Jerusalem the center of any rebellion, and if he controlled the high priest and the Sanhedrin, he would control all of his territory, including Samaria and Idumea as well as Judea. He kept five hundred soldiers with him as personal bodyguards.

On a winter night the Romans marched through the streets of Jerusalem and to the Fortress Antonia with banners bearing the image of Tiberius. They quietly replaced the Syrian unit and placed their banners on the southern battlement where sentries kept watch on the temple below.

At sunrise the next morning, some priests in the temple saw the banners and went running to tell the high priest, Caiaphas. Titus leaned back in his chair and smiled.

What's so funny? I asked.

I was just thinking of what happened next, Titus said.

"Master, master, come quickly. The Fortress," the young priest called to Caiaphas, who was preparing to leave his mansion for his morning services. The priest was trembling in fear. No one interrupted the high priest in his home, which was located near Herod's palace.

Caiaphas glared at the young man and then realized that something unusual had caused the outburst. "What is it? Why the disturbance?"

"The Romans have placed banners on the fortress wall," the priest replied.

"They usually do," Caiaphas said dryly.

"But these banners have the likeness of Caesar on them. The whole temple is in an uproar." "What! A violation, a violation. Sacrilegious."

Caiaphas was stunned. Why would the Roman fool do that? He had his servant finish dressing him quickly and hurried through the streets for the temple. People were already pointing at the banners. When he arrived, priests and Levites and Scribes surrounded him, shouting and waving their arms.

The insult called for immediate action.

Annas, as president, soon called the Sanhedrin into session, and the seventy-one members quickly assembled in their chamber in the south-west corner of the temple under the Royal Porch. Caiaphas sat at his right hand as vice-president. The high priest usually presided over the Sanhedrin, but Caiaphas had allowed his father-in-law to assume that position. Annas really controlled the power, so it was only proper to give him that position, the high priest knew. Caiaphas was pragmatic and an adept politician. He wanted to retain his position and knew that the Sanhedrin would have to make some decisions contrary to Roman wishes. Whatever conflict might develop, he would not be blamed.

Annas opened the special meeting and explained the problem. After the members had settled down, he spoke. "The Romans have violated the agreement they made with us when they seized Palestine during the reign of Hycranus. They promised to honor our religion and to bring no graven images into Jerusalem. Now they have broken that promise. Why?"

"To show their authority," someone said. "To humiliate us," added another.

"What it will do," Caiaphas said, signaling for no more responses, "is cause an uprising. We must send a message to Pilate in Caesarea to have the flags withdrawn immediately. And we must let the people in Jerusalem know that we have done so. We must keep a lid on the situation as quickly as possible before news of the incident spreads."

Annas knew that Caiaphas would have a logical answer, so he called for a general vote and received unanimous approval. A message was written, the Sanhedrin dismissed, and a rider sent on the sixty-mile journey. He should deliver the message later the next day.

Four days later when he returned with the news that Pilate refused to see him, the Jews were beside themselves with rage. They headed for Caesarea by the hundreds--priests, Levites, Scribes, common citizens. Their leaders had an audience with Pilate.

"It is against our laws to have any graven images in Jerusalem," one priest explained. "That judgment is written in the Law of Moses. It is a command of our God, Yahweh."

"Tiberius Caesar is ruler over all of this land," Pilate answered. "What we have done is in tribute to him. To remove his likeness from our fortress near the temple would belittle him. Would you defy your supreme ruler?"

"Yahweh is our only ruler," someone replied under his breath.

"We must protest because of our laws laid down by Moses," the priest responded.

"Begone with you," Pilate ordered. "My ruling stands. The banners remain."

The people in Jerusalem were outraged at Pilate's violation, and multitudes rushed to Caesarea to protest, Titus said. Pilate refused to budge, so the people went to the plaza and laid down in protest, demonstrating their refusal to give in to Pilate's contempt for their religion. They stayed there for five days, immovable, stubborn.

On the sixth day, Pilate had a chair carried to the plaza for him and sat in judgment over the spread-eagled Jews. Before he appeared for the tribunal, he had his soldiers secretly hidden from the protestors. Then he called out to the Jews now standing that he had come to give them a final answer. As he said that he signaled the soldiers to come forward and surround the Jews. They marched in and stood in three ranks, impassive, ready to obey the order of their leader.

Imagine the fear that must have caused those men waiting for Pilate to speak. The Roman soldiers held their hands on the hilts of their scabbarded swords. Then Pilate made his decision. You will be cut to pieces unless you submit to Caesar's images on the banners and shields of the Roman soldiers guarding you from enemy invasion. At his signal the soldiers drew their blades.

As one man, the Jews fell to the ground and exposed their necks, crying out in agony, their noise echoing through the streets of Caesarea. Kill us if you must, one of the chief priests cried out. We would rather die than see our laws violated. Our God is our salvation. We must obey him.

Pilate was surprised at their stubbornness, at the depth of their superstitious belief in their one God. He also knew that if he continued with his foolish action word would reach Rome and that his dreams of political advancement would be over. Pilate choked back his answer and smiled and signaled for the soldiers to re-sheath their swords.

You have persuaded me in your depth of loyalty to your God, he said. I will order the banners to be returned to Caesarea and for the images of Caesar on the shields to be replaced. The emperor's image is the insignia for the Twelfth Legion, and our young soldiers proudly carry it. My one desire as your governor is to keep the peace in Judea. All of you must also do your part to be good citizens of this great land and do your duty to your God and country. Obey your laws, but also obey ours. We are your protectors and are here to keep your enemies at bay. Now begone with you. My judgment is over.

The multitude returned to Jerusalem and to their homes rejoicing in their triumph. They felt good about the stand they had taken, but Pilate wasn't finished with them. They had little idea of how much he hated them and held them in contempt. He was hatching other plans.

12

Titus looked at me, his eyes like black pools under his heavy brows. Are you still with me? he asked. I have given you the background, the conditions of my suffering people, their deep desire for a savior. We have arrived at that point in my story. It begins with John the Baptist.

Yes, I answered.

John began baptizing in the year twenty-nine, fifteen years after the beginning of the reign of Tiberius. Jesus was thirty-five; I was fifty-five and beginning to feel my age.

John was born for his mission. His father, Zacharias, was a priest, and his mother, Elisabeth, was of a priestly family and a cousin to Mary, the mother of Jesus. John was ordained as a Nazarite, a position I need to explain to you. A Nazarite was commissioned before his birth by his parents for some special service to God. Sampson was a Nazarite. A Nazarite was to live apart from other people, never to drink wine or eat grapes, never to cut his hair before his mission was completed, and never to approach a dead body, even that of a parent. It was a condition of self-sacrifice.

John lived as a hermit in the Wilderness of Judea west of the Dead Sea, preparing himself for his mission. He wore a coat made from the hair of camels and girdled it with a leather belt. The coat was the type worn by some prophets of old, but it must have been a form of self-punishment because it was made out of coarse hair that constantly irritated the skin. He lived off the land and ate what it provided, stuff like locusts and wild honey and edible plants.

John had begun calling for repentance several months before he baptized Jesus.

> John came out of the wilderness preaching to anyone who would listen. His wild hair and sun burned body and coarse coat got the attention of people, and before long crowds were gathering to hear him preach. "Repent, salvation is at hand!" he would call out. He often quoted Isaiah, saying, "I am the voice of one crying out in the wilderness. Make straight the way of the Lord."
>
> "Maybe he is the Righteous One," someone said. Others agreed, desperate for relief from their oppressive lives.
>
> As John went north near Bethany east of the Jordan and the more populated areas near Jericho, more and more people came to see him and listen to him preach. People as far away as Jerusalem came to hear this fiery man prophesy, calling for a new age. He was mesmerizing with his fiery eyes and waving beard and bare arms raised to heaven.
>
> John stood in the cool water under a summer sun waiting for the next person to come to him. He looked at the crowd on the bank glaring at them, and then he gently took the apologetic convert by the shoulders and immersed him. The man came up gasping and wringing the water out of his hair, his clothes clinging to him. John's coat was soaked and heavy.
>
> "Who sent you crowd of sinners to me?" he asked the waiting people. "Who told you to run away from the coming judgment?" The people didn't answer.

"I know you call yourselves the sons of Abraham," John cried out, his strong voice carrying across the valley, "but you only believe that you are following his law."

"What should we do, then?" someone shouted.

"You are blinded by restrictions when you should be helping one another. If you have two coats, give one to someone who needs it. If you have food, share it." John's voice softened. "God doesn't want blind obedience. He wants children with good hearts."

"Rabbi, what should we do?" a tax collector asked him.

"Do what you are hired to do. Collect your taxes but no more than is due," John replied. "Be honest with others and yourself and God. Collect no more than is required."

Then a soldier asked him, "And what should we do?"

John hesitated for a moment because he knew that the man was a soldier under the command of Herod Antipas because they were east of the Jordan and in Perea. Soldiers were often called upon to beat people and sometimes help put them to death. Perhaps the question was a trap planted by someone who wanted John to soften his message. Perhaps he was sincere.

"Do not treat people unfairly," he answered. "Do not demand money from someone for not reporting some misdeed, and don't accuse people falsely. Be content with what your masters pay you." People were delighted with his answers. He was preaching for changes that gave them hope.

Perhaps he was fulfilling the prophecies about the end of days, the time when the Chosen One would lead them into a new path.

One day while John was preaching, someone interrupted him. "Are you the Messiah?" someone asked.

"I baptize you with water to wash away your sins, to help you be born again, but another is coming soon to baptize you with fire that will burn away the chaff"

Word of John's preaching and calling for repentance and his popularity began to concern the high priest, Caiaphas, and the president of the Sanhedrin, Annas. They didn't want to lose any control over the way Jews worshiped God, and they didn't want any disturbance that would get the attention of Pilate. They wanted to keep the people under control, to keep the peace. So they sent a delegation to question John.

One day several priests and Levites arrived in their distinctive robes.

"Who are you?" the leader of the group asked. "Some say you are the Messiah. Are you?"

"I am not," John answered curtly.

"If not the Chosen One, then are you Elijah returned?"

"No."

The group huddled, exasperated by John's brusque answers, by his lack of fear. They had to have some kind of workable answer to take back to the council. "Then give us an answer that we can take back to those who sent us. Just what is it that you are doing?"

Once again John quoted Isaiah. "I am the voice of one crying in the wilderness. Make straight the way of the Lord."

They returned with John's unsatisfactory answers, so the council sent some Pharisees to dig a little deeper. Baptism was a form of washing that was a little different from the ritual bathing mandated in Leviticus. But it was obvious to the Pharisees that it was a form of purification, an ablution, the washing away of sin in order to begin a new life. John had been questioned about that.

When the Pharisees approached John with their questions, he was ready for them.

"The priests say that you have told them that you are not the Messiah or Elijah or Isaiah. If that is so, with whose authority do you baptize?" they asked.

"I baptize with water," John replied, "but there is one living among you whose sandals I am not worthy to untie. I am preparing the way."

It was late summer when John baptized Jesus, Titus continued. Later some said that John recognized Jesus as the Messiah because God had told him that a dove descending on Jesus would be a sign that Jesus was the Chosen One while others said that when Jesus came up out of the water, a dove came out of the sky and landed on his shoulder, that it was the Holy Spirit descending. Those who wrote the Gospels had varying accounts, but one common theme was that God revealed that Jesus was the Christ, and at that moment Jesus was born again. In a way, he had died and had been resurrected into a new life. Of all of those watching Jesus being baptized, only John knew that Jesus was Christ, the Messiah. To others, he was just another person that a tame dove had landed on.

Through most of his life, Jesus knew that he had been born as a son of God, that his life had a divine purpose. Mary and Joseph would have told him of his special birth when he had reached the age for the services changing a Jewish boy into a man. But he had known from birth. He had spent his life learning the history of Israel and its people, observing the life of those around him.

As part of the family, he went to Jerusalem at Passover and saw how a sacred festival was becoming a side show, a tourist attraction, not really changing the lives of the people of Israel. After the death of Joseph, he had filled his proper role as head of the house, but later with his mother's blessing he let his younger brother James assume that position. He had spent a few months with the Essenes at their camp in Huleh reading from the sacred texts and from other sources like the Book of Enoch and the writings of the liberal Pharisee, Hillel. There he really discovered the direction that the true Messiah must take. God's desire was for men to live in peace.

Titus shifted in his chair and took another sip of water. I knew by then what some of his actions meant. Titus had reached a point in his story that he considered important and that he wanted to choose his words carefully.

Shortly after Jesus came out of the Jordan, he disappeared, Titus began. John was baptizing others, and the crowd was focused on him, not on Jesus, who they thought was just another pilgrim coming to be cleansed of sin. Jesus walked south to be alone with God. He headed for the desert, a place of solitude where visions of God seem to be clearer. The beginnings of the Israelites and their relationship with God were in the desert. Abraham and Jacob and Moses communicated with God in the desert and received his commands there in the stark loneliness of a harsh world. People were more focused in a land where a wrong decision could mean their death.

Jesus had to find his true path, a way to change the way people worshiped God. The laws laid down in the Torah needed to be challenged. Leviticus and the laws given in the beginning of Numbers had been oral traditions for centuries, accumulated by prophets and others who believed they were right in following God's commands, but those rules were not leading to an understanding of what God wanted from his children. They were rituals that had lost any meaning for most people, only a burden that they had to observe. How could he bring about that understanding?

If Jesus returned north declaring himself the Messiah, people would see him as just another person who would disappoint them. Several people had declared themselves messiahs, only to be ones who had wanted to fight against the Romans. They ended up on the cross. If he declared himself the Messiah, the Jewish leaders in Palestine would want to get rid of him because their personal interests tied them in with their Roman masters. Herod Antipas in Galilee was in constant touch with Sejanus, now in actual control of Tiberius. Antipas had his hands full with the Zealots in Galilee and wouldn't want someone stirring the religious pot. Caiaphas in Jerusalem had one personal goal and that was to remain high priest under Pontius Pilate. As procurator of Judea, Pilate had the power to name a high priest. Caiaphas wanted no disturbance, a challenge to Jewish law.

Jesus knew that he had to show himself as the Messiah through what he did and what he said, and he had to be careful of how he delivered his message. Preaching the changes which needed to be made would only bring down the wrath of the Jewish leaders. The changes would be a direct threat to their mandate to the people. They retained their power by insisting that people obey the laws, even those laws which no longer had any meaning. Jesus knew, for instance, that the laws governing how people observed the Sabbath were so restrictive that they were aggravations more than aids. How do you keep the good and throw away the bad? How do you separate the grain from the chaff?

Jesus prayed constantly for guidance, and he had many visions in that forbidding spot where he lived for forty days. He followed the direction that God had given him. He knew that when he spoke to crowds he must speak indirectly in parables so that those in power could not accuse him of blasphemy or of stirring up the people against the state. He knew that he had to show the power of God given to his Son by performing deeds far beyond the capacity of any other person. He knew that he had to show that God wanted men to live in peace. Hatred is a killer of the soul, and the world that Jesus grew up in and was about to re-enter was filled with hatred. How could he convince the people that God's messenger was one of peace, not war? The Jewish people wanted a messiah who would lead them in a successful war against the Romans. The Essenes had even written a document called the War Rule giving their plans for cleansing the land of foreign rule.

The old prophets had written of two saviors for the people of Israel-one a warrior, the other a prince of peace. Jesus knew that some would see what he did as a fulfillment of those old prophets. He would act and speak in such a way that he would reveal himself indirectly. The path had been prepared for him.

It was time for him to begin his ministry. On that last morning of his living with God in isolation, Jesus headed north. His new life was beginning.

13

To regain his strength, Jesus spent a few days with the Essenes at Qumran on his journey home. In the wilderness, he had fed his soul rather than his body. After leaving the area of the Dead Sea, he passed Jericho and took the road north on the west side of the Jordan, the traditional route of Jews traveling between Judea and Galilee. Like all people living in the southern part of Judea, Titus said, I had heard of John, the fiery preacher who was baptizing people near Bethany in Perea and of his baptism of Jesus, people reporting about the strange appearance of the dove. I knew the time had come for Jesus to begin his ministry, and so I left my family to follow him.

The harvest had been plentiful with all of the family working along with the day laborers. Titus was shaking a limb on one of the last olive trees that was being harvested, the ripened fruit cascading down onto cloths that had been placed beneath it. His brother, Joel, was shaking another branch, the traditional method of harvesting olives in Palestine.

"God has been good to us this year," Joel said, laughing, "but we're both getting a little old for this sort of thing."

"Speak for yourself, little brother," Titus replied. "Age is just a state of mind."

"Tell my body that."

"We will be finished soon. Then comes the real work of working the presses. I won't be here for that. It is time for me to follow the Nazarene." Titus stopped shaking the limb, his work done.

"Marianne and I will miss you, but we know that you have a mission that God has given you. Our two sons and their families are already doing most of the work, so the farm is in good hands, the sheep being well tended. Life has been good to Marianne and me. We have been blessed."

Titus and Joel began gathering the loose ends of the cloths and piling the olives into bunches. They left olives in the trees for gleaners. The sun was almost setting behind the hill near their home when they paid the day laborers and left the grove, the sons going to their homes and families. It was the first week in October, and all land owners in Palestine were harvesting their crops. Fall was a time for work and a time for dancing. Rains had come early and regularly that year, and the harvests had been huge. Already people were looking forward to the Feast of Tabernacles, which would begin on October 15.

Titus left early the next morning with his shepherd's coat rolled and slung across a shoulder and his bag filled with fig cakes and bread and fruit. He also carried a water bag slung across his other shoulder. Maybe I should travel like the Essenes, he thought. They carry nothing except their spade.

Instead of taking the main road west of Jerusalem and then the road to Jericho, he went to the

Hinnom Valley and then east around Jerusalem to the Kidron Valley. There seemed to be more than the usual number of beggars and unclean people outside the Fountain Gate where a Roman guard stood checking products entering and leaving the city. The guard ignored the tattered group, and so did most people using the gate, the cries of the poor yammering in the fetid air, their dirty hands held out in supplication. "They should be driven away from here," Titus heard someone mutter. "Why aren't they forced to use the Dung Gate?" For a moment, he thought of resting at the Pool of Siloam, but he turned north and stayed overnight in an orchard near Bethany.

The next morning Titus followed the twisting, deeply descending road into the Jordan River Valley, the cool air of the Holy City turning hot in the low-lying valley even though it was autumn. He had noticed that people on the road appeared more animated than usual, talking with one another in excited voices, waving their arms. "It is some kind of miracle, I tell you," he heard one old man say. The man was looking skyward, his body trembling. "Perhaps the Day of Days has come. Perhaps the Righteous One is with us. Perhaps the prophecies of old are being filled"

In the late afternoon, Titus passed Jericho and went into a date palm grove where a small group of people had a fire going and was making a stew. "Hello the camp," he called to announce his presence. The four men and two women turned to look at him, hoping that he was not the landlord. When they saw what Titus carried, they relaxed Their clothing was shabby and worn, but they were smiling and happy, a strange contradiction to their appearance, Titus thought.

"Welcome, traveler," one of the ragged men said. "We have room for another and some food to eat, thanks be to God."

"We have been gathering the portion the landlord set aside for the poor like us," a woman said. "Many people were here during the day doing the same. It seems like a miracle to me because we kept finding fruit when there should have been none."

"I was here to witness what happened," another man said. "The manager had laborers climbing ladders and cutting off all the clusters when a deeply tanned man stopped by to watch the work. He was a commanding figure, perhaps a follower of John, I thought. Then he spoke to the manager in a quiet but stern voice. 'Does your master obey the laws of God?' he asked. 'Yes,' the man answered, 'as do I.' 'The workers are cutting off all clusters, even the minor ones, hardly worth their effort. Is this your command?' 'No, my master ordered a full harvest,' the man replied 'Then both of you are not obeying the law of your God He said you must obey my laws and be careful to follow my decrees. I am the Lord your God.' The manager looked away, unable to look into the stranger's eyes. 'Who are you?' he asked. 'By what authority do you question me?' The stranger waited until the manager again looked at him, and he answered, 'I am Jesus of Nazareth. Here for the harvest.'"

The man stopped for a moment trying to tell his story accurately. "The manager seemed to shrink, his arrogance gone. 'What your master ordered you to do and what you are willing to do is a sin against God,' Jesus said. 'He wants his children to take care of one another, to help those in need When you harvest, you must remember those who have nothing. God said that when you reap the harvest of your land, do not reap to the very edges of your fields or gather the gleanings of your harvest. Do not go over your vineyard a second time or pick up the grapes that have fallen. Leave them for the poor. Your harvest is full. But it is not too late to pray for a bountiful harvest but also for the souls of you and your master and for those unfortunate ones in need.' Jesus put his hand on the man's head and prayed After he had finished, the man seemed transformed and ordered his workers to leave some of the clusters of dates. Poor people were here for two days gleaning, and there is still fruit to be harvested Something has happened here. I would call it a miracle."

"Praise be to God," several in the group said.

Titus joined the group in eating the stew, and he shared his fig and nut cakes with them. They talked of the harvest and of how their lives had changed because of ill fortune, losing land or loved ones through illness or being driven from a village for some infraction of a strict law. Titus did not share his story with the group or tell them that he knew that Jesus was the Messiah. He listened as they talked of their hatred of the Romans and of Jews who profited from the ill fortune of others and of their deep desire for change. As the group separated to sleep, and as Titus was unrolling his shepherd's coat for his bed, he heard one of the men mutter, "Perhaps this Jesus is the Chosen One."

The next morning Titus filled his bag with dates and took the main road going north, hoping to catch up with Jesus so that he could observe him as he began his ministry. The road followed the curves of the hills, and Titus passed small clusters of houses tucked against the eastern side of the hills with groves on the slopes and fields out into the valley No villages were built along the Jordan, but rather fields went to its banks that were lined with willows and poplars. The Jordan twisted and turned its way south, making it unsafe for building along its banks because of possible flooding. Titus noticed how many poor people were gleaning the orchards and fields of grapes. Landowners were harvesting pistachios and almonds as well as dates. Grape vines were being searched by gleaners for withered or bird-pecked bunches left by workers. Lentil bushes were being loaded onto carts, and flax was being cut. Some people were digging in gardens for late onions and picking melons and gourds. In all the fields, the laws about harvesting laid down in Leviticus were being followed. Some of the poor picking through the harvested groves and fields must have come from as far away as Jerusalem, Titus thought. He had never seen so much left in the fields for gleaners. It was almost like the produce was reproducing itself.

Later that afternoon as the sun was setting behind the range of hills, Titus crossed the Jozeleh Wadi, a small trickle of water in it heading for the Jordan, and climbed the grade leading to Coreae, a larger village on the southern edge of

Galilee but near the border with Samaria. That part of southern Galilee took up the portion of land between the range of hills bordering the western edge of the Jordan Valley and joined a border with Judea as its northern border. That arrangement made it possible for Jews to travel to and from Galilee and Judea without having to set foot on Samarian soil, an act that would require seven days of cleansing. It also caused Samaria to be landlocked and deprived of some valuable, fertile land.

Titus sighed and looked across the parking lot at the diminishing number of cars before speaking. Leaving Joel and the others was difficult for me because I knew I would probably never see them again. I knew that Jesus would attract the attention of authorities and of the Pharisees because the Messiah's mission was to return the people to God, and most of them had strayed away from God's commands. And I knew that I would fight against anyone attacking the Nazarene.

When I entered the Jordan River valley, I heard the good news about a bountiful harvest and of a rabbi who was commanding the landlords to obey God's laws about leaving some of the harvest for the poor. People were happier than I had ever seen them, talking of the strange man who had appeared among them and had blessed them, filling them with hope. I knew that Jesus had begun his work.

When I stopped at Coreae for the night, some men at the inn where I was staying invited me to go with them after dinner to the synagogue for their evening prayers. We had a traveling rabbi read the scripture yesterday evening, one of them said, and he did not follow the usual path of others. His message was different and urgent. We can hardly wait for this evening's meeting. He challenged us to think of God's laws as paths. Do they lead to good relationships with one another, or are they simply laws laid down to hold us back?

The rabbi looked over the assembled men and noticed a stranger among them, a man who had been deeply tanned by the desert sun. The rabbi had heard of him, of Jesus, the Galilean, who was blessing the harvests as he traveled north. People passing through Coreae on their way north could hardly talk of anything else.

"Good teacher, would you like to read from the Torah?" he asked Jesus. "We have heard of your work among the gleaners. And that you have blessed the harvest. You have honored us by sharing this sacred hour."

Jesus stood and thanked the rabbi and helped unroll the scroll. "May God's blessings be with you and that you follow his commands," Jesus began, "as it is written, 'You must obey my laws and be careful to follow my decrees. I am the Lord your God. Keep my decrees and laws, for the man who obeys them will live by them.'"

Jesus began reading from Psalm 112.

Blessed is the man . . .

who finds great delight in His commands . . .

Wealth and riches are in his house,

and his righteousness endures forever.

Even in darkness light dawns for the upright,

for the gracious and compassionate and righteous man.

Good will come to him who is generous and lends freely,

who conducts his affairs with justice.

Surely he will never be shaken;

a righteous man will be remembered forever.

He will have no fear of bad news;

his heart is steadfast, trusting in the Lord . . .

He has scattered abroad his gifts to the poor.

His righteousness endures forever.

Jesus left the table and sat in the chair that the rabbi had placed beside him. He looked at the men. Some were shifting uneasily.

"Teacher, you omitted some of the passages," the rabbi said, in a hesitant voice.

"Yes," Jesus said, "the passage about fearing the Lord."

"But why do so?" the rabbi asked.

"The man who obeys the law has no reason to fear, but rather he loves the Lord and takes great delight in obeying his commands." Jesus looked at the men and smiled. "Many of the laws are written with a threat of punishment if they are not obeyed. One should obey with a cheerful heart, not out of fear."

"But they are the commands of Yahweh given to Moses," one of the men said.

"How long ago?" Jesus asked.

"You know, teacher. Many years ago on the journey to the promised land."

"And they are good laws," Jesus said, "given in the desert to a tribal people who were near the sacred altars. Now the people are scattered in many different lands with no priests to sacrifice for them. How are they to follow the laws of redemption or restitution without a priest to conduct the ceremony?"

"They must find a way," the rabbi said.

"Times have changed, but the laws have not changed Do people obey out of love or fear? Does God want blind obedience or action from a loving heart? We need to separate the chaff from the grain."

"There is love in punishment," the rabbi insisted. "A father must be stern with his son so that he may grow into a proper man."

"True," Jesus answered. "But the son must know that he is being corrected because he is loved. And the punishment must fit the crime. How does a poor man bring to a priest a fatted male lamb with no blemish in order to fulfill a law of some infraction he might have done. It is written, 'If a person sins and does what is forbidden in any of the Lord's commands, even though he does not know it, he is guilty and will be held responsible. He is to bring to the priest as a guilt offering a ram from a flock, one without defect and of the proper value. In this way, the priest will make atonement for him for the wrong he has committed unintentionally, and he will be forgiven.' Who records the laws of God?

"The Scribes," the rabbi said. "They are the ones who know the law, who interpret the law and teach others."

"And did our Father in Heaven give these laws to Scribes?"

"No, to Moses and prophets of old. They were passed on by telling others of God's commands. They were written later by the Scribes into our sacred book."

"The Scribes take great pride in memorizing the laws. They teach of a distant and stern God who must be obeyed. They pay attention to the punishment of some sin but not the laws that help neighbor live with neighbor or ways to show our love for our Heavenly Father. Obey the law so that you will not have to accept the punishments as they are written."

"You have given us much to think about, teacher," the rabbi said, concluding the meeting.

Jesus stood. "The time is fulfilled, and the kingdom of God is at hand," he said. "Repent."

The men stood and began talking with one another, but Jesus raised his arms, and they stopped talking and looked at him. "I will leave you with something to think about for tomorrow," he said. "It is written, 'Do not seek revenge or bear a grudge against one of your people, but love your neighbor as yourself.' There are many laws that tell you what to do, as well as those that tell you what not to do. For tomorrow's meeting, bring with you those laws which tell you how to

live in peace with one another. Our Heavenly
Father is a loving God. Amen."

After dinner, I went with the group of men to the synagogue
for their evening meeting. The rabbi talked of the challenge Jesus had
given them the night before and warned them that to omit parts of
the law was a sin against God's commands. Jesus spoke with authority, he said, and much of what he said was correct, but atonement for
a sin must be followed because only God can forgive a sin. A heavily
bearded man interrupted. But the priest is the one who declares a sin
completed after the burnt offering, he said. He is speaking for God,
the rabbi answered.

Titus smiled at some inner thought. The rabbi seemed to fear
that if he questioned any of the laws either written or oral some word
of his doubt may be given to a Pharisee. But the men were ready
to discuss the ideas that Jesus had suggested. Almost all of the laws
begin with "do not," someone in the group said. Often they could be
given in a positive way. For instance, it is written, "Do not defraud
your neighbor or rob him." That could be said as "Treat your neighbor fairly."

Others joined in, Titus said, quoting some of their favorites.
Each of you must respect his mother and father, one said. Yes,
another put in. Rise in the presence of the elderly and revere your
God. Notice, that does not say fear your God, another answered.
That is true, an elderly man said. And the laws about harvesting
could be said, leave some for the poor.

Many of the "do not" laws cannot be said better, a man who
had remained quiet said. Many of them are said simply. Do not bear
false witness, do not steal, do not lie, do not turn to idols. But I like
to think of all laws in a positive way. What the Nazarene said affected
me deeply because I have an uncle who is a leper and must live away
from people. He is lucky because his family feeds him where he lives
outside the city, but there are many in the land who live alone and are
dying because no one seems to care. God wants us to love one another
just like Jesus said. We all know the laws about people with afflictions
are just because if they lived with others, they would spread their

disease. The laws were given to help us, not hinder us. The difficulty comes when we have to seek atonement for a sin.

Well, another said, one thing is certain about the Nazarene. He has brought us a message of hope that we haven't had for a long time. I have heard people talking of little else the last few days. He is a powerful speaker and talks with authority. The harvest in my fields has been the best in years, and the poor are gathering more than they can carry. This Jesus seems to be working miracles.

And he was, actually, Titus said. The one people were believing to be just another unusual person was the one they had been hoping for, the Messiah.

The next morning, I left the town and went on north to Scythopolis, one of the larger cities in that area, one of the most fertile in Palestine, the Valley of Jezreel. People were busy with the harvest, and the main road heading north and west was packed with travelers talking of the man who had passed through their land, speaking of hope and new beginnings.

Then as you know, Titus said, Jesus went on into Galilee and began preaching in the villages and giving people hope that a new beginning was at hand. He began healing and offering comfort to those who were trying to survive the corning winter. Later he returned to Nazareth to visit his mother Mary and his brothers and sisters, most now grown. One Sunday while he was there, he read from the Torah and read from the prophet Isaiah the passage about the work of the corning Messiah. Then he told them that he would do no healing in Nazareth. He told them that no prophet was accepted in his hometown. And he was right. They all saw him as the oldest son of Mary and Joseph, someone who had grown up in their midst but who had wandered off and had not been home for several years. They became angry and wanted to kill him, but he left and never returned to Nazareth, which must have hurt him deeply.

14

What is easy to forget, Titus said, was that Jesus grew up and taught in a time and place and was involved in the social, political, and religious activities of the day. He was a Jew and had to face the world controlled by the Roman empire, which was corrupt and violent.

And the Jews in Galilee and Judea hated both Herod Antipas and Pontius Pilate, both controlled by Lucius Sejanus, a powerful member of the senate in Rome. Sejanus had his sights set on power and conspired, some believed, to become the emperor of Rome. He even poisoned Tiberius's son Drusus in the year twenty-three in order to get rid of that opposition. Tiberius had total faith in Sejanus and suspected nothing. With the encouragement of Sejanus, Tiberius left Rome in the year twenty-six and moved to his palace on the island of Capri, leaving the running of the government up to Sejanus. As a result, Pilate and Antipas thought they could govern as they chose because any complaint against them would go to Sejanus instead of to Tiberius.

I have already told you about Pilate trying to bring banners bearing the image of Tiberius into Jerusalem soon after he became procurator in the year twenty-six and the uproar that caused. Pilate had contempt for the Jews, and that attitude was encouraged by Sejanus, who believed that Jews were granted special privileges like not having their young men conscripted into the Roman army.

Pilate's next move was even worse when in twenty-nine he began issuing Roman coins bearing the image of Tiberius on one side and an emblem symbolizing Roman emperor worship on the other. I can't really describe how much the Jews hated that. It was sacrilegious to bring a graven image into the Holy City, and Pilate forced the Jews to use that coin. Complaints sent to Tiberius wound up with Sejanus, who enjoyed the uproar that Pilate created just as long as it did not cause a rebellion.

Herod Antipas also curried favor with Sejanus and kept Sejanus informed about conditions in Judea. Antipas knew that he had to be careful about stirring up the Zealots in Galilee, so he spent much of his time in Perea, a province he governed on the east side of the Jordan. And John the Baptist was the agitator that he kept his eye on.

During the last months of the year twenty-nine and the first part of thirty, Jesus continued his work in Galilee and found his first four disciples-Simon and Andrew, brothers who were fishermen in Capernaum, and their fishing partners, James and John, the sons of Zebedee. All four of the disciples had families to care for, but they gave up all of that life to serve Jesus. It was during this time that he performed his first miracle by turning water into wine at the wedding feast in Cana after his mother, Mary, had asked him for some help. On a trip to Capernaum, he healed Simon's mother-in-law and drove an evil spirit out of a man in a synagogue. He healed a man with leprosy. He added more disciples like Nathaniel and Matthew as his reputation grew and crowds began to follow him.

He and his disciples left for Judea several weeks before the Passover where Jesus taught on the west side of the Jordan and where his disciples baptized people. John the Baptist was on the east bank in Perea and berating Antipas for his sins.

Jesus and his group went to Jerusalem for Passover where Jesus became angry at the commercialization of the holy place and the sacred feast. A few weeks later Antipas had John arrested and sent in chains to the hilltop fortress at Machaerus.

John was drawing large crowds by his fiery preaching and by his baptizing, giving people a hope for a better life. In the previous fall Herod Antipas had made a journey to Rome before the sea lanes were closed in November and stayed at the home of his half-brother Philip, who had been sent to Rome years earlier by Herod, his father.

This is complicated, Titus said, so stay with me. Herod Antipas had two half brothers named Philip. The Philip, who had been sent to Rome, was the son of Herod and the second Mariamme, the daughter of Simon the high priest and the third wife of Herod. Philip had married Herodias, the granddaughter of Herod and the daughter of Aristobulus whom Herod had executed in 7 BC. Philip and Herodias had a daughter named Salome. The other Philip was the son of Herod and Herod's fifth wife, Cleopatra of Jerusalem, and was the Tetrarch of Trachonitis, one of Palestine's northeastern provinces. That Philip was the only good Herod. He married Salome soon after her dance for Antipas and her mother, but he died in the year thirty-four and was replaced by Agrippa the Great, a brother of Herodias. The Herod family intermarried frequently.

While Herod Antipas was staying with Philip and Herodias in Rome, he fell in love with her and decided to marry her and send his present wife back home to her father, Aretas, king of Arabia. Word of the arrangement reached Antipas's wife, and she conspired to be permitted to visit Machaerus but intended to continue on into Arabia to her father's home. King Aretas and Antipas had been bickering over their common border of Petra, and the affair Antipas cooked up merely fueled the flames. Aretas vowed to get even.

When Antipas returned home from Rome in early March, he was faced with a fiery preacher and angry subjects. John was preaching that Antipas had violated the law of God and should be punished for his sins. No man is to approach any close relative to have sexual relations, he yelled, and do not have sexual relationships with your brother's wife, he added. These are the laws of God, he said. And then John would drive home his main point. Everyone who does any of these detestable things must be cut off from their people.

Herodias was more furious than her new husband at the desert prophet for stirring up trouble, and she insisted that Antipas put a stop to it. He was more than willing because he feared the Zealots in Galilee would side with the Jews in Perea, and so with some misgivings he had John arrested and put in the dungeon in Machaerus, the isolated fortress on the east side of the Dead Sea.

Upon hearing of John's imprisonment, Jesus left Judea and went back to Galilee through Samaria. He knew that if his mission was to be successful he would have to be careful not to be labeled as a troublemaker. His real work was just beginning.

15

L ike I said, Titus continued, Jesus went through Samaria on his way to Galilee, his disciples with him, but some of them were edgy because Jews, by tradition, were not supposed to travel through Samaria. The oral law had declared it a form of defilement to touch the soil of that land.

The sky was deep blue and the land still green from the earlier rains that had given the Samaritans a good harvest. Jesus could see workers in the fields gathering the last of the wheat harvest, and he noticed that they had left some of the crop standing at the edges of the field just as God had commanded.

He and his disciples had attended the Feast of Weeks, or Pentecost, as it would be known by future generations. It was a joyous gathering of the people celebrating the first fruits of the harvest fifty days after Passover. The courts in front of the altar at the Temple had been crowded with Jews laughing and filled with joy as they watched the priests make the presentation of two loaves of leavened bread being offered to God, but being leavened, they could not be laid upon the altar. The priests then waved two lambs before the altar as a peace offering, and then following the rules

laid down in Leviticus they offered a young bull-
ock, two rams, and seven lambs with a meal and
a drink offering, and, last, a kid as a sin offering.
After that ceremony, the joy spread out even into
the Court of the Gentiles because the people now
knew that they could begin using the barley and
wheat that they had harvested.

Jesus knew that the division between the
Samaritans and the Jews was deep and had continued for generations, but he also knew that
they worshiped the same God and that Samaria
had been the home of Jacob and his tribe, even if
only for a short time in the history of the people.

After Jacob had made peace with his brother Esau,
he had left northwest Mesopotamia and moved
with his wives Leah and Rachel and bought land
in Canaan near Shechem, the city where Hamor,
the ruler of that area, had his palace. Jacob built
an altar on top of Mt. Gerizim where blessings
were read to Yahweh. Many believed that it was
there that Abraham had been willing to sacrifice
his first-born son Isaac. Jacob also built a well at
the foot of the mountain. Being an adventurous
girl, Dinah, a daughter of Leah, left camp one
day to visit with the women in the city. While
Dinah was there, Shechem, the son of Hamor,
saw the beautiful girl and violated her because he
had fallen in love with her and wanted to marry
her. A deal was struck with Jacob that he would
agree to the marriage if all the males in Hamor's
kingdom would be circumcised. They agreed to
the terms of Jacob and his sons, Simeon and Levi.
On the third day while the men of Shechem were
still in pain and defenseless, Simeon and Levi and
a group of men attacked the city and killed every

male, including Hamor and Shechem, and took Dinah back to camp. As a result, Jacob knew they had to flee the area, and he moved his tribe south to Bethel.

Jesus was remembering that history as he and his group walked north. Ahead in the distance they could see Mount Gerizim, cone-shaped and rising above the surrounding hills. The mountain is 2,849 feet high and rises 800 feet above the valley floor.

"I can see where they leveled off the top of the mountain and built their temple," Simon said. It was the first time the disciples had been in Samaria, and they were interested in seeing part of the historic past of their people.

"Yes," John answered. "They built their temple after Ezra and Nehemiah refused to let them rebuild the temple in Jerusalem."

"And it was destroyed by John Hycranus, a Maccabean king when he laid siege to Shechem three or four lifetimes ago," Simon said, his temper rising, "but they still worship there."

Jesus listened to his disciples talk of old times and of everyday things and of their families, and he marveled at how common-place it all seemed as they walked along. He saw Samaria and its ancient, limestone-ribbed and scraggly hills and saw the flow of land around him as a creation of God, as it was in Galilee and Judea and Palestine and the greater area of land of Syria and Arabia and the Negev Desert as though he were seeing it from a vast height, spread out before him, indifferent to the creatures who lived on it and dug into it and built on it different edifices to various gods. He thought of the task before him, saddened by the baseless rift between the Jews and Samaritans, but delighted to see once again Mount Gerizim, the scruffy, cone-shaped hill and its leveled top where men felt closer to God. Many people in Samaria still observed the same feasts as the Jews even though they could no longer do it in the temple in Jerusalem. The Samaritans held their sacred sacrifices at Jacob's altar in the open air, some of the debris of their destroyed temple still around them.

As Jesus and his disciples got closer, they could see Mount Gerizim much more clearly, its steep sides bare of vegetation except for pockets of thorn bushes clinging to areas around the bands of limestone circling the mountain. It was not a handsome hill, but it did have a quality that made it stand out from its neighbor, Mount Eba, which was across a short valley to the north. Stubborn, maybe. Defiant. Enduring. But Samaritans who lived nearby were used to it, and it had become commonplace to them, part of the landscape that they climbed seven times a year to celebrate the various festivals.

"What an ugly hill," Andrew said.

"It is a holy place," Jesus answered. "Notice the hill is not terraced for orchards. It is holy."

Fields and orchards surrounded the hill, the green landscape in contrast to the browning mount. The valley was fertile and productive.

The road they traveled went around the east side of Mount Gerizim. Close against the mount were a few sycamore trees and a well. They had been walking since early morning, and it was almost noon, the temperature rising. They went into the cleared space around the well, an area kept clean by the women who came there for water. The shade and well made the place inviting.

"This is Jacob's Well," Jesus told them. "Let us rest for a time, and why don't all of you go into Shechem and buy some food We will find no better place than this."

As Jesus sat enjoying the shade and the solitude, a woman from Shechem carrying a jar for water came to the well. She was about the same age as Jesus. She looked at Jesus and then drew back the well's cover and began to lower the bucket into the well's depth.

"Will you give me a drink?" he asked her.

The woman looked at Jesus with an amused smile. "How can you ask me for a drink?" the woman asked. "I can tell that you are a Jew and I am a woman of Samaria. Jews and Samaritans aren't supposed to talk with one another."

The woman had no fear of Jesus and was somewhat flirtatious. Jesus said to her, "If you knew the gift God has for you and who it is that asks you for a drink, you would have asked him and he would have given you living water."

"The well is deep and you have nothing to draw with," the woman said laughing, but not understanding what Jesus had meant. "Where can you get this living water? Our ancestor Jacob built this well and drank from it, as did his sons and his flocks. Are you greater than him?"

"Everyone who drinks from this well will thirst again," Jesus answered, becoming serious and looking at the woman closely, "but whoever drinks the water I give him will never thirst. It will become a source of water leading to eternal life."

The woman noticed Jesus's tone of voice and answered seriously but not understanding, "Give me this water so I won't get thirsty and keep coming back here for water."

"Go call your husband and return," Jesus said.

"I have no husband."

"You speak the truth," Jesus replied. "The man you are living with is not your husband, but you have been married five times."

"I can see that you are a prophet," the woman replied, awed by what Jesus had said. "Our ancestors worshiped on this mountain, but you Jews claim we must worship in Jerusalem."

Jesus answered, "A time is coming when you will worship the Father neither on this mountain nor in Jerusalem. Samaritans worship what they do not know. Jews worship what they know, for salvation is from the Jews. The time is coming, and has come, when the true worshipers will worship the Father in spirit and in truth. They are the kind of worshipers the Father seeks. God is spirit, and his worshipers must worship in spirit and in truth."

"I know that the Messiah is coming," the woman answered, her mood changed to reverence. "When he comes, he will explain everything to us."

"I who speaks to you am he," Jesus said.

The disciples returned soon after and were surprised to find Jesus talking with the Samaritan woman. They were astonished to see their master violating one of the unwritten laws, but they said nothing to Jesus about their concern. Soon after the four arrived, the woman left her water jar and hurried back to town to report her conversation with the stranger.

The disciples urged Jesus to join them in eating, but he refused and told them that he had food to eat that they knew nothing about. He said to them, "You say that the harvest is four months away, but I say to you, look at the fields, they are ripe for harvest. Even now the reaper draws his wages and harvests the crop for eternal life so that the sower and the reaper can rejoice together. I sent you to reap what you have not worked for. While others have done the hard work, you have reaped the benefit of their hard labor."

The disciples did not understand what Jesus was saying to them.

The woman had hurried back to town and told people of her meeting with the stranger at the well. "He told me everything I ever did," the woman exclaimed. "Could he be the Messiah?" Many Samaritans returned with her to Jacob's Well to meet Jesus and his disciples for themselves. At first, many of them had believed in

Jesus because of the testimony of the woman,
but after seeing Jesus and listening to him, they
believed in him more strongly and urged him and
his disciples to stay with them. Jesus and his disciples stayed for two days, and many Samaritans
became believers. They said to the woman, "We
no longer believe just because of what you told
us, but we have heard him for ourselves, and we
know that this man really is the Messiah."

Because of the incident at Jacob's Well, Titus said, Jesus and his
disciples stayed in Shechem for two days and converted many people.
As far as I know, Titus concluded, when Jesus spoke with the woman
at the well, that was the first time that he had told anyone that he
was the Messiah, the Christ. Jesus and his disciples stayed in Samaria
until the middle of January in the year thirty-one. I believe he first
revealed himself to the Samaritans because he knew that they, too,
had been waiting centuries for the Chosen One and that he would be
safe there because Antipas and Caiaphas and the other Jewish leaders
and Pontius Pilate would not see him as a threat as long as he did not
make that statement in Judea or Galilee.

16

I'm a little surprised at the ministry of Jesus in Samaria, I said. I had always believed that the Jews and Samaritans hated one another, and I had never been taught that Jesus had spread the gospel in that land.

History has a way of remembering some events and forgetting others, Titus said. Thousands of people from Samaria believed that Jesus was the Messiah and followed him, but those who recorded what he did had concentrated on other areas, areas of their interest. Samaria was a part of Palestine, which we have a tendency to forget, and it was under the jurisdiction of Pontius Pilate. But the Jews in Judea and Galilee would never forgive the Jews in Samaria for their worshiping on Mount Gerizim or for their tolerance of foreign gods. There were idols for Roman and Greek gods in Sebaste, the capital of Samaria.

But to return to my story, Titus said, When Jesus and his disciples returned to Galilee after their stay in Samaria, there was a renewed energy in Jesus. He taught in many of the synagogues with an urgency, telling people to repent because the kingdom of heaven was near, preaching of the good news of the kingdom and healing people of their diseases. By this time I was one in a crowd who followed him, hungering for some hope for a better life. Most of them were poor and hungry, their clothes dirty and ragged, their bodies smelling of disease and neglect. A few who followed were well dressed and stood out from the crowd. Some of them were believers, others were spies.

In other words, the Pharisees had begun to take notice of Jesus and his popularity, and they were concerned that they would lose control because at that time the Pharisees were powerful and used every political means to retain that power. They also controlled the religion through their strict observance of the Law of Moses, but more importantly, by observing the oral laws which had developed over the centuries and were stifling the people. Violate a law, and the Pharisees would hold you strictly accountable.

Jesus was teaching people that the law of God was for them to come to God willingly in spirit and in love while the Pharisees forced an obedience of restrictive laws that stifled the soul. The Israelites were hemmed in by trifling oral laws which had lost all meaning, such as the ritualized washing before one could eat bread, or bathing after going to market, the rules for washing cups and pots and copper vessels, fasting twice a week, the method of tithing, and the ridiculous laws which had been passed concerning the Sabbath. The Pharisees had turned the Sabbath into a burden. Jesus was teaching that the Sabbath was a day of rest and for a return to God. The Pharisees were self-righteous and had contempt for anyone whose beliefs were different. The Pharisees taught repentance through ritual. Jesus taught repentance through confession and forgiveness and love.

Jesus was beginning to challenge some of the oral laws the Pharisees demanded that the people obey. For instance, when he and his disciples were on their way to Passover in the year thirty-one, they were passing through a grain-field of barley, and his disciples began picking ripened grain and began to eat it because they were hungry. Some Pharisees just looking for an error on the part of Jesus or his disciples accused them of breaking one of the laws of the Sabbath. Jesus reminded them that David and some of his followers ate consecrated bread, and priests on the Sabbath broke the law in the temple but were not held accountable. He then said that one greater than the temple is here. I desire mercy, not sacrifice, he told them, for the Son of Man is lord of the Sabbath. Then he and his disciples went into their synagogue where there was a man with a shriveled hand. The Pharisees, wanting to trap him, asked Jesus if it was lawful to heal on the Sabbath. Then Jesus asked them if they had a sheep that had fallen into a pit on the Sabbath, wouldn't they pull it out? How much more valuable is a man than a sheep, he asked them. And then he healed the crippled man. From that time on, the Pharisees wanted to get rid of Jesus, to see that he was killed.

> The Pharisees were well aware of the meaning of Jesus's referral to the Son of Man because it came from the prophet Daniel:
>
> "In my vision at night I looked, and there before me was one like a son of man, coming with the clouds of heaven. He approached the Ancient of Days and was led into his presence. He was given authority, glory, and sovereign power: all peoples, nations, and men of every language worshiped him. His dominion is an everlasting dominion that will not pass away, and his kingdom is one that will not be destroyed."

Another incident occurred which seemed to really anger Jesus, Titus said. One day some of the Pharisees who had been observing Jesus noticed that his disciples had begun eating without first washing their hands in the ceremonial way laid down in the oral law. When the Pharisees asked Jesus why his disciples did not follow the law, Jesus called them hypocrites. Isaiah was right about you, he said to them, when he wrote, These people honor me with their lips, but their hearts are far from me. They worship me in vain; their teachings are but the rules taught by men. You have forgotten the commands of God and follow the traditions laid down by men. Here is an example of how you have set aside the law of God and follow the teachings of men, he told them. Moses wrote that you must honor your father and mother, and anyone who curses his father or mother should be put to death. But you teach that a man might say to his parents whatever help you might have received from me is Corban and belongs to God, then that man is no longer obligated to help his parents, which is a violation of God's law. Then Jesus turned to the crowd and said,

Listen to me. Nothing outside a man can make him unclean by going into him. It is what comes out of him that makes him unclean.

Later, when his disciples asked Jesus what he meant by that, he explained to them that whatever enters a man from the outside doesn't go into his heart but goes into his stomach and then later comes out. It is what comes out of a man that can be unclean because from his heart can come evil thoughts and deeds. These are what make men unclean, he said.

After Passover, Jesus and his disciples returned to Galilee and the area east of the Sea of Galilee where Jesus taught and worked miracles like feeding the five thousand and healing many people and always warning them not to tell who he was. He knew that it was very dangerous for people to begin to call him the Messiah. But he had to continue his ministry in spite of the anger of the Pharisees.

John the Baptist, while in prison in Machaerus, heard of the conflict between Jesus and the Pharisees and began to have doubts about Jesus because John was a strict believer in obeying every law of God, those given in the Torah and those developed by men over the centuries. As a result, he sent two of his disciples to question Jesus, to ask him if he was the Messiah. Jesus knew that they had heard reports of his work, but he told them of his healing diseases and the sick, the blind receiving sight, lepers being cured, and raising the dead like the ruler's daughter and the widow's son at Nain. After John's disciples left, Jesus said to the crowd that there is no one better than John, yet the one least in the kingdom of God is greater than he. Titus explained. John, like most people, thought the Messiah would rid the land of its oppressors through war. He did not understand that the key to the kingdom was love.

But conditions were about to change in Judea and Galilee where both Pontius Pilate and Herod Antipas felt they could mistreat the Jews with impunity because whatever complaints people made to Tiberius were handled by Sejanus, who kept them from the emperor. Sejanus had high hopes of seizing power in Rome, but the widow of Drusus, a son of Tiberius who Sejanus had imprisoned, sent a letter to Tiberius, exposing the plot that Sejanus was planning. As a result, Tiberius appointed Naevius Macro as prefect of the Praetorian

Guard and tricked Sejanus into the belief that Tiberius was going to grant him authority over Roman civil affairs. Sejanus went happily to the senate believing they were going to confirm the appointment, but he was arrested and immediately executed. The date was October 18, of the year thirty-one. As a result, both Pilate and Antipas were no longer protected from mistreatment of the Jews. Sejanus, a hater of Jews, had even caused Tiberius to expel them from Rome a few years earlier, but Tiberius's attitude had softened.

But both men had become so arrogant that they did not realize they were headed for trouble, Titus said, laughing softly. Both of them made political mistakes that cost them dearly and had a direct bearing on the fate of Jesus and the history of the early church and of the Jews.

Herod Antipas had imprisoned John the Baptist for more than just the Baptist's denouncing him for marrying Herodias. Aretas, the king of Arabia, had raised an army against Antipas for the insult Antipas had given him by divorcing his daughter, and the two of them had also been embroiled in a border dispute. Antipas thought he was also faced with a rebellion from his own people in Galilee for imprisoning John, who was very popular on both sides of the Jordan. He feared he might be attacked by both groups, so he had imprisoned John to get him out of the way and hoped that tempers would cool off in Galilee.

In October of the year thirty-one, Antipas threw a birthday party for himself in Machaerus and invited his high officials and military commanders and influential men from Galilee to a lavish, Roman-style banquet. As part of the entertainment, Salome, the daughter of Herodias, danced, which was highly unusual for a princess to do because it must have been a sensual performance.

You know the story, Titus said. Antipas, so taken by her performance, promised her anything she requested, so her mother told her to ask for the head of John the Baptist, and Antipas fulfilled his promise immediately. Later, the army of Aretas destroyed Antipas's army in a pitched battle over the border of Gamalitis. And not long after that, the reign of Antipas came to an end, but that is another story.

The execution of John was also a warning to Jesus. He knew what a thin line it was between being allowed to confront the rigid doctrines of the Pharisees or violating one of the capricious laws of the Romans or one of the laws enforced by the Sanhedrin. It was shortly after hearing of John's death that Jesus conducted his mission on the east side of Galilee. He had been warned by some friendly Pharisees that Antipas wanted to kill him. From that time forward, he did much of his teaching in parables and began to prepare his disciples for his own death.

Pontius Pilate was also making decisions that were political blunders, Titus continued after taking a sip of water. He seemed to take pleasure in antagonizing the Jews in Jerusalem. Shortly after the execution of Sejanus, Pilate placed shields in the palace of Herod in Jerusalem bearing the name of Tiberius with the message that the emperor was lord of all men. I suppose he had the shields displayed to show that he was loyal to Tiberius Caesar, but, of course, the act infuriated the Jews. The image of Tiberius was not on the shields, but the message implied that he was divine. During the Feast of Dedication in December that year, the Jewish leaders appealed to Caesar to have them removed. Included in the group protesting were Antipas, Philip, Herod Philip, and Agrippa. What is interesting to me is that the four Herods could agree on anything. Tiberius ordered Pilate to remove the offending shields and have them placed in the temple of Augustus in Caesarea.

Both Antipas and Pilate were now trying to curry favor with Tiberius, and they were more than willing to pass along to Tiberius any mistakes that the other had made. Their antagonism helped shape history.

17

But I don't want to get ahead of my story, Titus said. I believe that in many ways the feeding of the five thousand was a turning point in the ministry of Jesus, but earlier during that long, hot summer of the year thirty-one, Jesus had been preparing for the final stage of his work. Crowds were following him wherever he went, desperate for help. But Jesus knew that they were not understanding his message, that they needed to change in order to return to God. For centuries, the Pharisees had ingrained in the Israelites the belief that obeying the laws of Moses and the oral laws was a pathway to salvation. The strict obedience to the law gave them a feeling of self-righteousness, a concern for self. Jesus was showing them that a love for others was what God wanted from his children, to live together as a family, helping one another. In his frustration, he stated that several of the cities where he had performed miracles had not changed and would go to Hades if they remained unrepentant, but he said that if he had performed the same miracles in sinful cities like Tyre and Sidon and Sodom, people there would have believed and changed.

Jesus continued delivering his message that the time was being fulfilled and that the kingdom of God was near. He continued healing but always warning those whom he helped not to tell who he was because by now he was being closely watched by the Pharisees and by Herod Antipas. But some others saw the work of Jesus as fulfilling the prophecy of Isaiah, who said that a chosen servant of God would work quietly for justice, and in his name the nations would put their hope.

Later that fall some people brought Jesus a blind man who was possessed by a demon. The man also could not speak. Jesus healed him so that the man could see and talk rationally. The people were astonished and said it must be the work of the Messiah. When the Pharisees heard of the miracle, they scoffed and said that Jesus was able to drive out demons only through Beelzebub, the prince of demons.

Satan's right-hand man, I said.

Right, Titus said. *Beelzebub*, translated, means "lord of the flies." And there is a reason why he had that name. A swarm of gad flies attacking a caravan out in the desert east of the Jordan was something Arabs feared in the summer time. The flies would come suddenly in huge swarms and attack any living thing in their search for water. They would bite every exposed part, especially the eyes, and their stings were maddening. They would drive camels into a frenzy, causing the beasts to run away and leave their masters stranded and at the mercy of the deadly, summer heat. Little wonder that a demon god was named after them.

Jesus was a little amused at their response. That doesn't make any sense, he told them. If evil drives out evil for the good, then it is fighting against itself. If I drive out evil with the help of Beelzebub, in whose name do you drive out evil, he asked them. Anything divided against itself will not stand, he said. Anyone who speaks against the Son of Man will be forgiven, but anyone who speaks against the Spirit will not be forgiven. On judgment day by your words you will be pardoned, or by your words you will be condemned, he told them.

Jesus went with his disciples on north and lived that winter in Capernaum and Bethsaida in the households of his disciples and continued teaching. He was trying to prepare his disciples to continue the work after his death because by now he knew that his time was limited. Wherever he went he was followed by large crowds eager for his healing and his words of comfort. One day by the lake he told a crowd the parable about sowing seeds. Later he had to explain to his disciples the meaning of the lesson. I have given you the secrets of

Heaven, he told them, but not to them. Whoever understands what I am teaching will be given more, but whoever has but a little, even that will be taken away. This is what the parable means. If someone hears the message and does not understand it, the evil one will come along and take away that which has been sown in his heart. That is like the seed sown along the path. The seed sown in a rocky place is like a man who hears the message with joy, but since it has no root, it soon withers. The seed sown in thorny places is like a man who hears the word, but worries about his life and a lust for wealth choke it. But the seed sown on good soil is the man who hears the word and understands it. He produces a bountiful crop.

Jesus knew that most of his disciples were working men, not scholars, so he was very patient in explaining to them the parables that he gave to the crowds. His problem was transforming people from thinking in terms of self in day-to-day living, conditioned by rules and rituals where there was safety in habit, where breaking away from the mold was dangerous. Yet the very work that God had given him was to take away the old and replace it with a new vision.

On a beautiful March day in the year thirty-two, Jesus and his disciples left the house of Philip in Bethsaida on the west side of the Jordan river where it empties into the Sea of Galilee and took a boat over to Bethsaida on the east side of the Jordan. The west Bethsaida was in Galilee and the east Bethsaida was in Gaulanitis. The west Bethsaida had remained a fishing village, but Herod Philip, tetrarch of Gaulanitis, had rebuilt the east Bethsaida into a beautiful, modern city as a resort for wealthy Jews and foreigners and had renamed it Bethsaida Julias after Julia, the daughter of Tiberius Caesar. The contrast between the two villages was sharp and a reminder to anyone observant of the problem which was plaguing Palestine. On the west bank lived the conservative, hard-working, God-fearing Galileans. On the east bank played the wealthy who had become hedonistic, living for the moment. The area was a strategic location for Jesus and his disciples because it offered a quick escape from the jurisdiction of Herod Antipas to the safe territory of Herod Philip.

Jesus and his disciples went a mile or two east of Bethsaida Julias where he fed the thousands who followed them there.

Titus stood in the boat that was following Jesus and his disciples as they left Bethsaida in Galilee to cross over into Gaulanitis. The lake was calm and the water a deep blue, and the only sounds were the splashing of the oars of the men rowing and of their grunts as they worked. The boat was filled with people following the Nazarene and his band of men, silent as they focused on the boat ahead and the man standing in its stern. Masses of people had been following Jesus wherever he went and had even followed four of his disciples as those men went about their business of fishing while they were in Capernaum and Bethsaida. The people had camped on the narrow beaches of the lake and in the orchards and had stirred at every rumor of the Nazarene's movement.

A breeze rippled the water, and Titus felt the boat rock slightly as people shifted to get a better look at the fishing boat they were following. They went past Bethsaida Julias and headed for a slight inlet a mile or two north and east of the town. The hills beyond were green from the winter rains and crowded in closely to the shore with just a few acres of land slanting down to the rock-strewn beach.

The boat Jesus was in beached. The disciples secured it and followed Jesus up the rising meadow to the hill where Jesus led them a hundred feet above the lake. The boats following also landed wherever they could, and people scrambled out and assembled below where Jesus was sitting and talking with his disciples.

Titus followed his fellow passengers to the crowd gathering below Jesus and saw how the grass had been trampled and many of the spring flowers crushed. Off to the west Titus could see the hills beyond the lake and the bank of white clouds above them. The air was warm and soothing, and the smell of the grass and lake was like a tonic. Several gulls circled them on brittle wings. Titus looked back toward Bethsaida Julias and saw several hundred people scrambling along the shoreline to join the thousands that were beginning to settle down in the meadow below where Jesus sat.

The people were happy and excited and were enjoying the outing. Titus listened to their conversations and their singing as they sat or lounged on the warm ground waiting patiently for Jesus to begin teaching them. Titus could see that Jesus was observing them as he sat quietly with his disciples who had sat in a semi-circle between Jesus and his followers. Some of the children with the people had gone off beyond the crowd to play and to gather wild flowers, running and chasing one another. They were watched closely by their mothers who also kept track of what their teacher might be doing, not wanting to miss one of his stories or one of his healing sessions.

Then Jesus rose and came forward and raised his hands and blessed the people and began talking to them about God's plan for them. And as he went among them, touching some who were ill and talking with others, the shadows lengthened as the afternoon wore on, people not aware of the passage of time as their master went among them, giving them hope, showing love and mercy.

Titus saw a small skiff with four oarsmen beach and two Pharisees leave the boat, being helped by two of the oarsmen so that the Pharisees would not have to wade ashore or wet their white cloaks. Titus knew that they had been sent by Antipas to observe the huge crowd and to report back to the governor what Jesus might do and say. The white garments meant that the Pharisees considered themselves pure, sinless, and superior to other people. The two stood apart from the mass of people below the disciples, but their oarsmen soon joined the crowd.

The sun was setting behind the darkening clouds piling above the hills west of the lake, and Jesus returned to his disciples who began talking with him and gesturing at the people. "I will not send them away," Titus heard Jesus say. "Feed them."

Simon and Philip opened a bag that they had brought with them, and Andrew spread a cloth on the grass. Titus saw them remove five loaves of leavened bread and two fish and gesture at the food, Simon shrugging his shoulders as if to say it is hopeless. "This is all we have." Jesus smiled at Simon, stood and placed his hand on the head of his disciple, and turned to the crowd.

He raised his arms and faced the five thousand below him. "Sons and daughters, children of God, the hour is getting late. My disciples will feed you with the help of my Father. Listen to them." The disciples then had the people arrange into groups of fifty and borrowed baskets from some of the women in the crowd and returned to Jesus, who raised his arms and blessed the food and the people.

Titus sat on his shepherd's cloak and placed his staff beside him. He took a drink from his water bag and passed it among some of those sitting beside him. He had never been in such a huge assembly that seemed so filled with joy, people laughing and singing, anticipating a meal. People seemed to be sharing their possessions with one another. The disciples walked among the people handing out pieces of bread and fish. Titus could hear thunder on the west side of the lake.

After they had eaten, some men in the crowd began to shout, "This man is the prophet who has been promised us! He has fed us and cared for us. We should make him our king!" Others took up the chant as people stood and reassembled from their groups of fifty. Some women began ululating, their voices shrill and penetrating. The mass of people did not see Jesus send his disciples back to their boat while he walked farther up the hill and to the west. The two Pharisees and their oarsmen also left to return to the city of Tiberius and report to Antipas.

Titus left the crowd and began walking back to Bethsaida Julias, walking carefully along the unfamiliar shoreline because darkness had come suddenly, the wind beginning to whip in stronger gusts from the west. Before long, Titus had to go to higher ground because waves had begun to whip against the rocky beaches. Fierce gusts whipped his cloak and made him tuck his emptied water bag and shepherd's cloak under his arm while he felt ahead with his shepherd's staff for safe footing. When he finally reached the city, he was lucky to find an inn still open and escaped the rain squall that swept across the lake.

You know the story, Titus said, of how he fed the five thousand with just five loaves of bread and two fish. In your age, doubters say that the people began sharing what they had. Maybe. Miracles happen. But I was there, and I saw the joy and hope the people had that day, and I saw the love in Jesus for those who had followed him. He fed them with more than bread and fish. He gave them a new spirit and showed them the true path back to God. But he also knew that most would not get the message, that they were living in that moment of time, being fed and loved, that the daily grind and reality of their lives would wash away the euphoria of the event.

What really troubled Jesus was their attempt to make him their king. He knew that the effort would be reported back to Herod Antipas and that Antipas was already plotting how to stop him. He spent a few more days in Bethsaida and Capernaum before he and his disciples went south through the flower-filled valley of Gennesaret on their way to Jerusalem. Crowds followed him and were healed simply by touching his cloak. Then they crossed the lake to the east side and went to Gamala, a city in the area known as Genesareth. There he healed a man possessed by demons.

18

That miracle created quite a sensation, Titus said, smiling as he remembered the event.

Titus was with a group of hardy souls who had crossed the Sea of Galilee following Jesus and his band of men. After they landed, he looked back across the lake, now calm after the sudden storm the night before. Some fishermen were working seines near an inlet, knowing that fish usually like to feed near where fresh water flowed into the lake. They left the dock area at Gamala and took the road south and east to join the crowd following the Nazarene.

Then Titus heard a howling coming from the limestone-lined hillside where the city's tombs were located just outside the city. He elbowed his way through the crowd to get a closer look at the commotion. He saw a naked man crouching before Jesus, hobbling back and forth and jabbering incoherently. The man's hair and beard were tangled and his hands torn and bleeding and he had cuts on his arms and chest. He had broken his chains and had escaped from confinement. He fell to his hands and knees and then raised up to a kneeling position, tilted his head, and howled.

Jesus looked at the man and pointed at him. "Come out of this man, you evil spirit," Jesus demanded sternly.

The man looked at Jesus, his eyes bulging, his mouth gaping. "What do you want with me, Jesus, Son of the Most High God?" the demon lodged inside the man said in a loud, braying voice. "Swear to God that you won't torment me!"

"What is your name?" Jesus asked.

"My name is Legion," the demon answered, "for we are many. Please, do not send us away. Send us to them, Master." He pointed to a large herd of pigs feeding near the lake.

"You may go to the pigs," Jesus replied, and the spirits left the man and entered the pigs, which went berserk and rushed into the lake and drowned. The swine herders ran for town.

The man was healed immediately and began to weep. The disciples helped get him bathed, his wounds dressed, his hair and beard combed, and found a cloak for him. By then a crowd of people had rushed from Gamala to see for themselves what the swine herders had reported They were amazed at the change in the possessed man and were awed and frightened at the power of Jesus. They asked Jesus and his disciples to leave.

After most of the people had gone back into the city, Jesus and his disciples prepared to leave. Jesus tenderly touched the man's head. "Master, let me go with you," the man pleaded, "I want to follow you and be your servant."

"Go home to your family," Jesus answered, "and tell them how much the Lord has done for you." Then Jesus and his disciples took the road south to Gadara in the Decapolis, where word of the demons entering the swineherd was already being told. Titus was one of the people telling the story.

When Jesus drove out the demons from the man, they entered the pigs, and the pigs rushed to the lake and drowned, Titus said. It was a large herd, and the men herding the pigs panicked and ran into town yelling out the news.

Jesus and his disciples spent a few days in Gadara and the ten Greek cities in the Decapolis healing and teaching and listening to the large crowds following him. Word had spread about how he had raised a young girl from the dead, a daughter of a ruler of a synagogue in Gennesaret, and had performed other miracles. I could see how much Jesus loved the people, Titus said, and how much compassion he had for them. But I could also see how much they drained from him. His eyes told me.

Jesus and his disciples crossed the Jordan River at Bethany beyond the Jordan and walked up the steep road to Bethany at the head of the Kidron Valley and across from Jerusalem where they stayed with friends waiting for Passover to begin. Passover came late that year and began at midnight on April 13 of the year thirty-two.

Titus knew that Jesus would stay at the home of Mary and Martha and their younger brother, Lazarus. Titus had heard some of the disciples talking about the family and that Mary was the one who jealously took personal care of the Nazarene. After he arrived and was greeted, Mary would wash and oil his feet, a sign of respect and welcome for a guest entering a Jewish household.

That evening Titus tried to find a camping spot in Gethsemane. The garden was crowded with pilgrims who had arrived for Passover, and Titus had to go higher up to the eastern edge of the garden with Mount Olivet looming above him. He could look down into the grove of ancient olive trees, and he could see hundreds of camp-fires dotting the Kidron Valley, some even among the tombs of the kings on the west side of the valley and near the temple's east wall. He knew that Jews from all parts of the world had made their annual pilgrimage back to Jerusalem and to their most sacred feast. A city of twenty-jive thousand was now surrounded by perhaps a hundred thousand.

As Titus was unrolling his shepherd's coat for his bed, two men walked through the trees and came to him, bowing slightly as a sign of friendship. One was an older man with a long beard and travel-stained clothes. The other was young, perhaps in his early twenties, and was just beginning to grow a beard. His hair was neatly combed.

"Mind if we stay with you, Pilgrim?" the older man asked with a Galilean accent. "We find the accommodations down below a little lacking." He chuckled at his own joke.

"Not at all," Titus replied, glad for their company and after sensing that they were harmless. Robbery during Passover was fairly common with so many people crammed into the area. There was enough light for Titus to get a better look at the two men. The older man was thin but wiry. The other one was athletic and sat without using his hands. Titus could tell that they were from northern Galilee by the way they were dressed.

"Have you come far?" Titus asked.

"From Gischala, northern Galilee," the older one said. "But today we have traveled from Corese, along with many others. Have you come from a distance?" he asked Titus, politely.

"Not really," Titus said. "I have been following Jesus, the Nazarene."

"We have heard of him," the old man said, "and of all the miracles he performs. Some say he is the Messiah that the prophets spoke of."

"Perhaps," Titus said, not wanting to reveal what he knew. "I have seen many wonderful things with my own eyes."

"I have forgotten my manners," the old man said. "My name is Rufus, and this younger man is Gestus."

"I am Titus from Bethlehem," Titus replied. "Born there many years ago."

"You are near home, yet you are here," Gestus said, not asking why but wondering.

Titus was a little amused at the statement. It wasn't polite to pry too deeply into someone's past or reasons for actions, but he didn't mind. "I haven't been home regularly for the last twenty years or so, "he said. "I have had it as my mission to follow the Nazarene, even when he was young. Long ago I went into Galilee to Nazareth and to Sepphoris where I saw a man condemned and executed for following Judas, the Gaulanite."

"The Zealot," Rufus said. "That is one reason the two of us are here. I shouldn't have said that, but I think we can trust you."

"We are going to join the protest tomorrow," Gestus said. "Pilate is using the wrong funds to build his aqueduct. He can't do that."

"Then you are Zealots?" Titus asked. They didn't look like revolutionists.

"Many men in Galilee sympathize with those who oppose the Romans and our own governor, Herod Antipas. No, we aren't fighters," Rufus said, "but we do believe that we must oppose Roman rule and those who collaborate with them, even people like our high priest, Caiaphas. We have strong men enough on our side, men like Barabbas, who will be one of the leaders tomorrow."

"You are old enough to remember Judas, the one who organized the movement," Titus said. "Did you ever meet him?"

"No, but I was a young man then and went along with some of them," Rufus said.

"I stayed with him and his men one night," Titus said. "He was one of the most courageous men I have ever met."

"Then are you a Zealot?" Rufus asked.

"No," Titus said. "I have fought against the Romans and have seen their swift punishment for those who oppose them. I suppose, in a way, I was a Zealot once, but I have learned there are other ways of fighting back against oppressors. Jesus is showing us a different path."

"Little good it does to turn the other cheek," Gestus said hotly. "Then you have heard some of his teachings," Titus said.

"Enough to know that it will never conquer the Romans," Gestus replied.

"Perhaps," Titus said, "but history will tell us which way is best. Jesus teaches with authority and is filled with God. What happens with your demonstration tomorrow may show us the right and wrong of ill-timed action. May there be nothing but peace on Passover."

"I'll agree with that," Rufus reflected.

"What I missed most tonight," Titus said wistfully, "was the Passover supper. It is a time for family and giving thanks to God for delivering us from slavery."

"May he deliver us again from what we are today," Gestus said.

"Let us thank God for this beautiful evening," Rufus said. "Tomorrow comes early."

At sunrise the next morning, Rufus started a small fire and added barley meal to a small pot of boiling water preparing a mush for them while Titus removed a cake of dates and nuts that he had purchased in Bethany beyond the Jordan before he had crossed over into Judea. The three of them dipped into the pot with their fingers and scraped out the cooked barley.

"So much for the ritual washing before a meal," Rufus laughed as he sucked mush from his fingers. "Those who wrote the rules never had to live like we do. Reality triumphs every time."

"Look at how the sun is striking the top of the Temple," Titus said. "It's like another sun."

The shadow of the Mount of Olives still covered most of the Temple, but the white stone of the magnificent building reflected the sun, sending out golden beams. The three men watched as the shadow receded revealing more of the Temple until it lit the golden plates and cluster of grapes above the grand doorway to the Temple. They were deeply moved by the sight.

"It is almost like a sign from God," Titus said.

"Let us go there and join the others," Rufus said. "Perhaps it is a message to us."

Titus and the two men entered Jerusalem through a gate that let them into the city just below the south wall of the temple where they could join the throng of people taking the ritual bath before entering the Double Gate. They took the stairs that went under Solomon's Porch and led up to the Court of the Gentiles. The court was already filled with people, and they pushed their way through past the booths lining the Soreg Wall where money changers were doing business and where men had pens of lambs and cages of doves for sale to anyone who wanted to offer them for sacrifice and went west and north toward the stairs leading up to Fort Antonia.

"They are here already," Rufus said, pointing. "See that man in the front, the one who is facing the others and waving his arms. That is Jesus Barabbas, our leader from northern Galilee."

Titus could barely see the person Rufus was trying to point out because of the milling crowd, but he noticed the Roman soldiers at the top of the stairs looking down at the mob.

Then the packed group of men began chanting, "Not the Corban, not the Corban," over and over and getting louder. The Corban was a special offering to God that was given with a special vow and purpose in mind by the giver. A tithe was Corban by the law laid down in Leviticus, but the practice of a special offering had been added where a person could give something to God with a special vow and purpose in mind. Thus a person could interdict himself by a vow not only by not using the object, like land, for instance, himself but from giving it to another person. It was sacred and owned by God. Jesus attacked the Pharisees once in a conversation with them about what hypocrites they were because the Pharisees approved of that type of Corban where a man did not have to take care of his parents in their old age by giving to God what he could have given to them.

And Pilate had taken money from the Corban to construct the aqueduct. People had discovered the misuse of their sacred offering a few months before and were furious. The temple also asked for a yearly donation from all Jews in order to run the temple, but that donation was a small amount. It added up, however, to vast sums because thousands paid. If that money would have been used to bring more water into Jerusalem, people would not have objected, but the Corban was God's. It was sacred money, and they were angry at Pilate for using it.

An aqueduct had been constructed in the eighth century BC by Hezekiah, one of Israel's great kings, bringing water from Solomon's Pool near Bethlehem, but in the summer time the amount of water from that source turned into a trickle. Pilate's aqueduct began at the springs near Hebron, twenty miles south, and wound around the hills to the city with a declining pitch of a foot for every two hundred yards. Romans were great engineers, but not much better than the ancient ones who had brought water to Jerusalem from Bethlehem with a series of canals and clay pipes and tunnels.

The Jews in Judea had complained but were afraid of Pilate and unwilling to accuse Caiaphas of collaboration with Pilate. The Galileans were more conservative and combative. They were the ones confronting the Romans, crowding near the stairs leading up to Antonia.

Their shouts were getting louder as more joined in Barabbas was leading the chanting. "No aqueduct! No Corban!" they yelled over and over. The Roman guards stood impassively at the top of the stairs, staring down at the growing crowd.

What the Galileans did not know was that Pilate was furious at their demonstration and that he had ordered a number of his soldiers to dress like Jews and mingle with the mob below. They were armed with daggers hidden under their cloaks, and they had been ordered to attack the demonstrators on his signal.

The mob milling at the foot of the stairs was unarmed because they had been searched for weapons by Roman soldiers at all the gates leading into the temple. Titus had to leave his shepherd's staff and even his shepherd's coat at the Double Gate.

After several minutes of watching the protesters, a centurion commanding the soldiers at the top of the stairs left and walked back into the fort. He had been ordered to report to Pilate when he judged the crowd had begun to reach a fever pitch. Part of the fort housed the procurator when he was in Jerusalem. After a few minutes the centurion returned with Pilate and several of Pilate's special guards. Pilate was dressed in his military uniform, looking regal as he stood at the top of the stairs staring down at the now-quiet protesters.

Barabbas looked up at Pilate and raised his arms. "It is a sin against our God to misuse the Corban," he yelled. "The aqueduct must not be built with sacred money."

"We have the approval of your high priest," Pilate replied. "And it has been approved by your highest court, the Sanhedrin. The city needs the water, and it is only right that it is paid for by the people who use it."

"No Corban!" Barabbas yelled as he turned away from Pilate and back to the protesters. "No Corban! No Corban!" he screamed, waving his arms as a signal to the Galileans who took up the chant. Pilate watched and then turned to the centurion, who drew his sword and raised it.

Pilate turned and walked back into the fort.

The soldiers dressed as civilians began stabbing the men standing near them. Titus could hear their grunts and yells and the screams of the defenseless Galileans. Most of them turned and tried to flee, but the crowd behind them kept them in danger. Many fell and were trampled.

When the action started, Rufus sprang forward away from Titus and Gestus and beat his way through the struggling mass. Titus saw a squad of Roman soldiers run down the stairs from the fort and tackle Barabbas, who struggled feebly against the mass of soldiers who had been ordered to take him alive. Rufus was trying to help his leader, but as he ran toward the group of soldiers surrounding Barabbas, a soldier turned toward the old man and ran him through with his sword. Blood welled from Rufus's lips as he slumped to the ground. The soldier calmly put his foot on Rufus's chest and withdrew the blade and wiped it on Rufus's cloak. The others dragged Barabbas up the steps and into the fort.

Titus and Gestus were standing near the Soreg Wall on the outer edge of the mass of bodies, but not out of harm's way. As they tried to flee, one of the Romans dressed as a Jew came by them slashing with his dagger at a Galilean who had put his arms up to ward off the attacker. The Roman slashed his arms, and then as the man attempted to push the Roman, the Roman lunged forward and drove his dagger into the Galilean's stomach.

Gestus leaped on the back of the Roman who turned, elbowing the young, inexperienced attacker and drove his dagger into Gestus, who gasped and fell away, his eyes wide with surprise and shock. Then the Roman turned toward the larger group of Galileans trying to flee.

Titus dragged Gestus against the Soreg Wall away from the milling crowd and began to tear away Gestus's cloak so that he could see the wound. The Roman had aimed for the stomach, but blood welled from Gestus's side and was soaking into the stones of the Court of the Gentiles. Titus tore off a piece of Gestus's cloak and tried to stop the flow.

"Is it bad?" Gestus asked. "I can't feel much right now."

"I'm not sure," Titus replied, "but I think you'll be all right if we can stop the bleeding. I think it's just in your side and missed an organ. Nothing is running out except blood."

By then the area was clear except for the dead and wounded. The Romans were chasing the other Galileans back into the mass of pilgrims in the center of the Court of the Gentiles. Some of the wounded Galileans ran to the east side of the Court of the Gentiles and through the Soreg Wall, through the Beautiful Gate, into the Court of the Women, up the stairs into the Court of the Men, and up the other flight of stairs onto the Porch where the altar was, where priests were sacrificing animals. Some of the wounded died there.

Titus tore another, longer strip of cloth from Gestus's cloak and wrapped it around the youth's waist to hold the compressed cloth in place that Titus had placed on the wound to stop the bleeding. He put one of Gestus's arms around his shoulder, holding onto it while he placed his other arm around Gestus and headed for the Sheep Gate and out of the temple and the city. Titus knew of a hideout on Mount Scopus just north of Jerusalem. He had heard that a mixture of olive oil and a resin called the Balm of Gilead could be put on the wound to stop the bleeding. He would later boil up some figs and make a poultice for the wound if it turned putrid.

Gestus limped along, sometimes dragging his feet, as Titus labored off the road and up the mountain to a ledge of limestone and followed it to the east until he found a shallow cave, the entrance hidden by some thorn bushes. Below them was a grove of olive trees, and Titus could look east to the low hills bordering and hiding the Jordan Valley. He laid Gestus down and then gathered some of the leaves on the thorn bushes and chewed them into a paste, unwrapped the wound that had stopped bleeding, and applied the wad of wet leaves to the bluish stab wound Gestus wanted to see it, so Titus held him up to look.

"Will I live?"

"Sure you will," Titus answered in a positive voice. "I'm going to apply a remedy right now, and then hunt us up some food and other stuff so that we can stay here for a while. In a day or two you will be ready to head for home."

Titus knew that they would have to have water and food, and he wanted to return to the gate into the city where he had to leave his staff and coat and water bag. After he had made Gestus as comfortable as possible and after the young man began to sleep, Titus left following the route they had taken to their hideout. Off to the south, he could see the Temple standing white and splendid above the temple grounds and Jerusalem and its solid walls. As though nothing had happened there earlier today, Titus thought.

While Titus had been helping Gestus escape the city and taking care of the wound, Caiaphas had called an emergency meeting of the Sanhedrin to discuss the murderous action Pilate had taken against the Galileans. The action of the Romans went against all laws of the Romans and the Jews, but for the Jews it was especially serious because it had taken place on the temple grounds and on one of their holiest festivals, Passover. No matter how angry the members of the great council were about the murders of the Galileans, there was not much they could do about it. They were under the control of the Romans, and they did not want to start a bigger revolt, which was possible if they asked the Jews to hold Pilate responsible for the deaths of the Galileans killed in the Court of the Gentiles. They also did not want to suspend Passover because, although none of them said it, they knew that Passover was the biggest contributor to the temple treasury and to the businessmen in Jerusalem. Money poured in from the thousands of pilgrims who were there.

"We must rope off the area where the Galileans died until the Levites clean up the spilled blood, " Caiaphas said in closing the meeting. "Most of our people did not see the disorder and will only hear about it through rumor. Many have traveled far to be here and to offer their sacrifices to God. We will send a protest to Tiberius Caesar and let the emperor discipline the procurator. And may God protect us from further harm. Return to your duties and your homes and pray for all of us." Caiaphas knew that if he wanted to remain the high priest, he must kowtow to Pilate, who kept the priestly robes he was now wearing locked up in Antonia and released them back to the high priest only for the major Jewish festivals. The Romans even controlled part of the Jewish religion.

I lost track of Jesus at Passover that year, Titus said, because I got caught up in a revolt the Galileans staged on the first day of Passover against the aqueduct that Pilate was building from Hebron to Jerusalem. He was using the temple's sacred treasury for the project, and the people were protesting against him. He could have used the general funds from the temple because those are not especially dedicated to God, but Pilate was arrogant and persisted.

During the melee, Roman soldiers, cloaked in civilian garb, began killing Galileans who were gathered below the stairs leading up from the Court of the Gentiles to Antonia, the fort overlooking the temple. Barabbas, who you have read about in the Gospels, was a leader and was taken prisoner by the Romans. I escaped and helped Gestus, a young man I had met and who had been wounded. We left the city and hid out on Mount Scopus for a few days. After his wound closed, I helped him return back north to his home in Galilee.

19

Not much is written in the Gospels about what was happening in Palestine during that period, I said. I never realized how much control the Romans had over the Jews back then. How could Pilate use temple money to build the aqueduct without the permission of the Jews?

Because he controlled the high priest, Caiaphas. The Romans selected the high priest and had done so ever since they began governing Judea in the year six, Titus said. They kept the high priest's robes locked up in Antonia and brought them out only for the major festivals. When Pilate demanded that the Jews pay for the aqueduct and that they should take the money out of the temple's special treasury, the Sanhedrin objected, but didn't want to disturb the peace. They had become soft. The Galileans were the ones who were conservative and combative, who were angry with the Judeans for being submissive. But the ones who wrote of Jesus and his work weren't interested in history. They wanted to tell of his miracles and record his parables and spread his message, to authenticate him as the Son of God, the Messiah.

Anyway, Jesus must have been deeply disturbed by the brutality of the Romans against the Galileans in the aqueduct riot in the temple, in his Father's house during the feast that observes the Jew's escape from slavery in Egypt. And how easily that action was forgiven by the spiritual leaders of the Israelites. How ironic it was for the Romans to kill Galileans to prove that they controlled the Jews during a solemn but joyous festival celebrating their freedom.

Jesus knew that the Pharisees wanted to get rid of him because his message of love went against their strict adherence to the Mishnah as a path to salvation. And the death of those brave Galileans at the foot of the stairs of Antonia clearly showed how much control Rome had over Caiaphas and the other Jewish leaders. If those collaborators could make Jesus's ministry look like an attempt to seize power, then they could have the Romans arrest Jesus for stirring up a revolt.

After Passover, Jesus and his disciples left Jerusalem and went north, taking the main road east of the Jordan River through Perea and the Decapolis and Gaulanitis, fleeing the crowds and the spies of the Pharisees who followed him. He needed time to plan how he would fulfill his mission because he knew that his time was short and that even his disciples had very little understanding of how God wanted men to live.

They took the road through Bethsaida and spent a few days in Capernaum, staying in the homes of some of the disciples and doing some fishing. Then Jesus and his group took the road north and west to Phoenicia. The road they were on was the main road from Capernaum to Tyre, and it went through Gischala. I had arrived there with Gestus a week or so before that, Titus said. The young rebel's wound had almost healed by the time we reached his family's home, so I was ready to move on. I had intended to go back home to Bethlehem and my own home, but when Jesus and his disciples stopped overnight in Gischala, I changed my mind. That evening the crowd was so large at evening services that instead of having it inside the synagogue, we met outside where Jesus talked about the redeeming spirit of love. I have but a little time left to be with you, he said. My Father calls me. Then he blessed us and healed many.

But Jesus did not want large crowds following him, so he and his group left early for Tyre, and I followed them just as the sun began to touch the snow-capped top of Mount Lebanon. We crossed through a mountain pass east of the city during late afternoon and saw the blue Mediterranean off in the distance. We could see the hill that housed the old city jutting out from the mainland and forming the harbor. The newer city built around the harbor cut off our view of the wharves. Since it was a major port, Tyre was probably the most cosmopolitan city in that part of the world. Jesus and his disciples went off the road and sat under some cedar trees, resting before descending down into the plain. The sight below was peaceful on that spring day with the sun gleaming off the white buildings in Tyre. I could only imagine what Jesus was thinking, what he was planning, why he had come to this home of Gentiles and heathen gods, where the main interest of people was making a profit and living hedonistic lives.

Jesus knew that he had only a short time to prepare his disciples for their mission after his death. The world they lived in was in turmoil, full of violence, torn by a nation that governed by a system of government that demanded obedience from its subjects through an empirical system that called for practical actions for desired results. Any deviation from the policies of Rome brought swift punishment. The Jews made difficult subjects because of their religion, and hated the Romans who governed them. They resented the taxes collected by the Romans which helped the Romans govern them, which kept two legions of Roman armies in Palestine and Syria. The Jews felt betrayed by their high priest who was put in office by the procurator of Judea. Through that system, Rome controlled the Jewish religion. Every Jew who saw Caiaphas in the beautiful blue robe worn by the high priest at the altar during the different Jewish holy festivals felt betrayed. And many of the wealthy Jews had begun to accept the life style of the Greek and Romans, ignoring many of the laws of Moses. Fighting against the hedonistic direction taken by many of the Jews, the Pharisees had become zealous in demanding that Jews strictly obey every law of Moses and all the Mishnah rules that had developed over the centuries. And their control over the religious rituals of the Jews kept people from God because the process of ritual had become habit. Do a certain thing, and your sins would be redeemed. The Jews were desperate for the Messiah, for a savior, but they were looking for a warrior king, someone who would drive out the Romans and restore their freedom.

They were looking for a leader that would restore the old system of land ownership and of electing their high priest and of a life that was patterned by the laws of their ancestors. Those crowds which had followed Jesus saw him heal the ill and raise some from the dead and feed multitudes. Many believed that he was the Messiah, the Christ, the Chosen One, who would restore them as the nation that would lead all other nations back to God. But they saw him as a leader of the people, who would defeat the Romans and restore their kingdom. When Jesus talked of loving one another or of giving a man your second cloak if he demanded your first or of loving your neighbor as yourself or of doing unto others as you would have them do unto you, they did not understand the difference between body and soul. They had no real understanding of the spirit.

The crowds were amazed by the miracles performed by the Nazarene. They saw him feed thousands of people, they could be healed simply by touching him, they listened to his stories and were comforted by his blessings, but they did not understand that every time he fed them or healed them or comforted them he was demonstrating love, the path that God wanted them to follow.

And his disciples had seen it all and had lived with him but still did not understand.

Jesus looked down at Tyre and the fields surrounding it. A few travelers hurried past them driving beasts loaded with merchandise or following wagons weighted down with goods for sale. He wanted his disciples to experience a Gentile city, a city centered on trade and not controlled by religion, except, perhaps, trade was their religion.

"It is a magnificent sight," Simon said, "a city of our ancient enemies, the Phoenicians, or Canaanites, as our ancestors called them. But it is Godless."

"The people there worship many different gods," Jesus said. "We will go to the synagogue this evening."

"All they think about is business," Matthew said.

"Or whoring," Andrew said angrily.

"We will not judge them," Jesus said quietly. "They are people of God whether they know it or not. Many of his children have gone astray."

"We spoke in haste, teacher," Simon said. "We should not speak ill of anyone."

As Jesus and his disciples entered Tyre, Titus followed a short distance behind, mingling with the crowd of other people who were anxious to get into the city and find food and shelter. When they entered the plaza, Titus saw the platform where Moloch had sat accepting his sacrificial gift many years ago. Jesus and his group had stopped before it, and Jesus was talking with them. Several people among those entering the city began pointing at Jesus. "It is the Nazarene and his men," someone said. "I wonder what they are doing here?"

Several shopkeepers on the edge of the plaza had begun to remove their merchandise and to close their booths. The sun had set behind the warehouses hiding the harbor from view. The last rays of sun touched the top of the temple of Diana to the north of the plaza. Jesus began to walk away from the platform when a woman approached him. She was a Greek but born in Phoenicia. She had heard that Jesus was in the plaza, and she had run from her home to meet him, desperate for his help. She stopped before him, wringing her hands.

"Lord, Son of David, have mercy on me!" she wailed. "My daughter suffers. She is possessed by demons, and I don't know what to do. Help us."

Jesus looked at the woman but did not answer. He walked away followed by his disciples. The woman sobbed and followed at a distance.

"She is following us," one of his disciples said. "Send her away because people are beginning to notice. She won't shut up."

Jesus stopped walking and looked at his disciples and then back at the woman who hurried forward and knelt in front of him, looking up at him, her hands pressed together. "Lord, help me," she pleaded.

"Let the children eat their bread," Jesus said to her, looking down at the woman. "It is not right to toss it to the dogs."

The woman opened her hands and reached for him. "Yes, my Lord," she said, her voice low, "but the dogs feast on the crumbs which fall from the table."

Jesus took her hands and lifted her and looked at her tear-stained face. "Woman, you have great faith," he said. "What you ask for has been granted."

The woman shouted with joy and turned and ran for home.

Titus knew that he had witnessed a turning point in Jesus's ministry. The Mishnah law had developed strict codes about contact with Gentiles that required complicated cleansing rituals. For Jesus to talk with the woman was a violation of the law. For him to touch her was an even more serious violation. Jews had such contempt for Gentiles that they often called them dogs. Even his disciples knew what he had said to her and what her answer meant. The Canaanite woman was the first Gentile who had been accepted into the new path back to God.

That evening in the synagogue Jesus remained silent while the local rabbi read from the Torah and offered evening prayers. Titus could see that several of the Jews had heard of the plea of the Syrophoenician woman and that they disapproved.

One fat Jew wearing expensive clothes and golden rings, his hair and beard trimmed and oiled, stood and looked at Jesus. "It is reported that this man, Jesus of Nazareth, healed a mad daughter of a Gentile woman just before we met in this house of God," the man said accusingly. "What he did is a violation of our laws."

Jesus stood and looked at the perfumed man, at his expensive and fashionable clothing. He smiled and turned to the others. "The law of Moses must be obeyed, and I have done so. Our Father in Heaven said to Moses that you must not do in Canaan as they do where I am bringing you. Do not follow their practices. You must obey my laws and follow my decrees."

The fat man sat down. Jesus looked at those assembled, noticing that most of them were merchants who lived in luxurious homes. Some averted their gaze, some smirked.

"Have not some of you adopted the habits of the Gentiles, disobeying the laws of Moses?" Jesus turned back to the rabbi. "The time is fulfilled, and the kingdom of God is at hand We are all children of God, and the woman who I helped is a child of God, as we are. She has more faith in God than many here tonight. One of the laws of Moses says that the alien living with you must be treated as one of your native-born. Love him as yourself, for you were aliens in Egypt. God also said that we are to love our neighbor as our self. It was our heavenly Father who healed the child, who drove out the demon." Jesus sat.

Titus sat silent for a moment, gathering his thoughts, remembering events two thousand years ago.

We entered the city on the road that led us into the plaza where Jesus stood talking with his disciples. A woman approached him and asked for help. At first he refused, but then he healed her demon-possessed daughter without even seeing the child. It was another miracle, and the real importance of the act was that he had healed a Gentile. Then I understood. Jesus had brought his disciples to Tyre to show them the spiritual differences between the Jews and the Gentiles and to include the Gentiles into the new relationship with God; to show them the difference between the omnipotent, omnipresent, omniscient God of the Jews and the anthropomorphic gods of the Greeks and Romans.

The what kind of gods of the Greeks and Romans? I asked.

Manlike gods, Titus explained. Man as the final aim of the universe. If you believe that, you create your gods out of supermen. Even emperors could become gods in the Roman world. Everything in creation was for man. To exploit, to use to his advantage. Our God created the universe with man as only a part of it, the caretaker. All life is equally important, and God intended for man to know that he was only a part of it, given knowledge to recognize and worship God, the creator of all life. Without knowledge, how would we judge the differences between right and wrong? Without knowledge, we would obey blindly. As it is, we must choose to follow God. That makes all the difference, but is also a curse because many men choose themselves over God. That was the problem Jesus was facing in his attempt to bring people back to God. Self-interest often comes before the interest of the group.

But I got off track in my story, Titus chuckled. Some of the Jews in Tyre resented the action Jesus had taken, but he showed them they were hypocrites and left the next morning, leaving the city through the pass east of the city and then taking the main road on east to Caesarea Philippi where he had more lessons in store for his disciples. I followed at a distance, but by then it didn't much matter. Jesus knew that I was one of them.

20

The land was so much more beautiful back then, Titus said. As we took the main road east toward Caesarea Philippi, we could see Mount Lebanon to our north and Mount Hermon to our north east, the snow-capped mountains looking like twins with lines of tree-covered hills and valleys in between, the valleys rich with grass and flowers. Farmers were busy harvesting barley and trimming grape vines and tending to their trees. Crops were beginning to sprout in gardens. It was early May, and wheat wasn't ready to harvest yet, but the fields were browning, the plants heavy with seed. Even though we were just a little over a hundred miles from Jerusalem, the climate along the southern edge of Mount Lebanon and Mount Hermon was much milder than it was in southern Judea.

Such a lovely day, Titus mused. One could believe the poet who said that God was in heaven and that all was right with the world.

> Jesus and his disciples took their time walking through the upland hills and valleys that lay between Tyre and the upper Jordan River valley. The day was cool, and not too many people were traveling the road they were on even though it went by Caesarea Philippi and on to Damascus. The road was built for commerce and curved around the shoulders of the hills jutting south out of the two high mountains, their peaks

snow-covered with their slopes looking blue-green in the distance.

As they walked, Jesus spoke to his disciples about the world that God had created in all its beauty and majesty, about the birds in the air being fed by a loving God and the beauty of flowers.

"Look at them," he told his group. "Birds don't worry about what they will eat. They know that our Father in heaven will feed them. They don't worry about tomorrow. And these flowers are robed better than Solomon. If he does this for flowers, which are here today and gone tomorrow, how much more will he do for you? People have such little faith. They fret and stew about what they will eat or drink and try to save up for themselves. Our Heavenly Father knows what we need, and he will provide. Have faith in him. Tomorrow will take care of itself."

They stayed that night in a small farming village tucked against one of the foothills of Mount Lebanon. After the evening services in the synagogue, Jesus and his disciples were invited to stay in several different homes while Titus found a place to spread his shepherd's coat in a stable that housed a donkey and two goats. The hay he slept on was fresh, and he slept well with the patient animals chewing, their jaws working methodically, and with the smell of fresh dung bringing back memories of his home and the times he slept with his sheep.

Early the next morning Jesus and his disciples returned to the road and within an hour descended from the upland benches to the Jordan valley. Titus lagged behind, trying to blend in with other early travelers. The morning air was cold enough that Titus wore his shepherd's coat but removed it and rolled it up as he descended down into the valley.

To the north was a narrow valley with Mount Hermon rising sharply on the east side while high foothills of the mountain were on the west. The valley was formed in ancient times by a cataclysmic earthquake that had split the earth from Mount Hermon, through the Red Sea, and into Africa. It is called the Rift Valley, and it is the largest crack in the Earth. Ribs of granite and limestone jutted from both almost-vertical slopes. One branch of the Jordan River began far up the valley at the Spring of Hashea on the northwest side of Mount Hermon at an elevation of seventeen hundred feet and flowed straight south into the marshes of Lake Huleh that Titus could see. He remembered the time he spent near the lake with the Essenes.

They crossed a ford and followed the road on east around a steep foothill jutting from the mountain and then crossed a stream that flowed from the Pool of Phiala, which was fed by water gushing out of a grotto. The Greeks had built a town nearby and had named the spring Panias in honor of their god Pan. The Jordan valley where the two streams met was about a mile wide and then spread out north of Lake Huleh to about five miles, enclosed by hills running south. South of Lake Huleh, the valley terraced down and became a gorge before the river entered the Sea of Galilee at more than six hundred feet below sea level.

Jesus and his disciples followed the stream and valley east and north. They stayed that night at Daphne, a town that had more Gentiles than Jews. The town was located on a narrow shelf of land that quickly sloped up to a rib of Mount Hermon. They were close enough to the mountain that Titus could not see the peak that evening as the setting sun turned the snow into a pink cap.

The next morning the group left Daphne and went down the steep slope and crossed the stream before following it on east and north to see the ancient and mysterious spring that was the main source of water for the Jordan River. The main road that they had been on the day before had crossed the stream at Daphne and gone on to Caesarea Philippi about a mile upstream. Jesus and his disciples, followed by Titus and a few others, followed a path that would take them to the Spring of Panias. The spring flowed from the base of a vertical cliff that was about thirty feet tall. The spring flowed out of the mouth of a cave.

Jesus stopped before a small temple that was built near the mouth of the spring and gave his disciples a chance to take in the scene. Titus could see part of Caesarea Philippi downstream and up on the higher bench of land. The Pool of Philo and the spring were shaded by trees, and it was quiet. Titus could hear the water rushing over stones that had been laid there in some ancient time because travelers from the desert had stopped at Panias for thousands of years to refresh themselves after emerging from the harsh deserts to the east.

A small, marble temple was built near the spring. It was old and in need of repair, the patio in front of it littered with leaves of some oaks and sycamores that shaded the area. "This is a temple to Pan," Jesus told his disciples, "built here by Alexander many years ago when the Macedonians conquered all our land."

"An abomination," Simon said. "Half goat, half man."

"Many have worshiped false gods," Jesus said.

Jesus walked around the building and went to the cliff face beside the spring. A layer of sandstone about ten feet high formed the base of the cliff. Layered above was limestone and above that granite, a conglomerate of rocks and pebbles.

Beside the spring, some ancient artists had chiseled into the sandstone and had carved out heads of some ancient gods, giving them the appearance of being placed on shelves. There were ones to Zeus and Diana and a much older one to Baal-Gad, a desert god to fortune. Jesus pointed them out to his disciples and discussed the stone heads with them, describing them.

"And who do people say that I am?" he asked them, smiling.

At first his disciples were puzzled by the question because his tone had been light, almost as though the question had been asked in jest.

Then some of them saw that Jesus was serious and answered. "Some say John the Baptist," one answered, remembering the fear of Herod

Antipas. Other disciples named off Elijah and Jeremiah and some of the other prophets.

"But what do you think?" Jesus asked, his tone now serious. "Who do you think I am?"

"You are the Messiah, the Son of the Living God," Simon answered, his voice loud and clear.

"Blessed are you, Simon, son of Jonah," Jesus replied, "for this was revealed to you by my Father in heaven. You are Peter, and upon this rock I shall build my church, and Hades will not overtake it. I will give to you the keys to the kingdom."

Jesus took his disciples to a spring that was located just beyond Caesarea Philippi, Titus said. It was the main source of the River Jordan and back then flowed a full stream. The spring was named Panias by the Greeks and had some pagan shrines near it. Jesus was giving the disciples a lesson by taking them there. The spring is located near the desert and had been a stopping point for caravans for centuries, giving life to both beast and man. The symbols of life and death were obvious. Water and the life it produced with the trees and grass and flowers growing where the water fed them and just beyond the bleak and forbidding wasteland of the desert. The differences between a living and creative god and stone images were clear. It was there that Peter knew that Jesus was the Messiah, and it was there that the ministry of Jesus changed.

They went to Caesarea Philippi, the capital of Herod Philip, tetrarch of Batanea, Trachonitis, Aurantitis, Gaulanitis, and part of Jamnia. Philip had recently married Salome, the girl who had danced for the head of John the Baptist, and they lived in a luxurious palace in the city that catered to the wealthy. Caesarea Philippi had been rebuilt by Philip and modeled after Roman towns. It had a bath and a theater and a forum and many palatial homes. Jesus and his disciples looked out of place as they wandered through the streets. But on the outskirts of town beggars still begged and desperate mothers still pleaded with people for some food for their children.

THE LAST SHEPHERD

Jesus was teaching his disciples about the world that did not follow the commands of God, about the corruption of the soul-- that greed and avarice and gluttony killed man's spirit, were the opposite of love. Caesarea Philippi was a perfect example. Jesus began telling them about his coming death, that he would die in Jerusalem and be raised in three days. They were dumbfounded and did not understand what he was saying. After all, he was the Messiah, the Son of God, and could do anything. He was immortal. They had seen him perform miracles.

For several days, Jesus visited the nearby villages healing the ill and teaching in the local synagogues. Crowds began following him and his disciples. Most of the people were Jews who were servants for the wealthy living in Caesarea Philippi or who were laborers working on farms on the valley floor or in the orchards on the lower slopes of the hills at the base of Mount Hermon.

One morning before daylight, Jesus left and took with him Peter and James and John. They were gone for more than a day, Titus said, and it wasn't until later that we found out that Jesus had taken the three high up on Mount Hermon and that he had been transfigured and had met with Moses and Elijah and that God had spoken to the three disciples. When they returned, they found the other disciples embroiled in a dispute.

People rushed to greet them, and I was astonished at the change in Jesus. Light seemed to radiate from him and his clothing and his head, an aureole, a change in him that is difficult to describe. His mission had been verified to Peter and James and John on that mountain. God had spoken to them. Jesus was ready to continue to heal and to teach and to prepare his disciples and his followers about the new world that God had prepared for them. He was preparing himself for his death.

His disciples were in a heated argument with some Pharisees and an agitated man who was waving his arms and yelling. When Jesus asked what was going on, the man said that he had brought his son to the disciples to be healed. The boy is possessed by an evil spirit, he said to Jesus. It throws the boy on the ground and causes

195

him to gnash his teeth and foam at the mouth. Your disciples tried to heal him, but they could do nothing.

You unbelievers, Jesus said. How long will I stay with you? Bring the boy to me.

When they brought the boy, the boy fell to the ground, rolling around and foaming at the mouth.

The boy has been like this since childhood, the father said to Jesus. Help him if you can.

Titus interrupted his story and smiled as he remembered the scene. I never saw Jesus react to a request as he did to that one. He seemed amused and a little angry at the same time.

If you can? Jesus repeated, emphasizing the word "if." Anything is possible to one who believes. I believe, the father said.

Jesus commanded the demon to come out of the boy. The boy convulsed, and people thought he was dead, but Jesus lifted him to his feet, and he was healed. The crowd that had come running to see the performance was astonished. Later when his disciples asked him why they couldn't heal the boy, he told them that prayer was the only cure for that type of disease.

The next day Jesus and his disciples left and returned to Galilee. While they were in Capernaum, some men collecting taxes for the temple approached Peter and asked him why Jesus didn't pay his temple tax. They had been sent by Caiaphas in an attempt to trap Jesus. When Peter returned home, Jesus asked him who kings collected taxes from. From others or from their sons, he questioned. From others, Peter answered. Then the sons are exempt, Jesus said. But we will pay. Go throw your line into the lake, and the first fish you catch, open its mouth where you will find a four-drachma coin. Take it and pay your taxes and mine. Peter caught the fish, took out the coin, and paid their taxes, worth around fifty cents, your money, Titus said. Priests in the temple kept trying to trap Jesus. But that time they completely missed another of his miracles.

All that summer Jesus taught and healed in lower Galilee and Samaria and east of the Jordan in the Decopolis and Perea. Early that fall, he made his last trip to the Feast of Tabernacles to confront the religious leaders and to begin to bring his ministry to a close.

21

Titus stood and stretched his arms above his head and then lowered them. Let's take a short walk while I continue my story, he said. You have been very patient with me and have listened well, but sitting this long is tiresome. My story is almost over. Fewer cars were in the parking lot with an occasional customer driving through the pickup line for a late cup of coffee. The arc lights seemed to shimmer, their glare casting no shadows.

As I was saying, Titus continued as we strolled by the coffee shop and then through the driveway to the sidewalk and back again, I knew that Jesus was ministering in the area in lower Galilee and Northern Judea and that part of Samaria and east of the Jordan, so when he sent out seventy of his disciples to spread the gospel and cure illnesses, I knew that he intended to stay there at least until the Feast of Tabernacles, so I went home to see Joel and his family once again and to work and stay with them for the rest of the summer.

Joel seemed overjoyed to see me once again and showed me his family, now grown, his two sons doing the work on the farm. They had built another house near the olive grove and had enlarged the orchard, adding some pear trees. The changes made me realize that I had aged since I had last seen Joel and his family. I was fifty-eight but didn't feel that old, but Joel's grandchildren reminded me when they kept calling Joel granddad. Working in the groves and the garden and fields and with the sheep that summer felt good, Titus said. For a time the Messiah almost faded.

We returned to our table and sat again as Titus paused and then began again.

But Joel and his sons and I went to the Feast of Tabernacles, which began on September 10 of the year thirty-three. I was certain that I would see Jesus there and that I was ready to follow him once again.

> Jesus knew that some Jews in Judea wanted to kill him, so he went secretly to the Feast of Tabernacles, one of the three important festivals. The Feast of Tabernacles was a joyous one, celebrating the ingathering of the people and timed to celebrate the harvesting of the fruits and grains and the making of wine and olive oil. This year's celebration was early, but the priests went by the traditional calendar, so not all crops had been harvested yet, but the Israelites came from all corners of the land anyway. The ceremonies were magnificent.

> On the third day of the festival, Jesus suddenly appeared and began teaching in an area on Solomon's Porch. People at the festival had been talking about him and were divided in their opinions. Some said he was a good man, but others said he deceived people. When Jesus began speaking, people flocked to hear him and were amazed at his understanding of the Torah and the Law of Moses and of the prophets. Jews had to study for years and prove their knowledge before they were accepted as Pharisees, and so the Pharisees listening to Jesus were upset. "How did this man get such learning without having to study?" one asked his companion.

> Jesus overheard the derogatory comment. "My teaching is not my own, but from Him who

sent me," he answered. "If anyone chooses to do God's will, he will find out whether my teaching comes from God or whether I speak on my own. He who speaks on his own does so to gain honor for himself, but he who works for the one who sent him is a man of truth. Hasn't Moses given you the law?" he asked the Pharisees. "Yet not one of you keeps the law. Why are you trying to kill me?"

"You are possessed by demons," the outraged Pharisee shouted. "Who is trying to kill you?"

"I did one miracle and you were all astonished," Jesus answered, referring to the time he healed a man on the Sabbath with Pharisees watching. "Yet because Moses gave you circumcision, although it wasn't really Moses but the Patriarchs, if you circumcise on the Sabbath so that the law of Moses may not be broken, why are you angry with me for healing the whole man on the Sabbath? Stop judging by mere appearances and make the right judgment."

People watching and listening to the exchange began talking about the confrontation. "Isn't this the man they are trying to kill?" one asked.

"Here he is talking, but the authorities have not tried to stop him," another said. "Perhaps even the leaders think that he is the Christ."

Jesus continued teaching, and many people came to listen, many from far away like Carthage and Rome and Greece and areas in Asia Minor and upper Egypt and Damascus and even the Euphrates. They had heard of him and wanted to see for themselves.

The Feast of Tabernacles was like the other major festivals. It helped bind their religion into a central unity, constantly reminding the people of their divine delivery from slavery. It promoted gratitude and trust and gave the people a central point of worship in the temple. It also gave priests and rabbis a constant reminder of how synagogue services should be conducted. An important reason for the ingathering of the Israelites at festivals was that it kept them unified so that they would not break into tribal units scattered around the known world. People who attended carried back stories of the beauty of the temple and the great wealth of the Jews. Festivals were a perfect place to exchange information about different places as the people exchanged stories. Festivals were also an important time to seek atonement for sins. Another important event for the priests was the collection of tithes and temple taxes. With several million people paying about twenty-five cents a year as a temple tax, no wonder the temple in Jerusalem was magnificent. It was wealthy.

And the Feast of Tabernacles also boosted the economy for Jerusalem and its enterprising citizens. The feast not only was a thanksgiving for a harvest but a commemoration of the escape from Egypt to freedom and a remembrance of when people lived in tents during their years in the desert. As a result, on the first day of the celebration, people left their homes and constructed huts, or booths as they were called, from the limbs of olive, pine, myrtle, or other heavily leafed trees and lived in them for the seven days of the festival. Merchants brought loads of palm branches up from the palm groves around Jericho, and farmers found that time of the year just right for

pruning their fruit and nut trees. Material for
building booths near Jerusalem was a little scarce
for thousands of worshipers.

Each day the people celebrated joyously. In the
early morning, priests would go to the Pool of
Siloam and fill a golden pitcher with water and
would bring it to the alter where Caiaphas would
pour it on the burnt offerings. In the evenings,
four huge lamps would be lit in the Women's
Court, and people would dance around them
while holding torches. Their singing echoed
across the city.

On the last morning of the festival Titus was in
the group of worshipers who followed the priests
to the Pool of Siloam where a white-robed priest
and his attendants went to the north end of the
pool and filled a golden pitcher from the water
flowing from Gihon Spring into the pool while
a choir of Levites sang, "With joy you will draw
water from the well of salvation." Like the other
pilgrims, in his right hand Titus carried a branch,
or lulab, a myrtle branch tied together with
a palm frond, and in his left hand he carried a
bough with a lemon.

As the priest and his attendants entered the Water
Gate, trumpets and cymbals sounded as the people shouted praises to God. A feeling of joy overwhelmed Titus, and he followed the water bear-
ers through the Court of the Gentiles into the
Court of the Women where the crowd pressed
together to see the ceremony.

Caiaphas, the high priest, stood at the altar
dressed in his ceremonial robe, which was kept in
Antonia by the Romans until the priest needed

it for festivals. The robe was a rich blue decorated with blue, purple, and scarlet pomegranates. Golden bells attached to the robe jingled when he moved His waist was circled with a band made of blue, purple, and scarlet threads laced with gold Across his chest was a breastplate of the same material. On it were twelves precious stones, symbolizing the twelve tribes of Israel. On his head he wore a linen turban wreathed with blue and encircled by a golden crown with the inscription "Holy is the Lord"

The high priest had laid the last of the sacrificial burnt offerings on the great altar just as the priest arrived with the golden pitcher. Caiaphas held the pitcher over the altar while a chorus of Levites began chanting the great Hallel, the praise to God in Psalms 113 to 118. Flutes accompanied the chanting. At the end of the songs of praise, the high priest poured the water over the offerings on the altar.

During the pouring of the water, the pilgrims were so quiet they could hear water splashing on the sacrificial objects and the stone.

At this moment, Jesus took a few steps up the stairs leading to the altar and turned to the crowd. "If any man is thirsty, let him come to me and drink," he cried out in a loud, clear voice. "Whoever believes in me as the Scripture has said, streams of living water will flow within him."

The people stared at Jesus, awestruck. They were silent. Titus saw Caiaphas flinch. Then Jesus walked through the crowd and disappeared Someone near Titus said quietly, "Surely this man is a prophet."

Another said, "He is the Messiah."

But the temple guards did not stop him.

During the last day of the festival, Jesus did reveal to all of us that he was the Messiah, the Christ, when the high priest poured the libation of sacred water on the great altar, but most people didn't really understand what had happened when Jesus said if any man is thirsty let him come to me and drink. Caiaphas knew and so did the Pharisees and rabbis. Nicodemus, that great teacher, knew.

All of those who had studied scripture would have known that the prophet Zechariah had said that everyone who survives of all the nations that have come up against Jerusalem shall go year after year to worship the lord of hosts and to keep the feast of booths.

Titus looked at me, his eyes black pools. The temple guards did not arrest Jesus as they had been instructed to do. They were in awe at the way Jesus had spoken and the way he had defied the temple leaders. When the Sanhedrin met to discuss the incident, Nicodemus defended Jesus by saying that he should have a fair hearing, but his fellow Pharisees were scornful. Are you from Galilee, they asked Nicodemus. No prophet can come from Galilee, they said.

Jesus and his disciples left and returned to teaching in Judea in the area around Jericho and across the river. He was preparing himself for the final months.

22

Titus paused. A young barista came out of the coffee shop and approached our table. We close in half an hour, he said. But if you would like to order something now, I will bring it out to you. Our drive through is open twenty-four hours because we are so near the freeway, he added.

Titus looked at him and smiled. I would like to try a cup of coffee, he said. Nothing added to it. Just plain.

Bring me a cup of ice water, I said. We could use a drink. I handed the young man a ten-dollar bill. Keep the change, I said.

Thanks, he said. It's been a long night and I have an exam tomorrow. He confirmed my suspicion. As a teacher, I knew that many students had to work to pay for their education.

In a short time he brought us our drinks, and Titus took a sip. Ah, he said, licking his lips. I had heard of this drink a long time ago. It was the drink of royalty deep in the southern Arabian Desert, and was used during rituals at Petra. How stimulating.

In December of that same year, Jesus went to Jerusalem to the Feast of Dedication in spite of the fears of his disciples, Titus said, getting back to his story. He knew his time was short, and he had begun to reveal himself as the Messiah. For him it was a symbolic act, the cleansing of the Temple that had become corrupted by the Jewish leaders. Because it was winter and the Romans had banned shipping on the Mediterranean during the stormy season, fewer Israelites attended the festival.

But it was an important festival celebrating the purging of the Temple and the rebuilding of the altar after Judas Maccabeus had driven out the Syrians in 164 BC. Can you imagine? Three years before that, Antiochus Epiphanes had placed a statue of Zeus on the Temple's sacred altar. So when Judas destroyed Zeus, that became the date for celebrating the heroic actions of a great Jewish leader.

The Feast of Dedication, or Hanukkah as it is now called, was a joyous occasion lasting eight days with people carrying branches and singing the Hallel as they did during the Feast of Tabernacles. I suppose it has lost most of its meaning, but back then it was a very important event. The Temple had been returned to God. And that was the mission of Jesus. To cleanse the Temple and return the people to God.

The Nazarene drew crowds of people wherever he went. On one of the days of the festival, a group of Pharisees gathered with him in an area of Solomon's Porch. If you are the Messiah, one said, tell us plainly. Don't keep us in suspense. As I listened to them, Titus said, I could see them smirking, trying to trap Jesus.

I did tell you, he said to them. The miracles I do, I do in my Father's name, but you do not believe me. My people follow me because they believe, and I give them eternal life, and they shall never perish. My Father who has given them to me is greatest of all, and no one can take them. My Father and I are one.

When Jesus said that, the Pharisees became enraged and picked up stones to kill Jesus. He looked at them calmly. I held my breath.

Why do you want to stone me, he asked them. I have shown you many miracles. Which of these do you find offensive?

Blasphemy, they shouted. You say you are God.

Jesus answered them. It is written in your law, you are gods, you are all sons of the Most High.

If the scripture cannot be broken, what about the one that God set apart as his very own son and sent into the world? Why do you accuse me of blasphemy because I said I am the Son of God? Even if you don't believe me, believe the miracles which come from God so that you will understand that the Father is in me and I am in the Father.

At that, they tried to seize him, but Jesus walked away from them. Titus took another sip of coffee. I have never seen anything like it, he said. It was as though they were frozen, their grasping hands useless. And Jesus was magnificent, erect, defiant, unafraid. Truly the Son of God.

When he left Jerusalem, he went to Bethany across the Jordan where many people believed in him.

In early January, Martha and Mary, his friends from Bethany near Jerusalem, sent word to Jesus that their brother, Lazarus, was deathly ill. When Jesus heard the news, he answered that Lazarus would live so that God's glory through him could be shown. He and his disciples stayed two more days across the river, and then Jesus said that he was ready to go to Bethany because Lazarus had died. I am going there to wake him up, he told his disciples.

His disciples pleaded with him not to go because the Jews wanted to kill him, but they decided to go with him, to die with him, his disciple Thomas said.

When they arrived in Bethany, Titus said, Martha, who had gone to meet Jesus, told him that Lazarus had been placed in his tomb four days before. Many people from Jerusalem were also with the sisters as they mourned their brother's death.

When Jesus told Martha that Lazarus would rise again, she said that she knew he would on resurrection day, but Jesus told her that those who believed in him would never die. He asked her if she believed that. She answered that she believed. You are the Messiah, she said humbly, the Son of God, who was to come into the world.

When Mary heard that Jesus had come, she hurried quickly to be with him and her sister. The Jews who were mourning with her followed, thinking that she was visiting her brother's tomb.

Mary fell at the feet of Jesus and wept. Had you been here, he would not have died, she said. Jesus, deeply moved, asked where they had buried Lazarus. The girls took him to the tomb followed by the Jews. Many other Jews from Jerusalem hurried to the scene, warned by others of what was happening. Many Pharisees were in the crowd.

I could tell that Titus was re-living the scene. He was clenching his hands, and his voice had softened, had become hoarse.

Jesus stood in front of the stone covering the entrance to the tomb, Titus said. He stood there for a few minutes and then asked for the stone to be moved. But, Lord, Martha said, Lazarus has been dead four days. He smells by now.

I told you that if you believed you would see the glory of God, Jesus told her. Some men removed the stone, and Jesus looked heavenward and said, I know that you always hear me, but I say this for the benefit of those gathered here that they may believe that you sent me.

And then he looked into the blackness of the tomb and called in a loud voice, Lazarus, come out! Then in a few moments an apparition wrapped in cloth and linens emerged from the darkness. Take those off and let him go, Jesus commanded. Lazarus was uncovered, blinking rapidly at the bright sunlight, confused by the surroundings and the stunned people staring at him, mouths open. Many of the Jews who witnessed this miracle believed, but when the report reached Caiaphas, he called a meeting of the Sanhedrin, where they realized that Jesus posed a real danger for them. The people will follow him, and the Romans will take away our power, Caiaphas told them. So they began to plot and lay plans for killing Jesus.

Jesus and his disciples went north to an area around Ephraim near the Samarian border. The chief priest and the Pharisees had issued orders that if anyone knew where Jesus was that they were to report it so that he could be arrested. But Jesus had many followers, and they kept his location a secret. Many now believed in him. The raising of Lazarus was a sobering miracle, beyond belief.

The people had little respect for their high priest, and you can only imagine how tom they were because of that. Caiaphas, their earthly link to God, was controlled by the Romans. And the Jews knew that they could be arrested if they knew where Jesus was but did not report it. Caiaphas was right in being concerned.

But just at this time, Titus said, a situation developed in Samaria that gave Caiaphas a chance to regain some power over Pontius Pilate. A religious movement had started in Samaria that caused Pilate to blunder.

The Samaritans also believed in a messianic messenger, the Taheb, who would lead them to the top of Mount Gerizim and show them where Moses had hidden the ark and other sacred vessels. A man appeared claiming to be the Taheb and said he would take them up the mountain. Of course it was all foolishness because Moses never crossed the Jordan, but the man had the people in a fever pitch and they assembled to journey up their sacred mountain.

Pontius Pilate was notified that the Samaritans had armed themselves and were assembling at a village called Tirathaba near Mount Gerizim. Fearing sedition, Pilate sent a cohort of the Twelfth Legion to stop the uprising. The commander had his horsemen and foot soldiers positioned on the roads, and when the thousands of pilgrims approached on their way up the mountain, the Romans attacked them and killed many. Others fled, but Pilate had the soldiers hunt down the leaders and had them executed.

This action by Pilate was the beginning of the end for him as procurator of Judea. The Samaritan senate sent an embassy to Vitellius, president of Syria, accusing Pilate of killing people who were on a religious pilgrimage, not revolting as reported by Pilate.

Titus smiled. And, of course, Caiaphas was pleased by the affair but also a little concerned about what might happen to him if Pilate was replaced as procurator. The high priest was thinking more about himself than he was about Jesus during those early months in the year thirty-four.

23

And now my story is drawing to a close, Titus said. Jesus returned to Jerusalem for Passover. He arrived at the home of Lazarus, Martha, and Mary in Bethany on March 28 in the year thirty-four. It was six days before Passover.

At that time, I was staying with my brother, Joel, on the farm near Bethlehem, and I went to the temple for the ritual cleansing before Passover. On Monday afternoon, I was standing on the bench which was built all along the wall on the east side of the Temple under the colonnaded area called Solomon's Porch looking out across the Kidron Valley at the Garden of Gethsemane and the Mount of Olives. On beyond to the east clouds hung over the Jordan River Valley. It was a peaceful scene but bustling with people putting up tents for their observance of Passover. By next week, more than a hundred thousand people would be in and around Jerusalem.

Then I began to hear shouts with people running toward the road leading from Bethany to Jerusalem. I leaned farther out onto the thick temple wall for a better look. I saw Jesus on a white donkey surrounded by his disciples. As they started up the grade toward the gate to Jerusalem, I could hear people shouting for joy, some women yodeling out their throaty cry in high-pitched voices. People began laying their coats as a path along the road and placing palm branches along it. I could hear them crying out hosanna and he has come in the name of the Lord and blessed be the king of the Jews. Jesus rode calmly, smiling. He had come to reveal himself.

I pushed my way through the crowd in the Court of the Gentiles to the stairs which came up from the Water Gate. Jesus came up the stairs into the temple, looking at the crowd pushing around him, and began walking to the booths lining the Soreg Wall.

Merchants were busy selling doves to the poor for their sacrificial offerings, and others were selling items as souvenirs or food. Money changers were exchanging Roman coins for Jewish money that was acceptable for gift offerings and tithing and temple taxes. Scribes were writing letters for those who needed their services. Jesus looked at them in disgust.

Then he walked up to the table of a money changer and tipped the table out onto the temple floor, coins cascading into the surrounding crowd, the startled money changer cringing against the Soreg Wall. Some people scrambled for the coins.

My house was built for prayer, not made for a den of thieves, Jesus cried out as he opened the cages holding the doves. The startled birds took flight for home. The crowd hung back, awed by his violent action. What they did not realize, nor did I at the time, was that he was cleansing God's house, the temple, for the most holy feast. Some Pharisees went running to the council chamber in search of Caiaphas to report the incident.

Jesus looked at the people for a moment and then walked among them, talking with them. They began crowding around him again, and he began touching those who begged for his help. He healed some who were being led to him because they could not see. And I saw him heal several cripples. But the hour was getting late, and he and his disciples left. No temple guards attempted to stop him.

Just as I was about to leave, someone called my name, and I turned to see young Gestus coming toward me through the jostling crowd.

Titus, old friend, he called out. I have been looking for you.

We hugged, remembering our short time together and the short rebellion in the temple over the building of the aqueduct. It's good to see you well, I said.

I wanted to find you to have you join us, Gestus said, whispering and looking about. I have come to Jerusalem with a special group, but I can't talk about it right now. There may be guards around that will hear me.

Well, then, I said, don't act so guilty. Anyone observing you would think you were up to no good. But we can talk later about whatever it is that you are up to. Right now I'll take you home with me for the night.

When we arrived at the farm, Joel welcomed Gestus warmly. At the supper table Gestus seemed a little uncomfortable, waiting for some of us to dip food or spoon our soup. He had spent most of his young life in northern Galilee and was aware of our differences. Judeans were supposed to be sophisticated, know social etiquette. He relaxed a little when he saw us using our right hands for holding food, an ancient custom born out of the deserts in the middle east where water for washing hands was scarce. Like other Galileans, he had a soft slur to Aramaic, but when Joel began talking about selecting the perfect lamb to take to the temple as a sacrificial offering, Gestus joined in, forgetting our differences.

That night, I borrowed a shepherd's coat for Gestus to use and took him through our olive grove to the sheep fold where the sheep were being held because of the weather. The sheep were ready for shearing, and I loved the smell of their wool dampened by the heavy night air. The moon was blocked out by lowering clouds. As we entered, the sheep looked at us with trusting eyes, new lambs snuggling in their mothers' wool. Gestus wrinkled his nose.

We entered the small, roofed shed, open on two sides. The other sides were stone walls in a comer of the sheep fold. There was enough hay left for us to make comfortable beds, much better, I thought, than a mat on the floor of the main house, sharing the space with Joel and Marianne and several grandkids.

We must leave early tomorrow morning, Gestus said. I am to meet some men in Modin, and I told them I would bring you with me. We feel the time is right to rid our land of the Romans, and we need your help. We know that you have been a follower of Jesus of Nazareth. We believe we have a plan that will force him to lead us to victory. We need you with us.

Don't be foolish, I said. The Messiah doesn't need our help. We need his. The Zealots are ready, Gestus said angrily. We must act.

I knew that I had to go to the meeting with him to find out what they planned to do and to try to talk them out of it.

We left early the next morning for Modin, more than twenty-five miles away, just as the sun was rising over the hills blocking out a view of the Dead Sea. But low clouds made the morning gloomy, the air cold and damp. We went north on the road to Jerusalem and then west on the Joppa Road. Early in the morning, very few people were on the road, but by afternoon as we went through the hills north of Emmaus, many people came by us on their way to Jerusalem for Passover. The small port at Joppa must have been busy bringing pilgrims up from Egypt.

That evening just outside Modin we managed to get a bowl of soup at an inn crowded with pilgrims who had already taken up all the rooms and the stable. Once again the night was dark, and I was not familiar with the area, so I felt uneasy. The gates to the city had been closed at sundown, and guards were posted to turn people away.

Plans have been made for us to enter through the Dung Gate, Gestus told me. He was told that we would find it on the south side of the city where a ravine slopes off to the south and west. I let him lead the way, but it took a while for my eyes to adjust to the darkness. We continued on the road for Modin and then turned left as we neared the city's wall and followed it south. There were some dwellings nearby and some groves of olive trees. A dog barked at one of the houses, and we froze until it settled down. As we reached the corner where the wall headed west, the land became barren and rocky with thorn bushes. Gestus cursed quietly when he stumbled into a bush, the thorns gouging him.

He turned to me. We must hurry, he said. The slaves bring out the refuse an hour after sundown, and plans have been made for us to enter the city with them after they have emptied their buckets. After a short time of feeling along the ancient wall, we came to the Dung Gate, which had no guard on the outside because it was not a gate used as an entry. We crept away from it a few yards, sat beside some thorn bushes, and waited.

After a short time, we heard voices on the other side of the gate and the gleam of a torch guttering in the mist that had become heavier. The gate opened and slaves emerged carrying buckets slung between them on a wooden beam. They were used to the routine and followed the worn path toward the ravine. After the last of them had passed, Gestus and I fell in behind. No guards were with the slaves because there was no fear that they would try to escape. Where would they go and not be recognized as slaves? They would be hunted down and flogged and put back to work or perhaps sold to some harsher master.

About a hundred yards along the trail, the last two slaves slowed down, and the rear one whispered, Put these on and quickly. My master is expecting you. They dropped cloaks for us.

The cloaks were the same type as the slaves were wearing, and I put mine on over my shepherd's coat, a tight fit, but passable, I hoped. We followed the group, almost gagging because the buckets were filled with human waste that had been collected from different parts of Modin during the day to be dumped outside the city.

The first group of the slaves reached the point where the rock face of the ravine was vertical and where a wall about two feet high had been built so that the buckets could be tipped there, spilling the contents down into a crevice. Gestus and I took one of the emptied buckets and acted as though we were dumping the foul load. I looked down into the blackness, but it was so dark I could see nothing. The mist had turned into a light shower, and we covered our heads with hoods attached to the cloaks. We continued carrying the bucket back to the gate and entered with the other slaves where we were cursed and told to hurry back to our quarters. I suppose the hoods helped hide Gestus and me from the slave master, who was only too glad to be done with the unpleasant job.

Someone had made careful plans for our secret entry into the city.

Modin was an ancient city, not influenced by Greek or Roman planning, and the streets were crooked, meandering around blocks of housing and businesses and trades where families or like minded people lived together. Gestus seemed to know where he was going, and after we had traveled inside the city for a short distance, he stopped and took off his cloak. I pulled mine over my head, and we put them in a doorway.

A little distance farther, Gestus stopped at a door to a compound and knocked softly, tapping three times, pausing and then tapping twice more.

Someone on the other side, said hoi in a hoarse voice.

There is no God but Yahweh, Gestus said, his lips pressed against the door latch. No tax but that of the temple, the hoarse voice whispered.

No friend but a Zealot, Gestus responded.

The door was opened but blocked by a giant of a man, wearing a sword around his massive waist. Welcome, friend, he said. The others are already here. He looked at me, measuring me with a practiced eye. He would be prized by any army, I thought.

This is Titus, Gestus said. The man I was to bring.

You look like an old fighter, the man said to me, smiling. We can use you.

We went across a short courtyard and entered a room typical of a Jewish middle-class home. About a dozen men were seated around the perimeter, some sitting on counter tops or benches built in along three walls. One man was standing ready to greet us. He was also large but more slender than the one guarding the door. He was tall and stood erect. He motioned for Gestus and me to have a seat. He raised his arms and said a short prayer, asking for God's blessing.

The room was warm, and I removed my coat.

So, you are the shepherd we have been looking for, the man said, looking at me and smiling.

We have need of your good advice, he added.

I nodded.

Then he turned to the assembled men. I am a Galilean, he said, a Zealot, ready to rid our land of the hated Romans. I use the name Judas in honor of Judas Maccabeus, who drove Antiochus Epiphanes out of Jerusalem and cleansed our sacred Temple after Antiochus had desecrated it with an idol of Zeus, as you all know. Modin was the home of Judas and his father, Matthius, and their graves are here.

Modin is a sacred city and a symbol of righteousness. We are ready to strike, and we believe the time is now. I call on Hiram, our friend from Jerusalem to explain.

A well-dressed man stood. His beard was carefully oiled, his hair combed. He contrasted sharply with the others, most of them dressed in drab robes. I am a Pharisee, he said, a Judean from Jerusalem, who has followed the Nazarene for some time. I believe he is the Messiah because I have witnessed several of his miracles and have listened to his stories. I wasn't totally convinced until several days ago when I saw him raise Lazarus from the dead. I had been present when Lazarus had been buried four days before Jesus brought him back to life. He did smell of death, and when he came stumbling out of his tomb, he brought that smell with him. When he was unwrapped, he had the look of death about him, and then he opened his eyes and began to live again. Only the chosen Son of God could do that.

And then yesterday Jesus fulfilled the prophecy of Zechariah when he rode a white donkey from Bethany to the gates of Jerusalem while thousands cheered and some calling him the king of the Jews. The old prophet helped restore our faith when Ezra rebuilt the temple and restored Jerusalem. He wrote about the coming of the Messiah. This is the passage from the Torah. "Rejoice greatly, 0 daughter of Zion; shout O daughter of Jerusalem: behold, thy king comes to you; he is just, and has salvation; lowly, and riding upon a donkey, and upon a colt the foal of a donkey." At last Jesus has revealed himself as the Messiah, even though he knows that Caiaphas and the Sanhedrin want him dead. I also know that the high priest has ordered that Jesus not be arrested in public because he knows that the people would rebel. He plans to have Jesus arrested secretly away from public view, and then he plans to turn him over to the Romans as someone who wants to seize control as king of the Jews. Caiaphas and the Sanhedrin want the Romans to do their dirty work for them. Because of this, I believe that Jesus would save himself from the Romans and lead our revolt to return the kingdom back to God.

As you know, most Pharisees want peace at any cost. They believe they can outlast the Romans and save Palestine, but they are becoming corrupted themselves with so many restrictions on the faithful that life is becoming unbearable for those trying to obey the laws. The Pharisees cannot see how the Romans have influenced our way of life, our priests living in luxury and more concerned with themselves than others. But many of us are ready to join a revolt. Nicodemus, a member of the Sanhedrin and my beloved teacher, is ready to get rid of Roman influence and return our highest court to its rightful function, a voice of God. Thank you for listening to me, he said and sat down.

Judas stood. Well said, brother Hiram, Judas said. From what you have heard, he said to us, it is apparent that Jesus wants people to know that he is the Messiah, the Chosen One. His entry into Jerusalem was his way of telling the world that he is ready to take his place as the Son of God. My men in Jerusalem have reported what brother Hiram has told us. The temple guards did not arrest him, but it is obvious that Caiaphas wants him arrested. Therefore, Hiram is correct. Caiaphas wants Jesus arrested in secret, just waiting for his chance. When Jesus is arrested will be the time for us to act.

And now I would like for us to listen to Josiah, an Essene from the camp at Qumran. A short, squat man stood, dressed in a plain cloak girdled by a rope.

As your leader said, I am Josiah from Qumran, the storehouse of our sacred scriptures. I am not used to speaking to a group outside our order, so bear with me if I falter. In our community, my role is that of a teacher, a Maskil, or master, who trains members to become part of our covenant. In that position I have to know the scriptures in the Torah, as do the Pharisees, and I also have to memorize our rules laid down by our Teacher of Righteousness. Many of you do not know of them, but we have the Community Rule, the Damascus Rule, the Messianic Rule, and the War Rule.

I believe that Jesus fulfills the qualifications for the Chosen One given in the Messianic Rule, and I believe that if we follow the plan in the War Rule, we can drive the Kittim from our land.

The Kittim, someone asked.

The Romans, Josiah answered. We refer to the Romans now when we use the word Kittim, but it could apply to anyone who attempts to rule the Jews.

We have heard that you are a sect of people who believe in peace, not war, someone said.

That is true, Josiah said. We do believe in peace but not peace at any price. We believe that when the Messiah has reached his rightful place he will bring peace to the world. That is why many of us are ready to join a war against the Romans. A world filled with hate will become a world ruled by love. Josiah remained standing for a few moments to see if anyone else had a question, and then he sat.

Thank you for joining us, Judas said, standing. We all know how strictly the Essenes obey the laws of God and their own laws. Banded together as a nation, we can rid ourselves of the Romans.

And then Judas turned to me, Titus said. His face was glowing. He was pacing the meeting very well up to that point, but I had listened, heartsick, almost struck dumb by their plans. They were wrong.

And now I would like to hear from our old shepherd, Judas said. People tell me that he has been a follower of the Nazarene for years, he added, looking at Gestus.

I stood, barely able to speak. I believe with all my heart and soul that Jesus of Nazareth is the Messiah, the Chosen One, the Son of God. I was a shepherd who visited the holy family soon after the birth of Jesus. I met them in the Negev Desert when they were fleeing to Egypt. I saw him as a young boy helping his father, Joseph, rebuild Sepphoris during the time of Judas from Gaulanitris who began the Zealot movement in Galilee. I have witnessed many of Jesus's miracles during the last four years and have heard many of his stories as he tried to lead his people back to God. I, too, saw his entry into Jerusalem and heard the shouts of joy of those following him. He is the Son of God.

But all of you know that there are two prophecies about the coming Messiah. One has him on a horse of war, another on a donkey, an animal of peace. Jesus has always taught that we should love one another just as scripture says. He has a plan and is fulfilling it, don't you see. We must not interfere the way you are suggesting. Only if he asks us for help. We should be ready, but we must not plan a war that Jesus may not want. I sat, hoping that I may have changed some minds.

Judas, who had remained standing, frowned. He had not expected me to be against their plan.

Thank you for your counsel, old warrior, Judas said. We have heard your warning and have considered the point that you have just made. But we believe it is God's plan for us to follow through with what we are doing.

Even now, Judas Iscariot is meeting with Annas and the high priest to betray Jesus so that the temple guards can arrest Jesus in secret, away from the crowds that surround him during the day. It will be two nights from now. It is our belief that Caiaphas will call a meeting of the Sanhedrin on Friday morning and charge Jesus with treason against the state. The usual time for a court session is the third hour, that is three hours after sunup. That charge would be a crime against Rome, so the Sanhedrin would tum Jesus over to the Romans for a trial, and according to Roman law treason is punishable by death. As a result, Caiaphas could not be accused of the execution, and the anger of the people would be directed against the Romans, not the high priest.

The time for us to attack would be during the transfer of the prisoner, Judas said. And then he turned to Gestus and me. That is where we use the two of you.

Titus sighed and folded his hands, his cup of cold coffee pushed aside.

I was so dumbfounded I could not respond, he continued. ·How arrogant they all were to assume that I would want to be a part of such a harebrained scheme. Gestus was leaning forward eager to hear what we were to do.

Judas ignored Gestus and me and began addressing the group of rebels. The Romans have brought a brigade of the Tenth Legion into Judea and have set up a camp for them in the Hinnom Valley on the southwest side of Jerusalem. A cohort of the Twelfth Legion has remained stationed at Caesarea, a brigade is quartered in Antonia, and a cohort of Syrians from the Twelfth Legion is guarding the area around Jericho. That means that they have about fifteen thousand soldiers in Judea to suppress any rebellion.

That sounds like a large army to me, someone interrupted. They would be hard to beat.

We are not alone, Judas said. How many Israelites will be in Jerusalem for Passover, he asked.

Thousands, Hiram, the Pharisee, answered. Some estimate that about a hundred thousand of us observe Passover in the temple.

Just so, Judas replied. Of that number, we estimate that many thousands of our people already here would join our fight. Besides that force, we have agents in Arabia who have contacted their king. He is expecting an attack from the Romans because of his defeat of the army of Herod Antipas. So he would be willing to fight the Syrian forces at Jericho. The Idumeans will join us from the south. We have heard that many Phrygians would join us because belief in Jesus as the Messiah is strong in that· land. I believe the whole area is ready to rid itself of Roman domination. Maybe even the Egyptians would fight to free themselves. Jesus could lead us all to freedom and return the world back to God. Judas paused, looking at his followers. We will win, he roared.

We will win, the men shouted, standing now with raised arms.

After a moment, Judas motioned for the men to sit.

This is the plan, he said. On the night of the paschal supper, two nights from now, Gestus and Titus will secure a Roman banner from the Tenth Legion and then the next morning unfurl it on the third hour on the Beautiful Gate, the entrance into the Holy of Holies. That will enrage the people so that the Roman soldiers will come down into the Court of the Gentiles to calm the crowd. This time our men will be ready, and the battle will begin. Last year when the Galileans were killed during the riot over the aqueduct, we weren't ready, and they captured our brave leader, Barabbas.

This timing is important because that is when the trial of Jesus would have begun, and Passover begins. He will be rescued from the council chambers of the Sanhedrin and will lead our army to victory and return our land and our people back to God. Judas raised his arms and said hallelujah and began singing the first few verses of the Hallel, praising God.

Then he sat and said in a tired voice, It is time for us to sleep. Tomorrow we have much to do.

Titus looked at me. I didn't sleep much that night, he said. And early in the morning Gestus and I took the road back to Jerusalem, I with a heavy heart, and for the first time in my life, feeling my age.

24

Titus stood and stretched his back, hesitating to continue his story, remembering events that were difficult. I could only imagine what he must be thinking. He closed his eyes and sighed and then sat across from me again. He folded his hands and looked at me, his face haggard, sad, tired.

I have been sent here to tell my story, and I must finish it, he said, although the last part is very difficult for me to live again. It is filled with unimaginable pain, not only in my body, but also my soul.

Gestus and I joined many other people heading for Jerusalem that Wednesday morning, and when we reached the Roman road that led to Jerusalem from Caesarea, the road became even more crowded with pilgrims coming from Italy and Greece and the nations of Asia Minor. Jews were coming home for their most important festival.

The Pharisee was right, Gestus said. Maybe there will be more than a hundred thousand at Passover. We do have a chance to defeat the Romans.

Have you noticed anything on the road, I asked him as we saw a patrol of twelve Roman soldiers marching in the opposite direction, people pushing aside to make room for them. The Romans are expecting trouble, and they will be prepared. Remember, they are trained for war. We are not. We fight out of anger, and that leads to mistakes. Armies are trained to fight as a unit, acting on command. A few of them can stand up against many who are acting as individuals. The only way to defeat them would be to fight before they could be organized.

God is on our side, Gestus said. We will win. But he did notice more Roman patrols keeping watch over the pilgrims heading for Jerusalem. They were soldiers from the Twelfth Legion stationed in Antonia overlooking the temple, and they were used to Jews and their devotion to their one god, Yahweh. For them, crowd control was routine, and keeping an eye on the crowds during the different feasts celebrated in the temple was part of their job, a little boring. But I noticed that the soldiers were more alert as they looked over the crowds heading for the city. It was as though they would welcome a little scuffle to break the monotony, give them a chance to show off their skills.

By evening we had reached the road that went south to Hebron and passed near Bethlehem. We followed it a short distance and stopped at a place to rest beside a food vendor where we bought a round of bread and some cheese. Just east of where we sat we could see the encampment of the Tenth Legion. It was on the southeastern slope of the Hinnom Valley with its eastern edge near the road that followed the valley on around the southern edge of the city. It was organized with military precision, neat and orderly. We could see guards stationed around its perimeter. The sun had set, but it was still light enough to see details.

That is where we are to get the banner, Gestus said.

Pay attention to details, I told him. Notice how the guards are spaced around the camp and how they go back and forth in their posts. Getting in without being seen would be impossible. We must find some other way.

We will find a way, Gestus replied stubbornly.

Perhaps, I said. Notice each cohort has a banner, and each block of tents is organized into cohorts, or battalions. Then each cohort is divided into maniples, or companies, with a hundred and twenty men, commanded by a centurion. A tribune is in charge of the cohort. Each maniple has its own banner. Those flags are used as rallying points in battle, raised high so that the soldiers in each group can see them and follow commands in the heat of battle.

Somehow, tomorrow night we need to slip into camp and steal one, Gestus said.

We sat a little longer studying the terrain and the area, seeing a footpath south of the camp that skirted the place where Moloch was said to have accepted sacrifices of children long ago when Hoshea was king of Judah. It was an area where Israelites refused to go, but the Romans had set up part of their camp on the spot. Down the hill through some shrubs and thorn bushes from the path was a low stone wall bordering the road that the guards were patrolling.

Maybe there is a place where we can be successful, I said to Gestus. In the meantime, let's go home. It will be well after dark by the time we reach the farm.

We reached the sheep fold and slept once again in the storage shed making our beds in the hay as we had two nights before. The night was dark, but a nearly full moon was above us. Tomorrow night, the Paschal Moon, a full moon, would signal the beginning of Passover. We were so tired that we fell asleep almost at once, Gestus not complaining about the smell of sheep.

The next morning Joel and Marianne welcomed us for breakfast of some curdled goat milk and bread and fruit. I had difficulty during the meal because I knew it was the last day I would be spending with them. Our attempt to get a banner could be successful, and that would mean the beginning of a revolution, and I knew that I would die in it. Also, we could fail in the attempt, and that would also be my death sentence.

During the day Gestus and I worked in the orchard with Joel and his sons. We trimmed barren and dead branches from the almond trees which were blooming and worked on some olive trees which would bloom in another week. The few pomegranate trees were also blooming, beautiful blossoms like the ones adorning the ornate robe of the high priest during the sacred festivals. But we spent most of the day working with the grapes, the vines just beginning to swell with their first leaves.

Early that morning, Joel's youngest son had taken a lamb to the temple to be sacrificed where the priests would have cut its throat, one priest holding its lower jaw so that it would emit no sound, and then it was skinned and its entrails removed and burned on the altar's fire. By midday the son returned, and Marianne began slowly roasting the lamb for the Passover meal. Following tradition, Joel took a sprig of hyssop and sprinkled the lintel and the two side posts of the door with the blood of the lamb, which the son had brought home in a small vial.

At sundown, the entire family gathered for the paschal meal. The table had been extended with planks, and planks placed on chunks of wood acted as seating. Joel sat at the head of the table. He filled our cups with wine, and he asked a blessing and blessed the wine. Then Marianne placed the bitter herbs on the table, and we all took a small taste, some of the smaller children grimacing. Then Marianne brought a large round of unleavened bread and Joel passed it around and each of us tore off a small portion. Then two of Joel's sons carried in the roasted paschal lamb and placed it in front of Joel. We all drank a second cup of wine, and the oldest son, following tradition, asked his father to explain the meaning of the feast. Joel told the story of how the families in Egypt had gathered in their own homes and had sprinkled blood on the lintel and the posts of the door to their homes so that the angel of death would pass over them as they slew the firstborn of all in Egypt except those marked as God had commanded Moses to have the people do. Then Joel with the help of his sons sang the first part of the Hallel in Psalms 113 and 114. Then Joel carved the lamb, and we all ate it as the ceremony demanded. No portion was to be left over. After that, Joel sang the second part of the Hallel, from Psalms 115 to 118. That ended the Passover meal. I had been greatly moved by it because I had not participated with my family for several years.

That evening after supper, I went alone to the tombs of my wife, Esther, and my son, Benjamin. I knelt and prayed and promised I would get revenge for their deaths. The sons of Herod will be punished for his sin, I said. I believe the Romans will punish them for allowing the Galileans to rebel. I stayed with them for some time knowing that I would never return. I also said goodbye to my mother and my father, Eli, parents that I had deserted.

The night had a full moon, and I was familiar with the farm and soon joined Gestus at the sheep fold. He was anxious to leave on our mission, but I tried to settle him down by explaining that it would take us just a little more than an hour to walk to the hill sloping down into the Hinnom Valley, the one that was our best approach to the Roman camp.

People will be stirring around until it is late, I told him. We must wait until the moon goes down and we can go near the camp without being seen. The Roman guards will be alert until much later in the night. We must be patient. We have only one chance, and that is slim.

I dozed a little while Gestus stayed awake trying to judge the hour. He woke me at about the beginning of the new day, Friday, the day that the temple would open for the beginning of Passover. The hour was late and the night dark with the moon in the west. The Paschal moon would begin the next night. No one was on the Hebron road that we took north, aware that there could be Roman soldiers patrolling it.

As we approached Jerusalem, we could see torches lighting Solomon's Porch and the great sanctuary in the temple. We could barely make out the path that left the road and skirted east along the brow of the hill forming the southeast ridge of the Hinnom Valley. And then as we quietly continued along the twisty path, we could see the Roman camp.

Farther down the path as it wound its way downhill to the floor of the valley, we had to be careful that we did not snag our clothes on the thorn bushes. I still wore my shepherd's coat and carried my shepherd's staff which helped me ward off the brambles. As we neared the low stone wall that we had observed the day before, I signaled to Gestus to keep quiet and began to crouch as I inched along. By that time we were near the point where a Roman sentry would be patrolling the border of their camp.

By the time we reached the wall and laid down out of sight, it must have been an hour into the new day. We planned to capture a sentry and use his clothes in order to get into the camp, a foolish plan but the only one we could think of. By that time, the sentries would be lulled into believing that their duty was senseless, that there certainly was no danger to the camp, and as a result they would be careless.

Before too many minutes had passed, one of the sentries, tired of walking his beat, sat on the wall just above us, his back turned to us as he looked back into camp dreaming of when he would be relieved and he could get some sleep. He removed his helmet to scratch his head, and I whacked him a good one, wanting to put him out of action before he could sound the alarm. Gestus grabbed him as he began to fall forward, and we dragged him over onto our side of the wall.

Quickly, I hissed at Gestus. Get him out of his uniform and put it on. We have very little time. I didn't know whether or not my blow had killed the soldier, but I tied him securely as Gestus donned the toga and put on the breastplate and the shin guards and the helmet.

You look every bit the part, I whispered. Now go get the other sentry and have him come toward you. I slipped along the wall and waited for Gestus to get the attention of the sentry whose post was next to the one we had clubbed. Gestus was brave enough to play his part, and after he got the other Roman's attention by beckoning him to come, I waited with my staff, and when the sentry, a bigger man, came up to Gestus, not sensing a trap because of the darkness, I hit him across the neck and probably did kill him. That was the only weak place in his defense. Hitting his helmet would not have worked, and crippling him by a leg shot would have only caused him to scream. I threw aside my shepherd's staff and pulled off my shepherd's coat and my cloak and donned the Roman's uniform, although it was a tight fit.

We were now committed. There was no turning back.

I began patrolling the perimeter of the sentries' posts while Gestus slipped across the road into an area of tents where the other Romans were sleeping. A banner was attached by a pole to one of the tents, and Gestus was able to remove it and slip it off its staff. He quickly folded it and slipped it under his cape. So far we had been very lucky. The Romans must have felt smug, confident in their strength that nothing could happen to them. They were complacent, a bad condition for any army. We left hurriedly, striding down the road at the bottom of the Hinnom Valley heading for the Fountain

Gate, the one that we thought would be the least guarded during the night.

When we arrived, we could see several people waiting for the guards to let them enter the city. They had accepted the situation, and most were sitting or lying down, waiting for dawn. Gestus and I went up to the Roman sentry guarding the gate, Gestus doing the talking to the temple guard keeping watch along with the Roman. We had been mistaken when we had thought that they would be sleepy, careless. Both were alert, ready for a confrontation.

Let us through, Gestus said, trying to push past the guards. We have been ordered to go to the Tyropean Bridge and Temple Street, where there has been a report of a disturbance.

We have heard of no such thing, the temple guard said. The Roman sentry looked at the two of us and laughed.

Who are these fools, he said in broken Aramaic. The one old enough to be my grandfather has a heavy beard and isn't dressed properly. Look how his shoes are laced and the shin guards wrong. And this young one sounds like he's straight out of Galilee.

Without waiting I tried to overpower the Roman while Gestus tried to run past the other guard. From inside the gate, several other guards rushed out and overwhelmed us. The banner fell out from beneath Gestus's tunic, the golden eagle standing out from the blue cloth.

Look at this, one Roman yelled. These are rebels dressed in Roman uniforms. You, he said to one of the young Romans, run up to camp and report this. We will take them to Antonia and hold them there. Whatever they had planned must be stopped.

They twisted our arms behind our backs and blindfolded us. We had failed in our mission, but in a way I was glad. Now maybe there would be no revolution involving Jesus.

They stripped the Roman uniforms off us, and a squad of soldiers took us naked up the Tyropean Valley to Antonia and hustled us down two or three flights of stairs where they tied us to posts and beat us with whips that had several strands of leather and had been soaked in water. Gestus screamed, and I could hardly stand the pain as the whip cut into our backs. I could feel blood running down my back and onto my legs. The soldiers who had brought us there stood around and laughed at us as we dangled from those posts, cursing us.

When they had finished, they took us to a room that reeked with human waste and unwashed bodies, two or three torches lighting the area as we entered. The prisoners who were there blinked in the sudden light and looked at us without much interest. Then one of them stood, and I saw that it was Barabbas, dirty, his hair matted, but still erect, ready to resist.

So, two others of us, he said. I thought that the guards had come to get me for my execution. I am to be crucified this morning, they tell me.

We were with you last year at the aqueduct revolt, I told him. We were caught trying to start another one, but failed.

Well, you don't have to worry about it here, Barabbas said. This is the end for you and for the rest of these miserable souls sharing this room.

Then on the other side of our barred door we heard a sudden stirring of our guards, some cursing, voices raised. One of them came to the door and glared at Gestus and me. We have a report on you two, he said. One of the sentries you hit on the head made it back to camp and reported your crime. The other sentry is dead. The two of you will die for this, and I hope I get to help crucify you. A life for a life.

Maybe you can join me, Barabbas said to us sarcastically. I could use some company.

Titus turned away from me for a moment and sighed. It seemed like hours to me in that dungeon, he said, waiting for my death. I finally found a place to sit and wait for my ending.

Later we heard our guards stirring on the other side of the barred door, and then one of them entered and approached Barabbas. You are to be freed, he said harshly. The Jews have talked our governor into crucifying some crackpot named Jesus in place of you. So be it, he said. We can always take care of you later. The Jewish court accused him of saying that he was king of the Jews, and Pilate would see that as treason. The king of the Jews is our emperor, Tiberius Caesar.

I lost all hope when I heard that. Judas had been successful in his part of the plan in betraying Jesus to the high priest and the Sanhedrin. And they had tried Jesus illegally and had tricked Pilate into ordering the Messiah's death. The Zealots had no chance to begin a revolt because the followers of Jesus were not aware of what had happened.

About midday, Gestus and I were brought out of the dungeon and up the stairs to an inner court of the fortress. Jesus was in the room dressed in a bright, red robe. I could hardly recognize him because he had been beaten, his face bruised and swollen. Someone had put a crown of thorns on his head and had pushed it down so that streams of blood had run down his face and into his beard. He looked at us in pity, but said nothing.

And then they brought out three beams of cypress wood about six feet long and three by five inches wide and high. They tied our hands together about six inches apart and put the beams on our shoulders and had us support them with our roped hands. Then they opened the outer door and drove us out into the street, Jesus leading the way, so beaten and exhausted that he could barely move. We entered the street that led to the Joppa road where people began staring at us, pulling away from soldiers guarding us, cowed by the sight of three criminals being led to their deaths.

And then some people began to recognize that one of us was Jesus, and a crowd began following us. Jesus stumbled and then fell, and one of the guards ordered another man to carry the beam for Jesus. As we neared the Gennath Gate, which opened to the road to Joppa, some women began wailing and crying out to Jesus.

Jesus stopped and looked at them and began speaking through puffed lips, hardly able to make himself heard. Daughters of Jerusalem, he said to them, do not weep for me. Weep for yourselves and for your children, for the time will come when you will say, blessed are the barren women, the wombs that never bore and the breasts that never nursed. Then they will say to the mountains, fall on us and to the hills, cover us. For if men do these things when the tree is green, what will happen when it is dry.

And then the guards forced us on through the city gate and the short distance to the short, steep grade up Golgotha, the hill of the skull, where we were to be crucified. The sky had layers of dark clouds with streaks of sunlight shining through. One lit the white marble of the Temple. I saw it as I laid down my beam at my guard's command.

Then a guard forced me down and had me lie with the back of my neck on the beam and stretch my arms out. Gestus was in the same position. A soldier removed the robe from Jesus and two others roughly forced him to the ground, and then I saw no more. A soldier on either side of me knelt and put their hobnailed shin guards across my arms at my elbows while two other held my wrists. Then I felt a sharp object feeling along my right hand where it joined the wrist, and then I felt the tearing pain of a nail being driven into my hand where it joined the wrist. I shuddered violently, my body arching, and then the same thing happened to my left hand. I heard Gestus screaming.

Two soldiers grabbed the beam and forced me to sit while two others joined them and lifted me up. Poles were fitted on the transverse beam, and they lifted me up to the vertical post that was permanent. The beam was put into the notch at the top of the vertical post. The weight of my body tore at my wrists, and I could barely breathe. And then two soldiers placed my feet on a narrow stand on the vertical beam. They crossed my feet and once again I felt the searing agony of a nail being driven through me. I stood and took a breath. As long as I could stand, I could breathe. When I slumped, the weight of my body pulled my chest tight, and I could not breathe. Jesus had been crucified between Gestus and me. I was to his right, Gestus to his left.

Jesus was looking down at the Roman soldiers, one holding the scarlet cloak that Herod Antipas had put on Jesus as a mockery when Jesus had been called king of the Jews to Pilate by his accusers. He looked at the crowd which stood a little way down the hill, some mocking him. He still wore his crown of thorns, and it had been thrust back onto his head, and fresh rivulets of blood trickled down his face.

A group of bolder ones drew nearer and began hitting his legs with reed switches and spitting on him. Father, forgive them, for they do not know what they are doing, he said, hardly able to speak. One Pharisee came forward near the foot of Jesus's cross and screamed, he saved others, let him save himself. He can if he is truly the Son of God, another Pharisee replied, his rings flashing in the beam of sunlight that suddenly lit the scene, falling squarely on Jesus.

Signs had been nailed to our crosses as was the custom. The ones for Gestus and me said we were robbers. The one above the head of Jesus said King of the Jews.

The group of people who hated Jesus left after they saw that they could not torment him any further. The mother of Jesus and two other women and one of his disciples, the one named John, approached the foot of the cross, the women wailing in grief. Jesus looked down at them in pity, knowing that they did not realize that he was fulfilling God's command. Dear woman, he said to his mother, Mary. Here is your son. And to John he said, here is your mother.

The sky darkened, and I lost feeling and only caught glimpses of activity. I would stand and breathe and then slump and could not breathe again. Agony had clouded me. But then I heard Gestus screaming at Jesus. If you are the Messiah, he yelled, save yourself and us.

That angered me. Jesus was doing what God had commanded him to do. He was enduring the worst kind of death for all of us. Don't you fear God, I said to Gestus. We deserve what we are getting, but this man has done no wrong. And then I turned my head and looked at Jesus, who was looking at me. Jesus, I said, remember me when you come into your kingly power.

Jesus looked at me, and I saw his eyes as they were as a baby back in Bethlehem as they looked that night in the Negev Desert. His face was filled with love. Truly, I say to you, Jesus said, today you will be with me in paradise.

We had been hanging on our crosses for about three hours when Jesus asked for a drink. A guard dipped a sponge in vinegar and then held it up to Jesus on a hyssop twig, but Jesus refused it. And then he prayed in a low voice, My God, my God, why have you forsaken me? And we hung on our crosses, slumping and then standing, filled with agony.

About three in the afternoon I heard Jesus cry out in a loud voice, Father, into your hands I commit my spirit, and then he slumped forward. The centurion in charge of the guards came to the foot of Jesus's cross and looked up at him. Jesus had died, but the centurion ordered one of the guards to make sure by running his spear upward into Jesus's side.

A soldier had come from Antonia about this time and whispered a message to the centurion. The officer turned to his soldiers. He said all of these men must die so that they do not disturb the Jews on their holy holiday. So break their legs, he told the burly soldier who had driven the nails.

At that moment a violent earthquake shook the ground and lasted for many seconds. Our crosses quivered. The guards backed up in awe, but after the tremor had finished, the guard with his heavy hammer, broke our legs below our knees, and we could no longer breathe.

That is all I remember, Titus told me. That is my story. Jesus had come into a world that was filled with hate, preaching love. He had fulfilled his holy Father's commands, showing people that the only hope for the world is one of love, not hate or war. That is why I have been sent back again to your world, Titus said to me. People must repent, if they wish to survive.

Tell my story, he said, looking at me, his black eyes deep, penetrating. Promise me.

I promise, I told him. I have read the Gospels, but I never knew what life was really like back then, how much people suffered. How much some people wanted Jesus dead.

Remember the promises he made, Titus said. He will return when you least expect it, but I am only the messenger sent back to alert you once again.

The bright lights of the parking lot suddenly dimmed, leaving our table in a sudden gloom. The only lights around the coffee shop were the ones lighting the drive-through entrance, the restaurant, and the back where the pickup window was located. I looked at the restaurant in time to see the young college student who had waited on us emerge from the front door with his bicycle, wave goodbye to the young man on duty, and lock the front door. He looked in our direction as he peddled away.

I turned to speak to Titus, but he had disappeared. I had looked away for no more than two or three seconds. I thought I saw a whitish blur across the dimmed parking lot, a warping, perhaps, of air.

The shepherd was gone. A cup partially filled with cold coffee sat across the table where he had been. I sat there alone for a minute more and then slowly walked away.

AFTERWORD

Sometimes history is based on facts, sometimes on events that are passed along orally and, as a result, may be changed. We have both written history, with dates given, and eye witness accounts that were recorded long after the events happened during the time that Jesus lived. In both cases, they are based upon the beliefs of those who recorded them. Two people seeing the same occurrence may report it with slight differences based on their perspective, their biases, their audience, and their reason for telling the story in the first place.

This happens in the Gospels where the different authors told of Christ's ministry, each from his own perspective and from the collection of stories remembered by people who had witnessed the miracles and heard the parables. As a result, deciding on an accurate timeline of those four years is almost impossible because of the emphasis different writers put on different events. Very little attention is paid to historical events in the Gospels, but some are given.

What is interesting is the tangled relationships of some of the major players named in the New Testament. What happened to the Herods ruling at that time, to the Roman leaders, to the high priest, and to the apostles illustrates how volatile the times were during the life of Jesus and following his resurrection.

Herod Philip II, the son of Herod the Great, died in AD 34, not long after he married Salome, the daughter of Philip I and Herodias. According to all accounts, he governed Batania, Trachonitis, Auranitis, Gaulanitis, and some part of Jamnia. Herod Agrippa I was made king of that tetrarchy in AD 37 by Gaius Caesar, better known as Caligula. Agrippa I, the brother of Herodias, was brought up in Rome and had been imprisoned by Tiberius, but when Tiberius died in AD 37, Caligula became emperor and soon rewarded his friend, Agrippa I with Philip II's tetrarchy.

Herodias was jealous of her brother Agippa's sudden rise to power and talked Herod Antipas into going to Rome with her to plead for a better position and have Caligula make him king of Galilee and the northern provinces. Earlier, Agrippa had written to Caligula accusing Antipas of conspiring against Tiberius with Sejanus, and in AD 39, Caligula banished both Herodias and Antipas to perpetual banishment in Spain where Antipas died. Caligula then made Agrippa I king of Galilee and Perea. Antipas had been the one who had beheaded John the Baptist at the demand of Herodias after Salome danced, and he had feared Jesus and had wanted him killed. At the end, Antipas mocked Jesus and sent him back to Pilate for the final sentence of death.

After Jesus was crucified, things didn't end well for Pontius Pilate, procurator of Judea, or Joseph Caiaphas, high priest and president of the Sanhedrin. The Samaritans had sent a petition to Tiberius to have Pilate removed because he had massacred many of them when they were on their pilgrimage to Mount Gerizim, believing that a prophet would take them up on their holy mountain to find the hiding place of sacred objects left there by Moses. In AD 36, Vitellius, then president of Syria, heard of their complaints and sent his friend Marcellus to take charge in Judea. Marcellus sent Pilate to Rome and removed Caiaphas as high priest. He replaced Caiaphas with Jonathan, a son of Annas. Several stories are told about the ending of Pilate, but the most popular one is that he committed suicide.

Soon after, Agrippa I was made king of Judea and Samaria, which meant that Palestine was ruled by one king for the first time since Herod the Great. Agrippa was a strict observer of the Law of Moses and sought favor with the Jews. Shortly before Passover in the year AD 44, Agrippa had the apostle James, the son of Zebedee and a cousin to Jesus, put to death. Soon after that, Agrippa also died suddenly. Caligula was murdered in Rome on January 24, AD 41.

All the apostles died as martyrs except Judas, who hanged himself in remorse for having betrayed Jesus. Most of the stories of their deaths are based on tradition. Simon Peter was a missionary among the Jews as far as Babylon and Rome, and the author of some epistles. He was crucified in Rome, head down, in AD 67. Andrew, the brother of Simon Peter, preached in Scythia, Greece, and Asia Minor. Tradition states that Andrew was crucified on a St. Andrew's cross shaped like an X.

James was executed in Jerusalem in AD 44, as previously stated. His brother John, author of a Gospel, letters, and Revelation, worked in Asia Minor, mainly Ephesus, and was banished to Patmos in AD 95. He lived to an old age, dying a natural death.

James the younger wrote an epistle and preached in Palestine and Egypt. Tradition has it that he was crucified in Egypt. Others say he was thrown off a pinnacle. His brother Jude also wrote an epistle and, according to tradition, preached in Assyria and Persia. He was martyred in Persia.

Philip preached in Phrygia where tradition says he was martyred. Bartholomew was flayed to death according to traditional accounts. Matthew died a martyr in Ethiopia according to some. Thomas was claimed by the Syrian Christians as the founder of their church, perhaps also in Persia and India. Tradition has it that he was shot by arrows while at prayer. And Simon, the Cananean, was crucified, according to tradition.

Through all of this, the message of Christ has continued. His message of love endures in a world where people seem to find it much easier to hate. And the historic time when he taught, hate centered, self-centered, living for the moment, doesn't seem all that much different than it does today or any time in history. That his message continues even now is the true miracle.

Sources Used

Alexander, David and Pat, editors. *Eerdman's Handbook of the Bible*. Consulting Editors David Field, Donald Guthrie, Gerald Hughes, Alan Millard, I. Howard Marshall. Grand Rapids, Michigan: William B. Eerdman's Publishing Co., 1973.

Alexander, Pat, consulting editor. *Encyclopedia of the Bible*. A Lion Book. Tring, Herts, England: Lion Publishing Corp., revised ed. 1986.

Bishop, Jim. *The Day Christ Died*. New York: Harper & Brothers, 1957.

Cary, M. ed. With others. The Oxford Classical Dictionary. Oxford: Oxford University Press, 1957. Condor, C. R., Maj. Illustrated Bible Geography and Atlas. London and New York: Collin's Clear-Type Press, no date.

Boehner, Harold W. *Chronological Aspects of the Life of Christ*. Grand Rapids, Michigan: Zondervan Publishing House, 1977.

The Holy Bible "The New International Version Containing the Old Testament and The New Testament. Colorado Springs, Colorado: International Bible Society, 1984.

The Internet on almost any subject.

Josephus, Flavius. *Josephus: The Complete Works*. Translated by William Whiston. Nashville, Tennessee: Thomas Nelson, 1998.

Moore, Rev. Pamela. Sermon containing the Panias scene.

Peloubet, F. N., assisted by Alice Adams. Peloubet's Bible Dictionary. Philadelphia: Universal Book And Bible House, 1925.

Potter, Dr. Charles Francis. *The Lost Years of Jesus Revealed.* Greenwich, Connecticut: Fawcett Publications, Inc., 1962.

Rowley, H. H. The Modem Reader's Bible Atlas. New York: A Reflection Book Giant Association Press, 1961.

The New Testament of Our Lord and Saviour Jesus Christ. King James Version with Pictures. New York: American Bible Society.

Schonfield, Hugh J. *The Passover Plot. "New Light on the History of Jesus."* New York: A Bantam Book, 5th printing 1967.

Ward, Kaari, ed. "Jesus and His Times." Pleasantville, N. Y.: The Reader's Digest Assoc., Inc., 1987. Vennes, G. The Dead Sea Scrolls in English. Baltimore, Maryland: Penguin Books, 1962.

Wright, Ernest G. Principal Adviser and Editorial Consultant. "Great People of the Bible and How They Lived." Pleasantville, New York: The Reader's Digest Association, 1974.